THE JEWEL AND THE SWORD

MARJORIE JONES

GOLD IMPRINT

Dedication,
For Keith, Jason, Staci-anne, and Heather.
I love you over the moon, around the stars and back again.

June 2004
Published by Medallion Press, Inc.
225 Seabreeze Ave.
Palm Beach, FL 33480

If you purchased this book without a cover you should be aware that this book is stolen property. It was reported as "unsold and destroyed" to the publisher, and neither the author nor the publisher has received any payment from this "stripped book."

Copyright © 2004 by Marjorie Jones
Cover Photographer: Sandy McPherson
Cover Illustrator: Adam Mock
Cover Heroine: Ali DeGray
Cover Hero: Sean O'Brien
Costumer: Connie Perry

All rights reserved. No part of this book may be reproduced or transmitted in any form or by an electronic or mechanical means, including photocopying, recording, or by any information storage and retrieval system, without written permission of the publisher, except where permitted by law.

ISBN 1-932815-06-6

Printed in the United States of America

For more great books visit www.medallionpress.com.

Acknowledgments

In the course of my life, I have been touched by many individuals. Some have brushed me with their wings, and all I have is the memory; others have stood beside me, held my hand and, at times, breathed for me.

My parents are true believers in dreams and have instilled that same passion in me. I don't know that I would have pursued the joy of writing if they hadn't been ever supportive of my aspirations.

I must acknowledge the impact of two teachers on my writing career and my life: Mrs. Mullarney-Yano for encouraging a young girl to write from her heart and Mr. Wicks for his vision and dedication to shaping teenagers into some semblance of adults.

Good critique partners are worth more than words can ever say, and they will be the first ones to highlight, edit, delete, scratch, alter and modify it if one ever did find the words. They can do this because they aren't just partners, they're friends. Thank you Kim, Tam, Tara, Marie, Melissa, Jami, Cindy, and Sonja for Romancing History.

Thanks so much to everyone at Medallion Press. Peggy, for letting me in, Helen for her kind words and faith, Pam, for her fabulous red pen, and Leslie for endless advice and reminding me that the world is not such a scary place. I feel truly blessed.

And also, thank you to the friends who have supported me in my quest for this moment. Your emails and notes have been a source of constant happiness for me. I read them often, and your words and faith lift me up everyday!

Preface

A forbidding castle poised atop a hillock. Riders, bearing colorful banners, charge ahead of their King. A lady awaits the return of her knight.

So fascinating do we find the age of glory and chivalry that even now theme restaurants reenact the tournaments to prove the best swordsman or horseman. Renaissance fairs dot the countryside every summer, and entire organizations are dedicated to preserving the culture and educating the general public about it.

The Jewel and the Sword takes place in the midst of these times. Devlin is a "Marcher Lord," that is, one who protects the King's borders. In the most authentic use of the word, the Marcher Barons resided on the border with Wales in the Western portion of Henry III's empire. I decided, however, to place Devlin on the border with Scotland because, of course, this is where his lady has lived her entire life.

King Henry III inherited his kingdom at the tender age of nine, though he did not come into power until he turned twenty-five. Throughout his reign, he dealt with the threat of expulsion from the throne, a dream sought by the rebel barons in his own country. Married to a member of the royal family of France, Henry found the French more to his liking than his own countrymen. A state of civil war existed in his homeland at the time he ascended the throne, and he spent a portion of his time putting down minor rebellions. Major hostilities had been brought to a halt prior to his coronation at Westminster Abby in 1220.[1]

In addition to his manner for governing his country, or not governing it in some barons' opinions, he also inherited the blame for his father's tax system; just as our current leaders may or may not be held responsible for events put in motion by the preceding official. Henry's father, King John,[2] came into power when his brother and Henry's uncle, Richard the Lionheart, left England in his pursuit to reclaim the Holy Land for Christendom. Richard never returned to England, succeeding only in emptying the empire's coffers in his foolish and arrogant quest. John, forced to raise existing taxes and establish new ones, became one of the most

---

1. This was Henry's second coronation. The first took place prior to the end of the conflict, October 28, 1216, at Gloucester Cathedral.
2. You may remember King John from the legends of Robin Hood. It was King John's tax system that prompted Robin of Locksley to "steal from the rich and give to the poor."

unpopular kings in the history of the empire. Henry, by default, inherited some of the animosity that should have been his father's alone, albeit at no time did Henry reduce the tax burden to his subjects.

During his reign, Henry agreed to the Provisions of Oxford, a modification of the Magna Carta, which granted his subjects a more democratic government. Several years later, after seeking dispensation from the Church, Henry disavowed his earlier agreement.

Because of this and his attitude toward the plight of his country, he became the target of at least one plot to usurp his crown. Simon de Montfort, Henry's own brother-in-law, successfully captured Henry and took control of the country for a period of five years, beginning in 1260. In a glorious and romantic moment in history, or so I prefer to see it, Henry escaped his captors,[3] mounted an army consisting of Marcher Barons and, with the help of his son, retook his throne. An interesting side note? Henry's son was none other than Edward the Longshanks, the King we all loved to hate in Mel Gibson's, *Braveheart*.

Henry ruled in relative peace, after reclaiming his throne, until his death in 1272. He is buried at Westminster Abby, the cathedral completely refurbished and renovated during his reign.

Devlin and Meghan lived during a time of great upheaval and treachery, chivalry and honor. I hope you enjoy reading of their adventurous courtship as much as I enjoyed writing it.

---

[3]. In some accounts, both Henry and his son, Edward, were captured, and it was Edward who escaped and defeated de Montfort, thereby effecting the release of his father.

PROLOGUE
Northern England, Ravenstone Castle – 1233

"I'll go."

The men in the room with him fell silent. A traitor resided in the household of King Henry, and the power of the monarchy was at stake.

Devlin felt the intensity of their gazes as several pairs of eyes raked through him. He stared them down, each of these knights older, wiser, but none braver than he. Finally, his eyes met those of his King. Henry stared back, his own dark orbs reflecting the impact of Devlin's offer. Devlin read the unspoken trust and appreciation in Henry's shuttered expression. Neither of them needed to speak the words to know how deeply one felt for the other. Henry was more than his liege. He was Devlin's closest friend.

Henry's piercing stare never left Devlin's as he

appeared deep in thought for a moment, his expression unchanging. "Very well. 'Tis decided then. Ravenstone will ride out in my stead, while I, with a small contingent, will ride west under another banner."

The dim light of the torches flickered along the walls, a foreboding reminder of the task at hand. The quiet flames reflected off the jeweled sword hanging from rounded hooks imbedded in the rock walls. A symbol of strength and bravery, it served as a catalyst for the one thing that would never falter in his life. Honor. Originally belonging to his father, it was now his. Devlin was steadfast in his desire to be worthy of such a prize.

Devlin squared his shoulders. As he prepared himself for the first of many tasks he must complete before the evil of this night was done, he bowed obediently to his liege, and then he turned to leave.

As he strode proudly toward the door, his father placed a strong hand on Devlin's shoulder. He started at the unexpected contact, lifting his chin and meeting his father's gaze. The older man's features, so much like his own, misted.

"You make me very proud, my son. You're certain?" Lionel Barnett's voice sounded full and rich in the dimness of the chamber and reminded Devlin of the trust his father had always placed in him. He would continue to honor that trust until his last breath.

He looked again at the sword. Mesmerized for a moment by the prize representing a legacy of honor, he responded, "Aye, Father."

Waiting for his father's next words, he half expected the old earl to try to talk him out of this fool's errand. But he knew, as did his father, there would be no retreat. They were alike, father and son. If Devlin held one shred of honor or decency, he'd gained it from the man before him.

Instead, his father carefully regarded the sword as well. "I knew I made the right decision all those years ago, choosing you over your brother."

Devlin grimaced at the mention of his elder half-brother. His father was determined there would be peace between his first son and his second, and despite his wish to destroy the Scottish clan over which his brother now ruled, he would laud those desires. Even though he suspected Morven's hand in this current treason.

"Honor is more than blood born, Father."

Lionel clapped him on the back. Displays of affection were difficult for his father, and the gesture was more powerful than an embrace.

"Then so be it." Lionel paused, as if the next words he spoke would strangle him. "Your wife shall remain with us, as our daughter, for as long as she wishes."

Devlin nodded. He knew what that meant. Until she remarried. The thought choked him as profoundly as if he'd been hung from the tower. Silently, he made his way from the stark room in search of the only person who could bring him peace.

In their chamber he found Allyson reclining easily in their bed and sipping wine. Her black hair wrapped around her naked shoulders and cascaded over her breasts. Smooth skin, the color of fresh cream, reflected the firelight. Her eyes bewitched him the moment he stepped into the room. He took comfort in them. Forcing a smile, he knew she had no idea that tonight would probably be their last.

"So, Husband. You have finished with the King's council at last." She purred.

How could he behave as if he hadn't just volunteered to die? His King was in danger, and he knew of a possible way out. What could he do besides offer it to him? But the thought of withholding information so grievous from his own wife pained him.

Though the hour was late, and the chance for Allyson to speak with anyone other than himself slim, he could not risk providing her with facts that could cost Henry his hard-won throne, and very possibly his life. Should Allyson unwittingly pass such details to the wrong party, he hesitated to think what might happen. And if the last of the rebel barons suspected she knew anything that could help them finally remove Henry from power, they would stop at nothing, including torture, to get the information from her.

"Aye. The council is done. Henry will return to London before the dawn, and I am to go with him." He removed his sword belt and leaned the wicked blade against the hard, chamber wall.

Allyson's eyes widened at the news, and he felt a twinge of guilt at her reaction. His heart seized. She deserved to know the truth. As his wife, she had every right to know she might never see him again. But he couldn't put her at risk. The very fact she married him already made her a target for Henry's enemies. The House of Ravenstone had remained loyal to the King throughout history, during the recent rebellions, and would remain so forever. The few rebels who continued their ignoble struggle knew this and hated him for it.

Still, he found it difficult to gaze into her dark eyes and lie. His back tensed as he stroked her cheek with the back of his hand. He would do it for his King. And for her safety.

"Why must you go? I thought your service to the crown ended in London this month past?"

"Nay, Wife. I am the King's man and I will serve him always. 'Tis my duty."

"Your duty is to me." Her voice trembled. "To us." She lowered her cup to the small table beside the bed and placed her slender hands upon her belly.

His heart began to race as he realized her meaning. "A babe?" he asked, his voice hoarse with emotion.

She rose from the bed, reaching for him with trembling limbs. As she entwined her arms around him, her dark head rested on his chest. He took her in the embrace, a movement so natural his heart soared, even as it plummeted to hell.

"Aye, a babe, Husband. You cannot go."

He stiffened at her words. "I must."

Devlin winced as her body began to shake. He could not withstand the assault of her tears. It was the only weakness he allowed himself. Tipping her chin upward with one finger as he swiped his thumb across her trembling lips, he whispered, "I'm sorry, sweetling. I have no choice."

He carried her to their bed and made love to her, taking her fully into his soul as he entered her. She wept aloud and cried out his name as she found her release, and when he joined her, he did so with her name heavy on his lips.

He held her, wrapped in thoughts of what should have been, until he could delay no more. She refused sleep for most of the long night. He spoke softly to her, stroking her hair until finally she drifted silently away from him. He dressed, and as he strapped his sword to his waist, he watched her slumber. Placing one hand on her belly, he pressed a warm kiss to her lips, and then, weighted regret warring with duty, marched quickly from the room.

† † †

His eyes came open slowly and met only inky darkness, like a shroud of black cloth. Devlin Barnett came fully awake, familiar agony meeting the fetid breath of his injuries. As full awareness of his continued torment dawned, he was instantly assaulted by his own fury.

They'd beaten him until he'd finally succumbed to blackness and put him back into this hellish box. He cursed.

The windowless steel walls of the finite prison were heated unto fire by the burning rays of the sun overhead.

THE JEWEL AND THE SWORD

His body thirsted for relief in the sweltering chamber. His throat ached from lack of water.

He groaned at the lack of space, even to roll onto his other hip. He wasn't quite lying down and was unable to sit up without crowning himself on the metal roof of the small box.

Worse. The lack of flooring meant he sat directly upon the earth. The sharp stones upon which he rested added to his misery, their pointed corners tearing his flesh with the slightest movements.

He breathed deeply in an attempt to control the raging agony clawing over him like hawk's talons, ignoring the strong stench that filled his nostrils. He gripped the rags hanging from his frame in filthy, odiferous strips from his cramped legs. They were all that remained of his breeches and clout. His mail had been taken from him the first day, in preparation for the flogging he'd received. What remained of his tunic lay fastened to the oozing lash marks on his back.

He prayed his fellow knights searched for him. If they did not free him soon, he would likely die.

He attempted to raise a bruised arm and wipe the sweat from his burning eyes. Nearly unbearable, the heat choked his lungs and seared his flesh. The box, made mostly from steel, was designed to bake a man slowly until he died. His captor, wicked and cruel, savored an even slower and more painful death. Devlin released a rueful chuckle. Given just enough water to keep him alive, he was taken from the torture chamber daily to be beaten before being returned to this private hell.

Devlin closed his eyes when his futile attempts to see failed and held to his memories–to the one who could remove him from this place with only a smile, at least in his mind. An image flashed. Allyson. Beautiful, strong, and kind, she was life to him, and he lived only for her. Newly married to this woman who loved him beyond reason, and whom he loved more than his own life, he was gloriously happy. He could see her in his mind's eye as she lay in their bed, satisfied and purring in the afterglow of their lovemaking. Her black hair would be mussed, and her body stretched languidly across the silk sheets he'd purchased in London just for her; she would smile and ask him to come to bed. Despite his desperate situation, he felt his body respond to the memory of the last night spent in their apartments before his knightly duty called him from her side.

For that is what he was; he renewed his vow. As knight, proud and honorable, in service to his King and heir to a title and large property, it had been his duty to protect and serve his liege. A spy resided in the household of King Henry, and that threat had nearly allowed a usurper to overthrow the monarchy. As the King's man, it had been his plan that had set this end in motion. Disguised as the King, he had ridden from the residence with a modest contingent of guards, while the King rode out alone, for all intents and purposes, in the opposite direction. The plan had worked, at least he hoped. The traitors had set upon his party, and he had been taken prisoner in Henry's stead. Being taken alive had been a surprise for he had been perfectly willing to, and expectant that he would, give his life in this fool's errand of a mission. The score of men who rode with him had paid that price.

But they had taken him in the dead of night and, of course, within only moments of their arrival in this desolate place, discovered they had the wrong man. More's the pity for them; they did not kill him. For days they had beaten and tortured him for the King's true whereabouts, for any counsel he could provide them. But the folly was theirs, since he had no idea where Henry was or how to reach him. And it would take more than their wickedness to make him betray his liege.

He stiffened his back as resolution filled his bones and mind. He had withstood more pain and abuse in the last five days than in his entire life. And he had lived. Nay, they would not defeat him. He would see this through and be free of it. He had too much to live for—his wife and unborn child. He would survive for them.

At two and twenty, he lived the perfection of his dreams. And now it would end? Nay. He would not die here!

The roof creaked open on rusted hinges. Blinding, searing daylight burned his eyes. He threw one filthy hand in front of his bearded face to block the light. He wondered what hellish torture they had planned for him today. Another flogging perhaps, or the rack? Mayhap they only planned to beat him yet again. He sighed. His body tensed of its own accord, but he would not surrender. If he would not allow them to take his life, neither would they take his pride. For his pride was of greater value. He scowled. "You again? I believe I left word I wasn't to be disturbed."

Rough hands dragged him from the rancid heat of the cell. His limbs screamed in protest as his bare feet found purchase on the rock-strewn ground, his head throbbing as he struggled to hold it high. They might see him bleed, but they would never see him cower.

The guards released him, and he stood proudly before the same merciless bastard he'd been forced to endure since that first night. The man stood approximately the same height as Devlin, but appeared stronger, considering Devlin's current condition.

Over the man's shoulder, the keep loomed into the blue sky. Square and strong, this place had been designed for war and offered nothing to soften the cold edges of stone. He'd never been to this place before, and didn't even know if he was still in England.

"Begin!" a deep voice cried from across the bailey.

Devlin recognized the order to begin his daily regimen of abuse. He hated the grating Scottish voice that gave it. The leader of this rebellious faction sat atop a roan gelding, never closer than the length of three or four wagons, as if he were afraid to dirty his hands.

Coward.

Too distant for Devlin to make out any of his features, the man's eyes, nevertheless, held Devlin's attention. Even from so far away, he could tell no decency resided there. Only hatred.

Devlin concentrated his attention on those cold,

lifeless orbs, committing them to memory. Someday, they would meet again. He vowed, when that day came, one of them would die. His lips twitched into a lopsided grin. But not today.

A hand struck Devlin's jaw with the force of a wave crashing upon him from the sea. Falling in a clump at the feet of his captor, he tried to remember if this would mark the eighth time, or the tenth. He'd lost count of the beatings now, so intense was the brutality.

The clipping gait of a horse's hoofs crossed the rocky earth toward him.

"I thought to kill ye today." The gravely voice fell on him like a brick. "But nay." A chuckle reached Devlin's ears. "I'm likin' this game."

Refusing to release even the smallest moan, he forced his battered body to its knees and stared up at his enemy. Blood filled his eyes, blinding him. Only the satisfaction of knowing, even as his own body might betray his will to live, his King remained safe, gave him the strength to reply, "Why, indeed?"

His answer came in the form of the back of a hand across his cheek, knocking him to the ground again.

A thunderous roar belied the clear, bright sky above.

Finally. What took them so long? Devlin squared his shoulders, and a smile etched his bruised face. He summoned strength he hadn't known he still possessed, rose to his feet before his enemy, and wiped the blood from his eyes.

Dozens of mounted soldiers stormed the castle, the

earth shaking beneath his feet from the approaching steeds. He seized the guard to his left, taking the sword from the man's grip, and easily dispatched both him and the guard to his right. Turning back to face his rival, Devlin found the rebel leader fleeing in terror through the bailey.

He cursed aloud at the missed chance for personal vengeance. Faced now with the enemy forces fully on guard, he could not give chase.

Within minutes the battle raged full force around him.

He smiled as he recognized many of the men who had so valiantly risked their own lives to save his, and he vowed to be a good leader to them when the day came. But for now he would do them honor by fighting at their side.

The will to fight and the excitement of the battle coursing through his veins gave him more strength than he should have had. Aye. He would survive this and return to his beloved Lady Wife. Of that he was certain.

His blood boiled with the heat of the fight. He was born for this. The sound of clashing steel beat through him as he met first one enemy, then another. He fought well, years of training making his thrusts perfect and his strokes sure. He ignored the pain coiling through him and denied the weakness threatening to overpower his limbs.

A sure thrust from his newest opponent ripped the sword from his hands. Cursing, he staggered to retrieve it. Grabbing the fierce weapon with both hands, Devlin straightened and slashed. He caught the man's unprotected midsection with the finely edged blade. Full of pride, he stood over the fallen man and held his sword above his head with one hand. He tilted his head back, relishing the coming victory, and released a battle cry. He smiled in triumph as his warriors answered him in kind.

A fierce, brilliant pain pierced his left side. He fell forward, wincing at the sharpness of the rocks on his unprotected knees. The intensity of this new agony was unfamiliar, yet without opening his eyes he knew what had happened. He placed his hand at his side and probed the hot, sticky moisture escaping around the arrow penetrating his torso just below his ribs.

Damn. He wasn't ready to die. His thoughts raced to Allyson again. His Allyson. His lover. His bride. How she would ache at his loss. Married but three months and widowed so quickly. Her beautiful face swam before his eyes as he fought to remain conscious. He fell to his back oblivious to the battle surrounding him as her image floated above him, lost every so often in the glare of the sun directly overhead.

The intense shouts of the men fighting around him faded from his mind as blackness crept into the sides of his vision. He only knew Allyson now, as her image soothed him. Her dark hair and comforting eyes smiled down at him. How he would miss holding her, her easy smile and fiery touch.

What would their child look like? A boy? Strong in body like his father, strong in faith like his mother?

A girl? Beautiful and kind?

Determination renewed itself in his veins. He would not die, he decided. He would survive, if only to find rapture in Allyson's arms and immortality in his children.

Allyson's laughing eyes, her charming smile, her perfect form. All of her settled above him as he struggled to breathe.

He reached for her face again, desperate to feel her soft skin beneath his fingers, and when he finally touched her she smiled again and then laughed. Not the soft chuckle that so endeared her to him, but a rich, hearty laugh filled with spite.

Then she was gone, and with her his reason for living.

† † †

Devlin came awake slowly. His side ached. His head swam. He could hear a familiar voice echoing through the otherwise silent chamber.

"I don't know, Will. I'm doing the best I can. If he wakes, he wakes. But . . ." The frustrated voice filled the room with tension so thick, one could slice it.

"He will. He's always been strong, and this will not kill him." Will's voice. Did they discuss him or some other wretch near death?

"I'll do my best by him, Lord Will."

"And you'll summon me the moment he wakes. I want to be here when he learns of it."

The voices fell to a strained whisper.

The Jewel and the Sword

With great effort, he forced his heavy eyelids open. The green velvet hanging from the bed spoke of Dunburough Castle. This was the largest of the properties in his manor, his birthright, and the King's northernmost defense against the Scottish clans that would raid and pillage into England. Still, he could not deny the tightness coiling through his battered and worn body.

"Oh, dear God," his mother cried. "He wakes. Will? Come quickly. Gowain. He's waking." Her voice strained with worry, but was tempered by relief.

Devlin cringed as the two men raced to his bedside, their heavy bootsteps scattering the rushes on the floor. He hated feeling helpless. He detested that anyone should suffer over him. He tried to push himself away from the mattress.

"Nay, milord. Don't try to move." Gowain pressed Devlin's shoulders against the pillows. It was this voice he'd been unable to place.

"He needs water." Lady Ravenstone reached for the cup and plied him with several heavenly drops. The soothing liquid freed his voice from its raspy prison.

"Allyson?" he could hear himself whisper, but did not know his own voice.

"Don't try to speak, my son. You're strong and you will recover. But 'twill take time. Oh, how I prayed that you would return to us." His father's voice boomed from the doorway as he entered the room, the sound thankful and hopeful at once.

"Captured. Taken. King."

" 'Tis all right now, Dev. The King is safe. The

plan worked. 'Twas brilliant." He could hear the pride in his father's words.

"The traitor?" Devlin croaked through his still dry throat. "Captured?"

"Aye." Will breathed heavily. Without knowing why, Devlin sensed no joy or relief coming from him. "We discovered the guilty party in the very act of meeting with the new leader of the rebellion."

"You took them both?"

"Nay. The leader escaped."

Devlin allowed the disappointing news to wash over him. The man was born of an eel, he'd wager, so slippery did he seem.

"And what has become of the man you captured?"

"Dead," Gowain answered, his expression filled with obvious spite and fury.

" 'Twas Marcus." Devlin narrowed his brow, confused. "Marcus betrayed us all." He thought of the groom who'd accompanied Henry to Ravenstone Keep.

Had he hefted the weight of twenty men on his shoulders, Will could not have appeared more weary. "Nay."

"Nay!" Lady Ravenstone cried, rushing to her feet. "Say it not. He isn't yet strong enough." Her husband's hand pressed upon her shoulders and guided her gently back to her seat beside the bed.

Devlin's eyes flew wide at the desperation in his mother's voice, sudden terror seizing his heart in evil premonition.

"Who was it? Who did this?" He sat up against

The Jewel and the Sword

his mother's efforts to keep him still. He needed to know who had lost his foolish, worthless life to the madness of treason.

Will stiffened as he looked at his cousin and liege, and then whispered a single name. "Allyson."

† † †

Devlin urged his charger through the Ravenstone Castle's portcullis without slowing the large beast's reckless pace. When he arrived inside the bailey, he reined in the horse until he skidded to a halt on the moist earth. He leapt from the saddle, dropped the reins, and stomped toward the hall.

In fourteen months he had discovered many things about his dear, late wife. Her treachery against the crown had been only the apex of a life steeped in crime and ambition. He'd learned she had more than one lover in her past. In fact, he'd discovered that the man behind the entire plot shared her bed as recently as the week before Henry arrived at Ravenstone. The same man who held and tortured him for those hellish days.

The same man he still could not find.

Ten days ago, he'd ridden from this very place with the purpose of discovering the man's identity, tracking him to hell if he had to, and cleaving the man's head from his body. But he'd failed.

Again.

The pain he'd grown accustomed to over the past months still burned. A pain named Allyson.

"Did you kill him?"

Devlin grunted at the sound of the familiar voice, but continued to march through the hall toward the stairs. His mood boded ill for anyone who crossed his path. Especially Will, who had taken it upon himself to visit Ravenstone Castle more frequently in the past several months. His presence did little more than annoy Devlin and remind him of how greatly he had failed his people. He never should have brought Allyson here. He never should have married the witch in the first place.

Like spears, Will's eyes focused on his back. Devlin could feel them as readily as steel. He stopped in the center of the hall, but did not turn. Will's bootsteps echoed toward him.

"It's not your fault."

Devlin knew without asking what guilt Will tried to erase. His duplicity, his stupidity, killed his own child.

"It is."

"How do you know she carried your child? How do you know it wasn't someone else's? How do you even know she carried a child at all?"

"I can feel it. A part of me is dead, Will."

Will sighed. "You have to stop blaming yourself. She did it all, Devlin, not you. She tricked you into marrying her. She slid inside all of our hearts like a serpent, watching and striking when she felt she could do the most damage."

" 'Twas my stupidity which nearly cost Henry his country."

" 'Twas Henry who approved the marriage contract. He knew who she was. Her own father was hung for treason. What of it? We all thought she was of a different heart. All of us. Not just you."

"But I convinced Henry to trust her. 'Twas I, and I alone, who promised him her fealty." Pain born of guilt and the remnants of love stabbed in the region of his missing heart. He ignored the impulse to clutch his chest and stiffened his spine against the attack. "Think you Henry will ever trust my judgment again?"

"Aye." Will closed the distance between them.

Devlin scoffed and made to turn.

Will caught his shoulder and held him still. "She's dead, Devlin. She cannot harm Henry, or you, anymore. You must cease this foolish quest to find her lover. You have grown obsessed. Your parents worry over you. Accept the fact he has disappeared. He may already be dead by another's hand."

Devlin pulled away and blinked back the weakness of his own tears. "Nay, Will. Someday, I will find him."

CHAPTER ONE
England – Spring, 1243

"There it sits, milord. Just waiting for ye." Ian Douglas sat atop his horse, inspecting the man beside him through half-lidded eyes. A sly grin etched his dirty, bearded face. "We've nae been ridin' hard for five days and nights to just look at it. Ravenstone's done this to his own, and ye should no' feel guilty about takin' what's yers."

"Do you think I don't know that?" Morven Barnett Douglas, Laird of Clan Douglas, snarled in reply.

Ian stared, eyes glazed with greed, toward the thick walls of Morven's former home. The tall, black walls made for an impressive profile against the gray sky. Sitting precariously on the edge of a cliff, the castle looked as if it would fall into the raging sea beyond. But he knew it wouldn't. He spat on the muddy earth.

THE JEWEL AND THE SWORD

Nearly impenetrable, the castle boasted only one entrance: a guarded portcullis.

Convincing the Douglas to raid the castle had been simple enough in the end. Ian had spent many months designing this raid and its certain effects on his own people. The death of Morven's father had been a catalyst he hadn't expected, but he'd used it well to his own ends. With the old earl dead, Morven had appeared more than eager to pay his homeland a visit they would not forget.

He hid a smirk as he adjusted his saddle in preparation for the attack. Devlin Barnett had taken his knights on campaign, foolishly leaving his home unprotected. Nay. Should he live a thousand years, there would never be a better day for this raid.

Finally, Morven stood in his stirrups and raised his sword above his head, releasing a fierce battle cry from deep in his throat. The column of horses and riders raced with breakneck speed toward the walls of the castle.

As Ian approached the solid walls, the sentry at the portcullis sounded an alarm. The gate creaked free of its restraints. Before it closed Ian jumped inside the outer defenses. Swiping his sword with practiced ease, he let the blade down on the single guard's shoulder. Instinctively, he closed his eyes. His blade found its mark. The warmth of blood on his cheeks soothed him. When he opened his eyes, the guard lay on the ground, his own sword only partly removed from its casing. He spat on the lifeless body. Gripping the heavy ropes attached to the gate, he pulled, clearing the way for his clansmen to follow him into the bailey. His attention shifted to his laird.

Morven rode like a man possessed. His face twisted with rage. His eyes reflected a wrath that could only be borne of hatred. The charger he rode matched his master's fury, stamping wildly at any unfortunate who crossed his path.

Ian smiled. Morven knew where to go, having been raised inside these bloody, English walls. Ian watched as Morven rode his destrier up the chapel steps and through the large doors.

Ian secured the gate open before turning his mount and following his laird.

His laird. He cursed to himself. He should be Laird of Clan Douglas. He would be Laird of Clan Douglas this very night.

"Ye!" Ian pointed his sword to one of his clansmen. "Find the Lady Ravenstone and bring her to me!"

He ignored the frightened pleas of the scurrying crowd. His clansmen herded them into a circle in the center of the bailey, as he made his way through the screaming women and old men toward the chapel.

Ian dismounted, dropping his leather rein. His blood seethed as he entered the dimly lit chamber, the sweet taste of victory hovering on his lips.

The jeweled sword.

It sat atop the altar, on display and unguarded. Like none he had ever seen, the hilt, made of gold and encrusted with gems from every part of the world, winked in the filtered sunlight pouring through the

THE JEWEL AND THE SWORD

stained glass windows. Pearls, rubies, and diamonds were set into the hilt and scabbard and even in the belt. It was worth a king's ransom, and Ian's mouth watered even as his fingers twitched to grasp it.

But more than gold and jewels, it held the power to slice through the heart of his enemies.

Morven, still seated upon his horse at the foot of the altar, stared at the sword as if he'd never seen it before. Ian grimaced. He'd never believed Morven worthy of such a prize. He believed it less now. The man oozed weakness. Morven's anger and thirst for vengeance were a boon only to Ian. But Ian harnessed the emotions. He breathed them in until his entire being thrummed with power. That very power cascaded through him now as he spoke.

"Take it," he growled.

Morven's body tensed, as if startled by the words. "Is all well without?"

"Aye. Now take the bloody thing."

Almost hesitantly, Morven reached for the golden hilt. When his hand clasped around it, his eyes fell shut. "When I was a boy, my father told me this sword was a gift from the Giants of the Northland for his bravery in battle."

" 'Tis only gold and steel."

Morven seemed not to hear him as he continued. "Then later, when the time for boyish fantasies passed, and I knew it had been a gift from the King, a human king, but king nonetheless, I loved him even more."

"Aye. And he betrayed ye. Denied ye."

Morven examined the blade carefully and then turned in his saddle to face Ian. "He loved Devlin more."

"'Tis not true, my son." Lady Ravenstone gasped. Ian spun sharply at the plaintive voice.

"'Tis true," Ian called toward her, approaching her with long, predatory strides. The heels of his boots echoed in the stone chamber like the bells of hell.

Ian watched the color drain from her face as she eyed the blade of his sword. Still covered with blood, it hung easily from his grip. He squeezed the hilt and raised it toward her face, twisting it so the light from the doorway reflected off the still-wet, life's blood of one of her own.

"Morven?" She whimpered.

"Enough, Ian."

Morven turned his anxious horse and approached them. His voice sounded tired. Good.

"We have what we came for. Gather the men."

"Why, Morven? Why have you hated us these many years?"

Ian grimaced at the weakness in the old woman's voice.

Finally, Ian witnessed the hate and anger he had spent years breeding inside Morven bubble to the surface. Morven's face twisted as he held the jeweled sword before his stepmother. "'Tis what bastards do, *Mother*. The day ye and my father tossed me aside was the day I vowed to hate ye forever."

"We never 'tossed you aside,' my son. You chose to leave, after . . ."

"After I was named a bastard instead of heir." Morven laughed, the sound hollow and without humor. "Aye, I left. And even the welcome I received by my true mother's people little quelled my fury."

Morven's mount stomped on the stone floor. A small shower of sparks shot out from the shod hoofs. "Once I married Elspeth, I believed 'twas enough to be accepted by the Douglas. But 'twas no'. The past still haunts me."

Once more, Ian hid a smile. He had never allowed Morven to forget the betrayal by his family. He fed the weeds of hate daily, as together they trained the men, making them as fierce as possible.

For this day.

For the day when their loyalty to Morven would give Ian the power he needed for this raid.

Morven, looking as if, were he pricked, regret would pour from him instead of blood, stiffened his spine and stopped the animal's nervous pacing. "I came for what should have been mine. 'Twas no' given to me, so I take it. Devlin can have the manor, but I *will* take this sword."

He placed the prize in a bag hanging from his saddle and urged his mount forward. Once his head cleared the framework, he and his horse leapt as one from the doorway, over the stone steps and into the bailey.

Lady Ravenstone turned to follow. Ian grasped her shoulder, forcing her to face him. A shiver of pleasure raced through him at the fear reflected in her tearful eyes. He longed to take her life, but refrained. He remained focused instead on his final goal. Killing Morven would have to be enough. He pushed her small frame out of his way and hurried to his own mount.

A cry from Morven's twisted lips told the clansmen the task was done and to make for the portcullis. Ian knew most of his clansmen had already fled, as he'd instructed them even before leaving Scotland. Those who remained fled the minute they heard their laird's cry of retreat.

Leaping into his saddle, Ian followed Morven out of the bailey. He laughed when one of the women behind him raised a hue and cry. The bulk of the Douglas's forces were well out of sight already. Ian and Morven rode side by side, their horses lathered and breathless from their exertion. Ian glanced back, the castle nearly a mile behind them now, and then shifted his narrowed eyes to his laird. Without warning, he lifted his sword and swung it down upon Morven's right shoulder.

Morven reacted instantly, blocking the blow with his own sword. Taken off guard, he was unhorsed after only a few, quick thrusts. Morven's arm bled where Ian's sword had found a gap in his armor. Ian absorbed the fear in his laird's expression as Morven scrambled backward, trying to avoid the next blow.

Ian made a move to dismount, then cursed. Shouts of alarm reached him through the early leaves on the trees. Several men, torn from their spring planting, had answered the hue and cry. He made them out through the branches, their faces set in determined lines. One or two opponents he could best, but there were too many. He cursed. He would be unable to finish what he had set out to do. Taking Morven's horse by the reins, he plunged into the forest.

At least he had the jeweled sword.

† † †

"Yer father's been captured!" Ian stormed into the solar, jerking Meghan's attention from the tapestry she'd been nervously stitching as she waited for her father to return.

"What?" She could feel the blood drain from her face just as the tapestry fell from her trembling fingertips to land silently at her feet. Mattie, her maid and closest friend, rushed to her side, placing her hand reassuringly on Meghan's arm.

"Ravenstone's men took him," Ian answered simply, as if that explained everything.

"And ye left him there?" The accusation was plain in her voice as her blue eyes narrowed toward her father's second-in-command.

"What would ye have me do, storm the keep alone? The others had fled. Nay, I'll no' take that risk when I promised yer Da I'd watch over ye."

The lustful gleam in his eyes made her shiver in disgust. Thank God, Mattie stood with her. She refused to think what might happen if she were ever alone in a room with Ian.

"I'll never marry ye, Ian." She stood and met his

hollow glare through sheer force of will, her heart racing in anticipation of his reaction. This topic of conversation never went well. "My father has no' decreed it, and as long as he is laird here, he will no'."

The furious outburst she had been expecting never came. Instead, Ian turned his massive back to her and moved with deliberate strides to the door. Without turning, he replied, "Yer father is no' here."

The door shut behind him, and Meghan felt her knees wobbling before Mattie lowered her back into her chair by the fire. "Dear God, he's right."

" 'Tis only a matter of time before Ian declares himself Laird of Clan Douglas." Mattie's voice, filled with fear, stated exactly what Meghan had been thinking. Ian and her grandfather were cousins, after all, and he was next in line.

Meghan patted Mattie's hand. She didn't know what she would do without Mattie for her friend. She relied on her for so much more than the services of a maid.

Mattie continued, "And he grows more forceful in his pursuit of ye, as well."

Meghan closed her eyes against the truth.

"He fails to understand ye do no' want him. Ye'd think after so many years, he'd learn it well."

"Aye," Meghan replied, pushing Ian's insinuations from her mind. "But I'm more concerned for Da. He's changed over the years since Mother died."

" 'Tis Ian's doing, milady."

Meghan stood and walked to the hearth, letting the heat from the fire warm her chilled bones.

"And now Da is held prisoner by that vile man."

"The Lord Ravenstone is that, milady. A monster from all I've heard."

Meghan released a quiet snort. "Ian is a monster. His hatred of my father's family is borne from a hatred of anything English." She paced away from the hearth to the window overlooking the tiltyard. "I'm no' naïve. I ken terrible things happen on both sides of the border. But for so long, Mattie, we'd lived in peace. Before Mother died." She wanted to stamp her foot. "I wish Ian had never convinced Da to go after that horrid sword."

Mattie approached her, wrapping her arms around her in a comforting embrace. "Do ye suppose we can get yer father back? Before 'tis too late?"

She shuddered at her next thought. 'Twas only a matter of time before Ian achieved his goal and became laird. He would try to rule her as well.

Worse, her father's unreasonable pride and Ian's unquenchable greed had placed them all in danger. From what she knew of her uncle, the Lord of Ravenstone, he would not take the news of this raid easily.

" 'Tis more than likely already too late, Mattie. If the stories we've heard of Lord Ravenstone hold even a feather's weight of truth, he already plans his revenge."

Meghan closed her eyes. Her father was held captive. Her life and the lives of her people were in peril. Ian's intentions for her were more than clear. It had been a very long time since Meghan had cried, and she hated the acidic bitterness rising in her throat.

† † †

"We were wont to put the man in the dungeon, but your Lady Mother insisted we keep him locked in his chamber, my lord, ever since the day of the attack. I am afraid his band escaped with your father's sword and scabbard." Oswald, the bailiff of Ravenstone Castle, followed Devlin through the feasting hall.

"I don't think he's listening, Oswald."

Will was wrong. Devlin had heard everything. He'd heard everything since he'd returned home, less than an hour before, to learn of Morven's raid. He heard the cries of his people as they mourned the dead. He heard the accusations in their voices when they greeted him upon his return. And he heard the guilt beating in the hollow of his chest.

Clenching his fists, which ached to destroy, he made his way toward the stone steps rising along the far wall. Morven reclined in one of the rooms above.

Fat as he pleases.

Devlin felt his face twist in disgust as he mounted the first step.

"Whoa, there." Will put a hand on Devlin's shoulder, with just enough force to spin him on the step.

Devlin did not speak. Instead, he looked at his cousin's hand, then raised his eyes to glare directly at Will's face. Only two years Devlin's junior, Will was nearly his twin in all aspects save one.

Temper.

THE JEWEL AND THE SWORD

"I don't think it wise for you to see Morven as yet. Take a few moments and put the events in perspective."

Devlin descended the step, placed his feet well apart, and folded his arms over his chest. "Three of my people lay dead."

And my family's greatest treasure has been stolen. As much as that bothered him, 'twas just a sword. Killing his people took matters too far.

"And what do you intend to do about it?"

Devlin's expression did not change. Will's comment, designed to make him think before he reacted, was well timed. Ever the cautious one, whether it be his emotions, battle, or selecting the right field to plant, Will acted now as Devlin's conscience.

"I'm going to *kill* Morven," Devlin responded plainly, shrugging.

"And this will solve what? You would enter into a border war over this?"

"Aye." He nodded, turning on the landing and mounting the steps again. The rage sweeping through him racked him to his core.

"And the sword?" Will's voice lowered at the mention of Devlin's father's prize.

"Make no mistake, Will. I will get it back."

Will sighed. "Well then. I suppose I'll have to go with you. You'll just get yourself killed if I don't."

When Devlin reached the door of his traitorous brother's chamber, Will only a step behind, he turned the key in the lock.

"Easy, Cousin. You don't really want to kill him."

"Aye, I do."

But heeding Will's advice, he took several deep breaths and ran his fingers through his hair before pushing the heavy wood away from him. "You wait out here."

He ignored Will's heavy sigh.

"Brother?" The deep voice came from the farthest corner of the room. Devlin turned to the sound and found Morven sitting in a cushioned chair before a well-tended fire.

Devlin did not answer, except to close the door behind him and stride across the room, his temper barely checked. Morven shifted in his seat to follow Devlin's movements. Pity he hadn't been killed during the madness instead of suffering what had amounted to a mere scratch when compared with the deaths of his people, according to Oswald.

"What have ye to say, Devlin? Nothing? That's no' like ye. I would think ye would be railing by now."

"You have made a grave mistake, Morven, harming these people. They have naught to do with our quarrel. These people have done nothing to you."

"Ye mean *yer* people!" Morven rose to his feet, raising one trembling hand to point at Devlin. "Say what ye mean without honey for my sake. They should be my people. Instead I choked on lies fed to me with a golden spoon and was cast aside like a hunting hound, too weak for the chase!"

" 'Cast aside?' You chose to return to your mother's people. At no time were you ever promised the title or the lands. You assumed too much. But Father never treated you like a bastard, and Mother treated you like her own despite her knowledge otherwise. Did you think the decision easy for her? Taking in her husband's by-blow? Yet you were always welcome here, and you knew that. Nay, you chose to stay away for nothing more substantial than wounded pride. And then you do this. Father barely in the ground, and you make war? A coward's war at that. 'Tis obvious I should have expected no less from you."

Morven's face contorted with rage, and he crossed the room in two long strides, throwing himself at Devlin's head. Morven swung his uninjured arm furiously, landing a powerful blow against Devlin's jaw.

Devlin reacted instantly, his movements honed by years on the battlefield, and knocked Morven to the floor with one neatly placed fist in his stomach. His blood boiled in his veins, and he dived onto Morven. He released his fury on his brother for another full minute before he heard a scream from the doorway, and several pairs of hands pulled him free.

"Now see, Cousin. I told you not to come up here. I told you to wait, but do you heed my word? Nay." Will stepped in front of Devlin, his equal height and weight making an effective shield for Morven.

Devlin's temper ached for release. His eyes darted from Will to Morven, standing offensively behind one of the guards, to his mother, who he hadn't realized stood in the doorway.

Lowering his head for a moment, he steadied himself

with a deep breath. When he spoke, the unquestionable authority of his title filled the chamber. "This man is not my brother and deserves no quarter from anyone here. Take him to the dungeon." Leveling a glare toward Will, he silently dared him to argue. Will didn't. The release of a heavy sigh spoke well enough to indicate Will's disagreement. "And prepare a garrison to ride. We leave at dawn for Scotland."

Chapter Two

An hour later, Devlin strode into the hall to partake of the evening meal with his men. A bath and a change of clothing had done little to improve his mood. He caught the sound of whispering females as he passed three serving girls from the village, their lust-filled gazes settling on him. Ignoring them, he took his place next to his mother at the high table. His father's chair. Nay, he reminded himself.

My chair.

The responsibility of leading these people weighed heavily upon him. He took it very seriously. From the time he'd won his spurs, he'd vowed to protect them. He'd failed them, and the bitterness slithered through his limbs like hell's own serpent. In the years since Allyson's treachery and death, he'd managed to come to terms with the fact he could change nothing of his past. The fact that even his sworn duty to protect Henry's lands had opened his home and family to an attack filled him with a heavy guilt.

But he was used to guilt. He'd allowed his lust for a woman he barely knew to influence him. He'd gone to Henry personally to beg for Allyson's hand, promising Henry the dowerless girl had none of her traitorous father's ambitions. When he'd met Allyson in London, just days after her father's execution, he'd let the dark beauty capture his heart. Her sad eyes fell on him in the marketplace, and he was lost. A fortnight later, he married her in Henry's chapel and brought her to Ravenstone. He'd brought the enemy through the gate and had given her the keys to a kingdom. Even now, the irony of his involvement in the ruination of her schemes made him weak.

Never again.

"I must speak with you, Devlin," his mother whispered, catching his attention with her secretive, frightened voice. "How did you know?"

"I'm hungry and tired, Mother. Please, do not speak to me in riddles." He was impatient, but met her eyes fully. He loved his mother above all else.

A frown crossed his features at the thought. She alone of all her gender had ever earned his trust.

"How did you know Morven is not your brother?"

He sighed. "What are you talking about?" He placed several pieces of pork on his mother's half of their trencher.

"You didn't know? But upstairs, you told your men the truth, you share no blood with him?" Her curious expression concerned him.

"I meant that but figuratively, Mother. He has not been my brother these past many years, and I merely put a name on it." He placed his eating dagger on the table, his eyebrows lowered in a scowl. "What are you saying?"

"Come. We must speak privately."

He pushed his trencher away with a heavy sigh. Hunger clawed at his stomach. Mayhap he could take his meal later, in his chamber. 'Twas just as well. Were he to eat now, the meal would sit upon his gut like a lodestone, more likely as not.

He escorted his mother to his counting room, since privacy could not be found in the full feasting hall. Placing his mother in a cushioned chair before the blazing hearth, he took the bench across from her.

Of all the rooms in his castle, or any of his many properties, this one held a favored place in his heart. 'Twas here his father sat Devlin upon his knees, preparing him for a future of service, protection, and right.

And I failed him.

He shook away the sobering thought and brushed a frustrated hand through his hair.

"Mother?" Devlin prompted, when she did little but stare into the fire.

She cleared her throat, as if she had something of dire importance to discuss, but did not raise her eyes from the flames.

"You know I have loved Morven like my own child

since his birth. And you know that he is not my child."

"Yes, Mother. 'Tis testament to your kind nature that you loved your own husband's bastard. It can't have been an easy thing, having lost babes of your own repeatedly."

"Morven was such a lovely babe. He was quiet and cheerful, and even when he was at that age when most children become selfish and horrid for a time, he never did. No, my son, Morven was very easy to love."

Devlin made no comment, sensing whatever was to be said was not easy for her. He hid the incredulous expression vying for escape at the description. Although he couldn't remember a young Morven, he suspected a child very different from the one she described.

"The violent angry man he has become is as much my doing as anyone's. You see, I harbored the lies with the rest of them."

The hairs on the back of Devlin's neck stirred as he realized she was not speaking of the lies he already knew. But more lies. "To what lies do you refer, Mother?" he asked, his voice cold, even to himself.

"It was not hard to love Morven because your father was never unfaithful to me. He did not dally with servants. We may have had an arranged marriage, but circumstances arose which made us fall deeply in love and we remained so these many years. You see, Morven is not your brother, at all."

"I am beginning to realize that, although I don't fully understand."

"God save me, but I do love you both. I suppose it is just as well now that you know the full truth. His true father was a peasant, the man of some lesser knight. This peasant did a great service to your father and died in the course of it." She shuddered and then took a steadying breath. "He left a young Scottish bride, heavy with child. Your father felt so indebted to the man, he decided to bring this child, should it be male, into his home to train as a squire. When the woman died giving birth, he chose to foster Morven instead. We both grew to love him and, well, time slipped away. Before we knew it, he was a man full-grown, still needing to hear the truth. When the time came to name an heir, we both knew we could not cheat you of your birthright. But, Lord Ravenstone hadn't the heart to disown Morven completely, and so the story turned still farther from the truth."

Devlin's hands itched as he wiped the sheen of sweat from his palms. Blood rushed through his temples. All images of his father, decent and honorable, flashed in his mind. He scowled. Noble intentions be damned. They had conspired together, all of them, ultimately destroying a man's reality. His life.

His mother wrung her hands in her lap, looking at him with moist eyes the color of twilight. He knew her well enough to know she feared what Devlin would think of his father. And Morven.

Finally catching his breath, Devlin questioned slowly. "You actually believed Morven would be satisfied, nay even grateful, in thinking Lionel his father instead of inheriting the manor?"

Devlin stood, every muscle in his body tense as a bowstring. He ran both hands through his hair and turned away, unable to bring himself to face his mother. "You took away his title, his land, and his mother, with one swift stroke, and you expected him to be happy about it?"

" 'Twas your father's decision, Devlin. I am but a woman. I had no say in any of it." He heard the defensive tone in her voice and sensed her straighten in the high-backed chair.

He swallowed, knowing she would continue with her sordid tale. "Go on." His mother's heavy breathing reached his ears.

"Then Morven decided to leave us. He simply couldn't bear the thought of not belonging to this family. He chose to go where he felt he had a greater bond, to his mother's people. We would have fought for him, but the Douglas welcomed him so readily. Very soon after he arrived there, he married the laird's daughter who bore him a child of his own. He is laird there now, as you know, since the Old Douglas had no living sons, and all seemed well."

Devlin detested the wry chuckle that escaped him as he spun on his heel to reply. "Well, apparently it wasn't. He has festered with this hatred of us for years. And as much as I have never liked Morven, I can certainly understand his loathing. He has believed he was deceived, and rightly so, even more than he knew. And that hatred alone is what has brought us to war." He

The Jewel and the Sword

stepped in front of her, gripping the chair on either side of her. "War, Mother. Don't you see? I cannot allow him to attack and steal from us without retaliation. It would be an open invitation for anyone to attack us. And for what? For lies." He pushed off the elegant piece of furniture, its very richness a reminder of all Morven must feel he'd lost.

"Morven is but a misguided man. He is not evil. You must let him return home with the promise he will return what he has taken."

"I will do no such thing, because he will do no such thing. This isn't a child's feud. You cannot mend this with sweetmeats and pastry. He will not agree to return the items to me. I will go after them in the morning as planned. When I return with the sword and scabbard, I *might* set him free. But he is not to know that. I want him to believe he will be lucky to see the light of day again."

"But that is malicious, Devlin. You can't mean to be so *cruel* to your own brother."

"As you have said already, Mother, he is not my brother."

† † †

Silence, save the crackling of the fire and the occasional groan from the hounds asleep before the hearth, echoed in the nearly empty hall. Most of his men had retired to their beds with willing companions. He should probably do the same, he thought, taking a large sip of ale.

"I thought I might find you here."

"What do you want," he asked Will over the rim of the cup.

"I spoke with your Lady Mother. She is concerned for you." Will threw one leg over the bench on the opposite side of the trestle table.

Devlin raised an eyebrow. "Make yourself comfortable."

"My thanks, Dev. I knew you were pining away down here, alone, just hoping for someone to talk to. Figured I'd make myself available."

Devlin growled. "What did my mother tell you?"

"Everything."

"So you know that bastard upstairs had his entire life stolen from him?" He took another sip of ale.

Will reached for the pitcher and poured a cup for himself. Devlin took the pitcher from Will and refreshed his own cup.

"Aye. Nasty business, that."

Devlin sighed. "I suppose I understand my father's reasons for what he did, but not his methods."

"You must have known something was amiss. How could a child be reared in a household full of gossiping women and dispassionate men and never hear the word *bastard*?" Will asked, his eyebrows raised.

"I never gave it any thought, Will. We were but children when he left." He pushed himself away from the table, the legs of his bench screeching on the hard floor. "It matters naught now."

What mattered was the Douglas had crossed the

border and raided. What mattered was three of Devlin's own serfs had died because Devlin had failed to protect them.

A legacy of lies.

An ancestry of deceit.

And for the price of a golden sword, Devlin would make war.

† † †

Meghan looked out the window of her solar and scanned the horizon.

Nothing.

Turning, she crossed back to the fireplace and stirred the flames. They needed no tending, but she had to do something.

Anything. This endless waiting would drive her mad.

"Milady, this constant pacing will wear straight through the fine floor cover yer father purchased for ye. 'Tis been nearly seven full days, and nothing has happened."

"Nay, Mattie. 'Tis a vile hatred these men share. A raid will mean only one thing. War." Meghan made her way back to the window. The dawning rays of the sun finally peaked over the trees. She squinted into the glare.

"Mattie," she called, sucking in her breath and placing white-knuckled hands on the cold stone window ledge. "They come, Mattie. Too many to count. Quickly, we must warn Malcolm."

She took Mattie's hand and tore from the solar. They ran as swiftly as they could down the long hallway to the stairs. She raced down the steps, lifting her skirts to her knees, and screamed for the quartermaster.

"He's here, Malcolm. He approaches from the east."

"We know, my lady. We have sent riders to meet him. Ye must hie yerselves to the cellar, but quickly."

"I'll not hide in my own home, Malcolm."

The old man grinned at her despite the desperate hour. "Ye've the look of yer mother when ye get yer dander up, dearest. But I am afraid ye must. If Lord Ravenstone breaches the outer defenses, he'll come for ye, for certain."

"Ye will go to the cellars, woman. Now." Ian marched into the room, followed by several of his fiercest fighters, his personal guard.

Meghan sneered at them, no more than thugs and criminals, the lot of them. Her father had never allowed Ian to bring that sort of mercenary into the keep. It only proved how badly Ian hoped her father would never return.

"Come, milady. Please, do as he says," Mattie whined. Meghan stiffened herself against the plea.

Mattie feared Ian. Meghan did as well, but refused to show such weakness when her duty to protect her clan clamored for attention. Her back straightened further, even as her insides quivered.

He moved to take her by the arm. She flung herself away with a hiss.

"Never touch me, Ian. I've said that before." To

Malcolm she answered, leveling an icy glare at Ian, "I'll go to the cellar for yer sake, Malcolm, and no other."

Ian followed her to the scullery door, catching her shoulders from behind. Pulling her against his wide chest, his mouth but a hair's breadth from her ear, he whispered, "I will touch ye when I please, Lady Meghan, and soon. I *will* have my fill of ye. Do no' mistake me on this."

Revulsion shivered down the length of her spine. Bile rose to her throat when she felt the moist heat of his tongue trace her earlobe.

She swallowed deliberately. She would not cower before him. Pulling away, she spat, "Do ye no' have a keep to defend?"

Hiding the hesitation crawling through her, she faced him with her shoulders back, her chin held high.

"Aye, milady. I have *my* keep to defend."

Malcolm gasped at the traitorous words. Not surprised by Ian's bold claim, Meghan signaled Malcolm to be silent.

"My father will return to us, Ian. Ye will never be laird here."

"I am already laird here," Ian replied. The smug confidence sat upon his shoulders like a mantle.

"Tell the clansmen ye declare their laird dead, Ian. Tell them ye would rule us." While several of the clansmen would have no dispute with it, most of the men were loyal to her father. She saw his understanding as the color first drained, then rose high in his cheeks.

"In time, Meghan. In a very short time."

† † †

Devlin rode his black charger, Midnight, at the head of the attacking column. The men followed him without question, many from the experience of battles already won, which had proved their leader vigilant and wise. He did not look behind to make sure they followed. He didn't need to.

Will raced by his side, his own horse blowing in the cool air of dawn.

"Is that Roger of Downsworth?" Will cried above the thundering hoofs, narrowing his eyes in the direction of the oncoming forces.

"Aye," Devlin spat.

"He's one of your favorite people, isn't he? Since you bedded his wife?"

Devlin glared sideways at Will. With an uncanny ability to see humor in nearly any situation, Devlin sometimes admired the skill. But not today. The presence of Roger of Downsworth meant only one thing.

Mercenaries.

These were not Douglas clansmen. These were men who lived to fight for any cause, or none at all, if they were paid well. He knew the Douglas clan would prepare for retaliation, but he hadn't realized Morven had such a large following, or enough coin to buy one.

A trap.

The sobering thought shot through his mind.

Devlin's horse stomped and struck at the enemy, his

The Jewel and the Sword

breath leaving trails of mist in the cold air of the dawn. The horse reared, but Devlin remained in the saddle as his mount twisted and attacked anew. He and Will hacked their way through the seemingly endless barrage of rivals. By the time he passed the gate, he felt more confident. This may have been a trap, but he and his soldiers verged upon taking the keep. Quickly, he urged his horse over the rough, uneven ground of the bailey.

A deafening thunder sounded around him. He turned in his saddle, his sword at the ready, and searched for the source of the noise. From each direction around the castle itself came reinforcements. He cursed. *Where the devil had Morven come by such a force as this?*

"Jesu, Devlin. Where have they come from?"

"Hell," replied Devlin.

"What do we do?" Will asked him, his voice serious.

"Go back. Tell the men to retreat. They are well trained, but no mortal man can be expected to best these kinds of odds."

Devlin scanned the bailey and peered through the gate as best he could. Each of his men was set upon by at least five opponents. He had to think of his men's safety. His father, God rest him, would not want any more lives lost for an object, regardless of its value.

"Aye, Will. We leave." He confirmed the order, more to himself than Will, whose charger had already turned to carry him back to where the bulk of the men defended themselves. Bile rose in the back of his throat at the very thought of retreat.

Devlin continued to fight several opponents until he saw his forces making their escape. He turned Midnight's head in the direction of freedom.

A sharp, burning sensation rent his left side. The impact threw him from Midnight's high back to the hard earth below. He looked into the midday sky and saw only the silhouette of a man with a sword standing over him. By the looks of him, he was a Douglas clansman, and not one of the paid mercenaries. 'Twas the only reason he still lived.

In the distance, he could hear the portcullis gate creaking closed. He prayed all of his men, those that still lived, had escaped. Then he watched as the sun's rays dimmed above him, and the world went dark.

Allyson's black heart, his own heart ripped from his chest, leaving a hole devoid of breath, of life. Betrayal. He could not go back. He would not go back. He had spent too many months trapped in that emptiness. How had he been returned to the hell of that existence? Allyson was dead. She was dead and could not work her witch's magic on him again. He had seen her in death and was free of her forever. And never would he allow a woman that close to him again. He had vowed he would never again forfeit his heart.

† † †

"How long has it been, milady?" Bonnie, a maid of no more than ten summers, asked Meghan.

Meghan turned to face the child, whose wide blue

eyes spoke her fear even more plainly than her quaking voice. Her gaze then crossed over the fifteen women hiding in the cellar with her. Each of them expressed the same fear so clearly written on Bonnie's young features.

"These things take time, Bonnie," Meghan answered, hoping her smile did not tremble.

"Do ye ken they've come inside the walls?" another maid asked.

"Mayhap, but I do no' ken they've entered the keep. Fear no'. The Douglas men shall defend us to their dying breaths."

She prayed silently for her words to be more than a naïve wish. Her father's men were well trained, but her uncle was the King's champion. Ravenstone's forces also held the advantage of experience. On the other hand, Ian had supplemented their side with enough men to guarantee superior numbers.

Still, the waiting wore on her nerves as the distant sounds of battle made their way closer to the keep.

For probably the tenth time in as many minutes, she climbed the steep wooden steps and reached for the bolted latch. She hated not knowing what was going on as much as her maids did. But the fight seemed to be waning now.

Chewing her bottom lip, she debated whether to open the cellar door.

Mattie pulled at her skirts from the cellar floor. "Nay, milady. What if *his* men have come inside the keep?"

Caution for the maids with her in the dank space

won, and she retreated down the steps again. "I suppose yer right, Mattie," she replied, unconvinced. What was happening? Why hadn't Malcolm come for them?

Finally, when no sound of violence had reached her ears for several moments, she could stand the suspense no longer. With bold, determined strides, she climbed the steps a final time. She opened the cellar door cautiously and peered into the scullery.

"There is no one lurking, Mattie. Wait here, and I'll see what is about," she whispered.

Mattie and several of the other maids urged her again to stay in safety. She smiled reassuringly at them and exited the dark, damp space.

The fire in the scullery hearth had been extinguished as a precaution against disaster, so little light shone through the room. Only the sun peering in the high windows helped her see where she walked. She moved stealthily toward the hall, praying again that she would find only her own clansmen inside.

Just as she peeked into the hall, Malcolm collided with her, catching her about the shoulders. His face was flushed with excitement. His old eyes danced in the afternoon light.

"My lady, the intruders have been vanquished." He smiled at her as if he had slain them personally.

"Thank God." She hugged her dear friend. "But we must see to the wounded immediately. Have those unscathed bring the less fortunate into the hall." She moved to the cellar door and lifted the heavy wood. To her ladies, she added, " 'Tis finished, lasses. Come out

The Jewel and the Sword

now. Bring my herbs and bandages. I fear we have many wounds to dress this day."

As her father's soldiers brought the wounded inside, she determined who were the most seriously injured. She was well accustomed to treating a myriad of injuries, since she'd spent many happy days following her mother from house to house, helping her tend to the clansmen's various wounds or illnesses. Upon her mother's death she had assumed the responsibility. This day would be no different.

But how she hated it. So much blood.

She swallowed past the bitterness rising in her throat as she set about the long task of putting her father's men back together. Disgusted by the waste of so many men for naught more than glory and greed, she grit her teeth to the task.

Four hours later, she finished stitching the cheek of a young clansman. She released a deep breath. 'Twas the last. Most of the maids served the evening meal. It had been a very long day, and she wanted nothing more than to slip into her bed and sleep.

A quiet moan caught her attention. She listened carefully, trying to ascertain its source. The sound reached her ears again, and this time she recognized it clearly. Her head turned in the direction of the front doors.

'Twas the sound of a man in pain.

CHAPTER THREE

A man lay across the steps. Nearly dead.

Meghan immediately knelt beside him and lifted the blood-encrusted hauberk from a raw, festering wound. Beginning just under his ribs on the left side, it laid open an expanse of flesh half the length of her forearm. Wincing, she dropped the torn mail back in place.

The sun rested low in the sky now, but for hours he had been subject to its brutality as he lay alone in his suffering.

She eyed his mane of dark hair, neatly cut to his shoulders. His square jaw fell slack as he slept, his closed eyes fringed with thick lashes the color of new wheat. Beneath his hauberk, he wore a padded tunic of deep blue. The stitches spoke of pride in the hands of his tailor. Fine leather formed his heavy boots.

THE JEWEL AND THE SWORD

He wasn't one of her father's men, of this she was certain. And his rich attire did not indicate he belonged to the hideous collaborators Ian had invited into her home. Nay, this man came from wealth and could only be one of Ravenstone's number.

He moaned again, and his head shifted against the steps as his body shook in agony.

"Why was this man not treated among the first!" she yelled inside to several men with superficial scrapes to which she'd already attended.

If she didn't act quickly, he would die. She didn't know why this possibility disturbed her, yet letting him die seemed somehow . . . wrong.

Six men, ranging from newly baptized to battle to seasoned warriors, answered her call.

"He's one of Ravenstone's men, milady. The invaders," answered the eldest and fiercest of the group.

"I do no' care who he is, he is still a man." Meghan knelt at his side to further inspect the oozing gash, several ghastly inches in length. It had stopped bleeding, the edges raw and dirty.

Ian's rough voice cut through the still air of the bailey. "Let him die."

He towered over her as she knelt beside the stranger.

"I will no' let him die, Ian," she defied, spitting the words through her teeth. "He looks important. He is likely one of my uncle's captains and could be ransomed for my father. Help me get him inside."

The crowd surrounding them grew. Meghan

watched as her father's loyal clansmen came to see what was happening.

"He is no' worth the effort."

She raised her voice as she glanced at the ever-increasing audience. "Ian! Would ye toss aside a chance to reclaim yer laird?"

He fell silent for a moment. She recognized the brooding, thoughtful glint in his eyes. He debated her hidden challenge. "Nay. I would no'!"

He'd spoken loud enough for everyone to hear, and then knelt beside her, pressing his bulging frame against hers.

"Yet," he whispered.

Her mouth dry, she ignored the frightened paralysis suddenly making its way through her limbs.

"Take him inside," she ordered with more confidence than she felt.

Two men-at-arms removed his hauberk, and between them lifted the warrior's battered body. He winced on the very edge of consciousness. Were he awake, the pain would be unbearable. She followed the awkward movements of the men as they struggled to carry the large man through the keep.

She found Mattie spreading fresh rushes on the floor.

"Mattie? Find Elaine. Have her fetch fresh water. I've used the buckets she brought earlier. And more bandages. Then bring my herb bag and follow me. It should still be on the table in the scullery. Be quick about it."

"Who is that, milady?"

"A soldier. I do no' ken who he is. Go, please hurry."

Mattie scurried away to do her bidding as Meghan quickened her steps to follow the men up the stairs.

She hoped her skills alone were enough to save the man. She couldn't allow him to die. He was perhaps her only chance to get her father back. She loved her father greatly, but she needed to ransom him quickly for the sake of her people as well. 'Twas only a matter of time before Ian gained enough power by working his convincing plea over the clansmen. If he wanted to be laird, she knew he would be.

Ian's ability to sway others to his will astounded her. Most of the clansmen would remain loyal to her father in their hearts, but they were simple farmers. When faced with a powerful leader such as Ian, would they have the strength to resist him? And the garrison of soldiers under her father's command. How many of them had already sided with the current, if not official, leader? She knew of several, including Raibeart and Ailean, who would forever defend her father's rights. But with the influx of renegades and the banished of neighboring clans, she suspected Ian already had the power he needed to make a legitimate bid for her father's chair. And if she were, through some miracle, able to keep him from wooing her clansmen into acceptance, he would take it by force.

"Where should we place him, milady?" Raibeart asked, his breathing labored under the weight of his burden.

She thought for a brief moment. "My father's chamber."

"Nay!" her father's men balked in unison. "No' the Douglas's bed."

"Aye. 'The Douglas's bed'," she mimicked. " 'Tis the closest, and I want this man alive. Ye must hurry."

Several arguments followed, but in the end they heeded her word and brought the man to her father's chamber.

"Lay him there, on the bed." She stepped out of the way to give them access. Her eyes widened. At least a head taller than her father, the man's booted feet barely managed to stay on the bed, while his head brushed the wood of the massive headboard. Other than Ian, she'd never seen a man quite so large.

"Ye may go, now. Please leave one guard on the door," Meghan instructed.

The man groaned, drawing her attention to him as if he'd called her name.

With trembling fingers, she began to undress him. She stopped and shook her hands to suppress the shaking. She'd never before experienced nervousness while treating a wound. Yet, the prospect of this man's death loomed over her, and she suddenly believed herself inadequate.

Nonsense.

'Tis a man with a sword wound. She'd treated dozens in her life. This would be no different.

She removed his boots, making a mental note they would need cleaning before he could be allowed to wear them in the keep.

If he recovered. The omen threatened to obscure the tiny shreds of hope she'd found in the presence of this stranger.

Determined to succeed, she removed the remains of his clothing, save his trews. Her movements were quick, sure. Unwilling to let the virility of this man deter her, she ignored the obvious power he possessed, even as he lay perfectly still.

Her fingers itched to trace the lines of his strong jaw, the finely formed fullness of his lips. Even his brow spoke of superiority in his bearing as his forehead knotted in a wave of pain. The muscles of his legs, outlined by the tight fitting breeches, tensed and appeared ready to defend their master even in sleep. Suddenly self-conscious at the direction her thoughts were taking, she wished the maids would arrive with the water. She would be less tempted by his masculine perfection with others in the room.

She grunted, trying to remove his tunic. Thank goodness someone had seen fit to remove his mail before he had been brought inside. She decided finally, since the expensive, deep blue tunic was ruined anyway, that she would simply have to rip the remainder from him. She grasped the shreds of fabric near the wound and tore it away.

Her breath caught in her chest as her eyes roamed the most perfect expanse of male beauty she had ever seen. Though paled from pain and blood loss, his flesh promised a rich, sun-kissed bronze when he regained his strength.

Trying to keep her mind solely on the task at hand, she scolded herself. She had seen men's chests before, of course. She'd seen the men working in her father's fields. She had tended to guests' needs when she and her Lady Mother welcomed them into their home. But never had she been affected by a man more so than at this moment.

"Here's water, milady." Mattie set a bucket of water on the floor next to Meghan's feet and looked up. "Oh, my . . ." she breathed, the meaning of her astonishment obvious to Meghan.

So, 'tis no' only me. He truly was beautiful.

She narrowed her brows. "That's quite eno', Mattie," Meghan commanded, clearing her throat when she realized it had gone dry. "This man is injured and may no' recover if we do no' act quickly. We will need to clean and sew the wound carefully if we can even hope he will live. *Ye* are going to help me."

"Aye, milady," Mattie responded, without taking her eyes from the man in the bed. Not until this moment had Mattie's penchant for distraction ever irritated Meghan. Her friend's constant perusal of the man's unclothed form, however, irritated her beyond words.

Doing her best to ignore Mattie's sidelong glances toward the handsome knight, Meghan picked up a coarse cloth and moistened it in the bucket. Dirt crept through the cut's raw edges. She winced on his behalf as she scrubbed the mud and oozing poisons away from the wound.

Please, do no' awaken now.

When the wound appeared as clean as she could manage, Meghan mixed a poultice meant to heal torn flesh.

When Meghan finished closing the wound, she applied a thick slathering of the Yalluc blend to the cut. "I'm afraid he's too heavy to lift, Mattie. Ye'll have to roll him toward ye, so I can slip the bandage beneath him. We'll bring it out the other side and secure it in the front."

Mattie grasped his shoulders and did as instructed.

Meghan gasped.

"Milady?" the maid asked curiously. "What's wrong?"

Meghan took a step backward and covered her open mouth with a trembling hand. Old scars riddled the man's flesh, from the base of his neck to the small of his back.

Mattie craned her neck over the man's shoulder. "Good Lord, milady. What happened to him?"

She steadied herself, but her voice remained barely above a whisper as she replied, "He's been flogged, Mattie. The poor man."

Meghan could no longer resist the temptation to comfort him. The knowledge these scars were years old relegated itself to the back of her mind. She traced a path over the puckered flesh. She whispered, more to herself than to Mattie, "How can a man be made to suffer so grievously?"

Her heart wept for him, for the pain he must have endured, pain no human should ever have to suffer.

Inhaling deeply in an attempt to settle her stomach, she reached for the clean linen. "I'm sorry, Mattie. He must be heavy." She pushed the bandage under him, allowing Mattie to drop him gently to the mattress.

"Why would a knight be treated so horribly, milady? I wonder what he did to deserve such an awful beating?"

"No one deserves such a beating," Meghan chided. "Nay. This man has been tortured."

"Oh, my."

"There. That should do." Meghan sighed as she finished wrapping the bandage around the man's chest. Hints of bronzed flesh beneath the pallor caused by his wounds contrasted with the muted white of the bandage.

"Help me straighten the bedclothes, Mattie, and then if ye would, please, tend the fire. We need to keep him as warm as possible."

Now that they were finished, Meghan found herself mesmerized again by the sculpted planes of his jaw and cheeks. She'd yet to see his eyes, she realized, and wondered what shining color they might be. Dark, like his hair, or bright, like a moon hidden among the branches of a tree? Her fingers itched to move a stray lock of his hair from his forehead, for no reason other than to feel the tendrils between them.

"Milady? I'll watch over him," Mattie called from the hearth.

Meghan's mind snapped out of its reverie. She turned to leave, though she did not wish to. Her soul wept, begging to remain by his side.

He is the enemy. He will get my father back for me. For the clan.

"Of course, Mattie. Thank ye. Call me if he wakes." She couldn't stop herself from pausing by the door for one last look at her prisoner. "Or if he worsens."

She closed her eyes in a silent prayer. *Let him live!* She didn't know if she prayed for her people, herself, or her father.

Or him.

† † †

Meghan did not find sleep. Her bones ached as she lay among her fur blankets, exhausted. But it wasn't the ache of exhaustion keeping her from slumber; it was the longing in her heart. Each time she closed her eyes, she saw the prisoner as he must look in life.

Virile.

Powerful.

Wielding his sword above his head, a battle cry on his fierce lips. Galloping toward his rivals with a cry of, "Vanquish or die!"

Nonsense.

She rolled over, determined to put the stranger from her mind. He was a tool. That was all. And what's more, he was the very one she would see vanquished. And, she suspected, he would like to see her defeated as well. She must remember that. The foolish cravings of her body were fanciful dreams, nothing more. She closed her eyes again.

Stubborn images!

She threw the covers off and slid from the bed. Pouring herself a cup of mulled wine, she tossed the soothing liquid down her throat, hoping to assuage the restlessness inside her. She sighed, glancing toward the door. While soothing her body, the wine did little to settle her mind. At this rate, she'd never fall asleep.

Mayhap she should verify his well-being? Surely, once she convinced herself he would recover, so that she could trade his miserable life for that of her father's, she would then be calm enough to sleep.

Aye, she but worried for his welfare. And the impact his health would have on her father's release, she amended quickly.

If her father even lived. She hugged herself as she stood looking out her chamber window.

She took a step toward the door and stopped short, making a fist to keep herself from reaching for the latch.

She shook her head. Mattie sat with him. She would cry out if aught were amiss. Wouldn't she?

Of course she would. Unclenching her fist, she returned to her bed.

Climbing back amongst the covers, she lay on her back, with both hands flat upon the bed at her sides, and stared at the blank darkness of the canopy. Slowly, she began to relax. The wine wound its way through her, until finally her lids drifted closed.

A shriek and the sound of something heavy crashing to the floor rent through her chamber. Instantly alert, she instinctively ran to her father's room.

The Jewel and the Sword

The dark chamber, lit only by the dying fire in the hearth, appeared much as she had left it, except her maid's forearm twisted in the iron fist of the man in the bed. The table holding her mortar, pestle, and herbs lay on its side, and the yalluc poultice she'd brewed was smeared across the rush-covered floor. His eyes were open and the crystal blue orbs flashed fire and ice, but she could tell they witnessed nothing. His mind moved in another world, but his body posed a deadly threat in this one. A low growl came from his chest, the rumbling nearly shaking the earth with its vehemence.

"No!" Meghan screamed, and placed herself between the man and the guard as she realized her clansman intended to kill the prisoner to release the maid. "Nay, he does no' ken what he does." She turned her attention to the man, more powerful than she could have imagined.

" 'Tis all right, my lord. We'll no' harm ye. Release the lass and return to yer slumber. Aye, Sir Knight, just let her be now." Meghan knew she sounded foolish, talking to a wounded, attacking warrior as if he were a pup or a babe, but she hoped the soothing sound of her voice would put him more at ease.

It took several minutes of coaxing, but he did release Mattie, who dashed out of reach.

"I do no' ken why he behaves so, milady," Mattie cried. "He slept soundly but a few moments ago."

Slowly, he laid his head back upon the pillow. He reached his strong hand toward her face.

Mattie tried to pull Meghan away from the bedside.

"Ware, milady, he means to do ye harm now."

Meghan gently shook her off. He touched her lips with the tips of his fingers. Hard and callused, they branded her with tenderness. His flesh felt warm.

"Nay, he makes no move of violence now."

Still, she made no move of her own, lest he perceive a threat and renew his fight.

His hand fell to his side, but his eyes held hers for a brief moment before the heavily lashed lids drifted closed. His breathing returned to a ragged cadence.

Meghan released a whoosh of breath she hadn't known she'd held. "He sleeps again."

She spread the twisted bedclothes evenly about his frame. In the process, her hand brushed against his flat, muscled stomach. Snatching it back, she moved it to his brow.

The unfamiliar urgency of panic surged through her.

He burned alive with fever.

CHAPTER FOUR

"He's burning unto death, Mattie. Why did ye no' summon me?"

"I did no' ken he fevered, milady," Mattie explained.

Of course she wouldn't. Unless she'd touched him, and Meghan preferred to think her maid hadn't been exploring the man's body. No matter how great a temptation he presented for that very activity.

She urged Mattie toward the door. "We must have cold water, straight from the well, Mattie. And the feverfew from the cellar. I'll need more yalluc as well. And ye must hurry," she added when Mattie did not respond quickly enough.

Meghan rushed to the hearth, moving the kettle of water she'd left hanging there over the dying embers.

She stirred the blackened peat until a small flame caught, and then placed more fuel beneath the kettle. In moments, a roaring blaze heated the water.

Where was Mattie? How long had she been gone?

She rushed back to the bedside, ripping the heavy blanket from the man's restless limbs. He lay naked before her.

Her eyes fastened on his masculine parts, nestled in a bed of curling dark hair. She tilted her head, certain she must be imagining the size and shape of . . . it. She'd seen men's parts before, in her role as clan healer. But never one quite so . . .

Large.

Her breath left her. She quickly covered his midsection with a square of muslin, lest Mattie discover her ogling his naked form. Instead, she busied herself putting the table to rights and wiping the spilled poultice from the floor. She placed her mortar back on the table, even as her eyes moved stealthily back to the muslin hiding him from her view. She knew well enough what a man's parts were capable of, though as a maiden and a lady, she'd never experienced the act of physical love. In fact, she'd never before even known the desire for it. But when she looked at him, she felt the fingers of temptation whisper up her spine. What would it be like to be loved by a man such as this? She imagined him as virile in the act of love as he had been in the act of war. Heat suffused her cheeks, as she forced her eyes away again before she succumbed to her curiosity and lifted the muslin away.

"Here, milady. 'Tis straight from the well as ye requested."

Mattie's voice stole into her mind and ripped her from her lustful thoughts.

Meghan spun around and took the bucket of frigid water from Mattie, hoping the heat in her cheeks was not visible to her maid. "My thanks, Mattie," she whispered. "Will ye tend the kettle and let me know when the water boils?"

"Aye. I placed the herbs ye wanted on the table, there."

Meghan nodded her understanding and set about the task of lowering the man's dangerously high fever.

Using a soft cloth, Meghan bathed the man's entire body with it. The first icy contact brought groans of agony from the knight, who tossed his head viciously upon the pillow.

"I know, it hurts, it does. But 'twill help break the fever," she cooed to her patient.

"The water boils, milady," Mattie called from the hearth.

"Here, Mattie." She handed her maid the cloth and sat her next to the bed, the bucket of water at her feet. "Ye continue to bathe him, whilst I brew the tea."

Meghan mixed the feverfew with some of the boiling water, stirring for a moment, and then covered the cup with her hand. The steam rose up through her fingers and burned them, but she merely sucked in her breath, refusing to let the heat escape. After a few moments, she checked the brew and, satisfied she'd allowed the tea to steep long enough, carried the cup to the bed.

She lifted his head with one hand, alarmed by the dry heat coming from it. He groaned again, and she imagined his entire body ached with the fever. She touched the cup to his lips. As the hot liquid trickled past his full lips, he coughed. The droplets slid from his mouth. She plied him again. This time several precious drops fell into his mouth, and he swallowed.

"We'll have to keep trying, Mattie. He must drink the entire cup as quickly as we can get it down his throat," she whispered.

"Aye, milady," Mattie answered.

"There ye be, my lord," she whispered when he managed to swallow another few drops of the healing mixture. " 'Twill make ye well again." She added under her breath, "I hope."

"I told ye to let him die." Ian's voice penetrated the darkness like a dagger in her back. The hair on her arms twitched.

"Be gone from this place, Ian. I will no' let him die."

"Ye have need to obey me, woman." Ian stepped closer to her, indicating to Mattie with one hand she should leave the room.

If Meghan usurped the silent command and insisted Mattie remain, Ian would undoubtedly punish Mattie for it. Meghan watched her leave the chamber. The thick air choked her lungs with each breath. Darkness crept over her, darker still where Ian stood by the door. He crossed to her, slowly, like a cat stalking its prey.

"What do ye want, Ian?" Meghan placed the still

full cup of feverfew on the table.

His eyes narrowed, the deep creases shadowing his forehead making him appear sinister in the firelight.

" 'Tis no' yer concern what I want, Meghan. Ye knowin' I will get it, 'tis all that matters to me."

She sighed. She should be afraid, but exhaustion stole the fear. He could terrify her tomorrow. "I ken ye wish to rule the clan, Ian. I ken ye will do whatever ye must to achieve it."

"Aye. And this man steps in my way."

"I will save him, Ian. Ye will no' take this chance away from us." She turned to bathe the man's brow with cool water. "What do ye ken the clansmen would do if I told them of yer plans?"

"They are a simple lot, Meggie. They would no' believe ye, a mere lass, over me, their leader."

She considered his words for a moment. The clan might not believe her yet, but Ian's pride and anger would cause him to make a mistake. And when he did, she would be there to see him fall.

"Get out, Ian. Ye've no business here," she replied.

The guard she'd posted outside the door, a man she knew loyal to her father stepped inside. "Is aught amiss, milady?"

"Aye, Raibeart." She straightened her back and peered at Ian. "Lord Ian was just leaving and can no' seem to find the door."

Ian sneered. "Have yer way now, lass. It will no' last forever," he said, before turning away and leaving the chamber.

"Raibeart," she commanded in a hushed whisper, "make certain only those loyal to yer laird guard this man's bed."

"Why, Meggie? Has Lord Ian threatened ye, or the prisoner?"

"He means to rule us, Raibeart, and would kill this man easily eno' to suit his purpose."

Raibeart's expression grew hard. His jaw clenched as he looked toward the door through which Ian had just left. "Aye, milady. I ken ye have reason to fear for him then. Only myself, Moan, or Ailean will guard him. Ye have my word."

"My thanks, Raibeart." Meghan smiled, as she turned her attention back to her patient. "In this man's life lies our only chance to see yer laird returned."

"Aye. We'll no' let Ian have his way. There are many of us still loyal to yer da."

Meghan hoped Raibeart's confidence rooted itself in truth. If not, Ian could very well destroy them all.

† † †

Ian slammed his cup on the scarred table. Several drops of ale flew from it to land on the back of his hand. Lachann, captain of Ian's personal guard and most trusted ally, eyed him in silence. The rest of the patrons in the dark tavern minded their business or played with the serving wench. A peat fire offered little light, and Ian liked the shelter offered by the shadows. He was in no mood to be recognized or questioned tonight. His mind focused on one problem, and one problem alone.

Ravenstone.

The man was ever a thorn in his side. He should slit the bastard's throat while he slept. How had he survived? Ian had seen Lachann's blade meet its mark during the battle, seen the blood spill from the cracks in Ravenstone's ruined armor. Any other man would be dead now, not fighting through a raging fever.

"What will ye do?" Lachann pressed him.

What could he do? Meghan held the favor of the clan. Morven could very well return at any moment, should Lady Ravenstone's weak, charitable heart decide to release him. Nay, he would bide his time. As much as he would like to kill Ravenstone now, he would wait until more of his clansmen sided with him. When he had the support of the majority of the clan, he would purge the clan's memory of Morven as if he had never existed.

And then he would renew his bid for England.

The long dead Lord Reginald and Ian had spent many hours perfecting their designs to remove Henry from power. They would have succeeded had it not been for the old lord's love of whoring. In a fit of drunken lust, Reginald had bragged to some wench of his traitorous desires, and she'd promptly turned him over to the royal guard. Only his refusal to divulge Ian's name had saved Ian from the hangman's noose as well.

After his execution, his daughter, Allyson, had begged for the chance to avenge her father. His expression moved from grimace to smile. Young

Ravenstone, the perfect besotted fool, had actually loved the whore. It had been Ian's idea for Allyson to marry into the house of Ravenstone, a favorite of the King. Allyson had protested, of course, but in the end he had had his way. He always did.

And soon, he would be in a position to see those old plans renewed. He would be Laird of Clan Douglas, married to Meghan, and in favor with the very King he would see denied. He would unite the Lowland clans until he gained the power he needed to rule the whole of England, and then he would tame the Highlanders as well. The entire island would be his, and his alone.

Then, he would finish young Lord Ravenstone.

"What will I do, Lachann?" Ian smiled. "I will kill him."

† † †

Devlin dreamt he was dying. Not only was he dying, but he died by the fires of hell itself, racked by the torture and pain of a thousand Hades. His body ached. Unable to move, he suffered with the soreness of his muscles. The forsaken feeling of being trapped flashed unbidden through his memory.

Nay!

He remembered vague images of his death. Betrayal. A flashing sword. Left for dead amongst the fallen. Calling for help with no voice.

And then heaven.

An angel had come for him. An angel with streaks

of gold in her red hair and a voice sweet enough to soothe the most jaded of souls. She must have changed her mind about taking him to heaven. As soon as she looked into his eyes, she had bid him leave her, relinquishing him to the fires of Satan.

Thirst. He was so very, very thirsty. He tried to move his hand across his lips, but he failed.

Trapped. The worst hell of all.

† † †

Meghan hadn't left the knight's bedside for three days. Despite her knowledge of healing and herbs, she'd not been able to break the fever raging through his body like a fire out of control. He slept unnaturally deep, and his breathing became shallow, often ragged. Every hour she removed the bandage and applied more of the healing poultice meant to repair torn flesh, and every hour she renewed her prayers he would survive.

Though the oozing from the wound had lessened over the past days and the healing herbs seemed to be working, his fever had yet to break.

Her fears worked on her mind like a distilled spirit, convincing her that her father's life lay entwined with the man who burned under her fingertips. If she failed to save him, she knew her father would die. Terrified by the thought, she spoke. "Mattie, please boil water for tea."

" 'Tis no use, milady. Ye've put eno' feverfew into him for five people, and still his body burns."

"I do no' care. Please, just do it. If he dies—" She choked back a sob. "We'll have no chance for the return of yer laird. My uncle is a beast. Ye've heard the stories as well as I have. He would blame us for this man's death. He may even kill my father."

"Oh, milady." The pitiful set of her maid's features made Meghan want to cry. Meghan did not want pity. "Mayhap, Laird Douglas is already dead. What will we do?"

"Nay, Mattie." Meghan rushed to her feet, her voice firmer than she'd intended. "He is no' dead. I will no' believe it. We will get him back."

Trying to regain her composure, Meghan reclaimed her stool beside the bed. Something about her prisoner, just looking at the firm muscles beneath his flesh, which promised a deep bronze once he recovered, fostered in her a sense of peace. She felt her limbs relax as she nurtured him.

Running the soft, wet cloth across his bare chest and arms, she wondered again who he might be. Was he a high-ranking soldier, or perhaps a soldier for hire, or even a close friend of her uncle's? And if so, why would he be left behind? Might he have been too far inside the walls for them to reach him during their retreat? Did they believe his wounds had been mortal? The rules of war were beyond her understanding as much now as they had always been.

Sighing, she moved the cloth up to the man's arms, stretched taut from one side of the bed to the other where her men had tied him. She had adamantly refused when Malcolm first suggested the idea. But Malcolm's tone moved from suggestion to insistence. He'd argued that the man's fever alone could very well cause him to become violent again. He was also an enemy of this house, and she had been forced to admit Malcolm's logic held some validity. She finally, reluctantly, saw his reasoning and allowed the leather bindings to be fastened to the man's arms and legs. She reached for the ointment she'd mixed to soothe the chafes encircling his wrists. He had struggled against the straps many times in the last few days.

As she spread the ointment over his skin, still hot but not emanating the ferocious heat of the previous days and nights, she couldn't help but admire his sleek form. She took up the cloth again. Muscles, corded from what she was certain had been years spent training with a sword, rippled provocatively under his flesh at the slightest movement. He was a beautiful man for as much as a man could be beautiful, all raw power and inherent grace. She bathed his legs and torso, and between his legs. Her hands trembled slightly as the sight of his naked masculinity generated forbidden thoughts.

"Milady? Is all well? Ye've stopped bathing him."

Meghan sputtered, " 'Tis fine, Mattie."

She tried to think of this man as her patient, her prisoner, but the more intimately she bathed him, the more his wounded soul moved into her heart.

† † †

The fires receded. Hell didn't seem as hot as before. His thirst still waged war upon him, however, and he found it difficult to swallow.

His eyelids heavy, even his lashes aching, he tried futilely to open them. He could feel the soft caress of a woman's hand on his chest, and he groaned at the familiar pleasure. The last thing he needed right now was another pain, but the touch devastated him. His body responded of its own accord. The hand left him, and he sensed the loss to the very core of his being. Waiting impatiently for the gentle caress to resume, his reward instead involved an amount of water forced down his throat. He shook his head and sputtered, finally raising his lids in defense.

Two delicate hands, red and chafed, were raised above his head, wringing a cloth over his mouth, letting the excess water drip onto his slightly parted lips. What felt like someone trying to drown him was actually a woman trying to satisfy his thirst. He opened his mouth, allowing the cool moisture past his cracked and dried lips. When the droplets stopped coming, his brow furrowed in confusion, and he turned his head in the direction of his obvious savior.

"Yer awake." The woman's voice sang, barely above a whisper.

'Twas she. The angel from his dream. His fingers itched to trace her lips. How did he know they would feel like rose petals beneath his fingers?

Am I? He mouthed the words, but no sound escaped his lips.

"Do no' try to speak. Yer still weak, but yer safe eno'. So rest now."

When Devlin came awake again, the shadows in the room had moved. He sensed the lateness of the hour. The woman he had seen earlier sat beside his bed with her head on her arms. He vaguely remembered seeing her that morning, her red hair an explosion of riotous curls in the morning sunlight. Now it shone a burnished mass of red, gold, and amber in the fading twilight. He reached for it, unable to resist feeling it slide though his fingers. When his arm did not respond, he assumed he must be dreaming her again, so he tried once more to reach toward her. His arms were willing to respond to his commands, but could not.

He snapped up his head, ignoring the throbbing pain that shot through his neck, and saw the leather bindings holding him fast. He kicked his legs and found them bound just as securely. Anger surfaced inside him like none he'd known in years. He fought against his bonds. He grunted as his immediate panic subsided, and he tried using a slow, steady force to free himself, to no avail. He pulled at his legs again.

No use.

Devlin kicked and thrashed, his temper hiding the painful burning where leather met flesh.

His angel awoke.

Throwing her small weight over him, her surprisingly strong hands pushed against his shoulders.

"Stop, ye must stop!" she cried, just as an armed guard entered the room.

"Get off of me. Release me!" Devlin growled between gritted teeth as he continued to pull on the leather straps.

"Nay. Stop before ye injure yerself. The bindings will hold, but yer stitches will no' if ye insist on thrashing about."

The scent of roses came from the woman's hair, filling his lungs. Her breasts pressed against his naked chest as she fought valiantly to hold him down. The longer she held him, the more his body craved her warmth. He wanted her. Cursing silently toward his own traitorous body, he tried once more to free himself.

His side throbbed. His body ached as if feverish. He could never tear the leather straps in his condition. Reluctantly, he settled himself into a quiet, but ready position on the bed.

"That's better, my lord." The girl pushed herself off his chest, leaving cold emptiness in her wake. She immediately checked the bandage on his side. "Good, the stitches held fairly eno'. But the less we have of that sort of behavior the better."

She scolded him?

The pulsing in his groin did little to ease his mind as he watched her. In any other place, in any other time, the thought of having this woman control him, with complete access to his body, would please him. But now was not any other time.

"Why am I bound?"

† † †

The Jewel and the Sword

Meghan's heart raced as his penetrating blue eyes remained fastened upon hers. The deep tenor of his voice alarmed her. It reminded her of the forest in the fall, dark and despairing. She swallowed as its richness washed over her. Maintaining eye contact with him proved more difficult than it should have.

She'd lived among warring men her entire life, and she recognized the barely checked violence in his expression.

Her heart pounded so loudly she feared he could hear it. The simple act of speech seemed impossible. Clearing her throat, she found the voice she used with the servants.

"Ye were a danger to yerself and others. Ye attacked my maid whilst ye slept, and I feared for yer wounds." There. She'd said it without swallowing her tongue. 'Twas a fair eno' beginning.

"Am I still a threat that you refuse to loosen me?"

Suddenly, she believed him more of a threat than ever before. "Aye," she answered firmly.

"And where, exactly, am I?"

She didn't know where she found the strength to answer him. She only knew this man would not cow her.

Straightening her back, she replied, "Yer in my home. I expect ye to behave accordingly. If the decision to release ye is made, ye'll do well t'–"

"If?" He interrupted her well-rehearsed speech. Without raising his voice, he was able to cut her off as effectively as if he had bellowed from a mountaintop.

"Aye. 'If.' Who ye are and yer relationship with Lord Ravenstone are of great importance to me."

"Who are you?" He growled so deeply in his throat she couldn't be certain he'd spoken aloud. *He is no' a very pleasant man.*

"I am Lady Meghan Douglas. Ye are my prisoner. Now give me yer name." She leaned over him and placed the back of her hand against his cheek. His fever had broken, thank God.

"Nay."

His answer was firm, resolute, as he pulled his face away from her touch. She wanted to stomp her foot. "What do ye mean, 'nay'? Ye have to give me yer name."

"Nay. I do not."

Meghan watched his pulse beat steadily in his jaw, and the rise and fall of his breathing. She must be very careful with this man. She was suddenly thankful Malcolm had insisted he be bound.

"Sir Whoever-ye-are," she began. "In order for me to effect yer release, ye need to tell me who ye are and yer relationship to Lord Ravenstone. 'Tis the way these things are done."

"You hold knights for ransom often, do you? I would expect such from the daughter of a *Scottish* laird."

The words were a curse. Meghan's heart fell in her chest, the beating suddenly sluggish, as if it would stop altogether.

The man turned his head to peer at the leather straps on his wrists. He shifted his eyes, looking at her sideways. She shuddered. His sober gaze screamed vengeance. She liked him better when he thrashed and railed without thought. The promise of retribution in his silence frightened her.

"I'll have some broth brought to ye," she stated firmly. "Mayhap ye'll feel more cooperative once ye've broken yer fast."

An excuse. She only knew she had to quit the chamber before she cried in front of this man. For days she'd studied his closed eyes, ringed by thick lashes, the planes of his cheeks, the taut muscles of his shoulders and arms. She realized she'd built this man into a noble and proud creature, determined to make him her hero.

'Twas absurd. In service to her uncle, the knight, by his very choice in company, could not be trusted. She refused to meet his eyes as she turned and left him alone in the chamber.

She would have no problem remembering his true nature in the future. No knightly savior, he.

He despised her.

† † †

Devlin gritted his teeth as the door swung closed.

His head fell back onto the pillow as he cursed himself a fool. He'd been captured by a woman. A beautiful woman who, despite his convictions otherwise, tempted him.

Morven's daughter.

You are a fool.

Flashes of memory rushed into his mind. He'd thought her an angel come to claim him. He laughed. He could still hear her voice, purring just on the other side of sleep, urging him to wake. He had no indication of how many hours, or even days, he'd been racked by fever. He only knew she had been with him. She'd nursed him. Even sung to him, he suddenly remembered. She'd plied him with sweet, life-giving water. She'd bathed him with soft fingers, stroking him, teasing him to life.

He closed his eyes as his body betrayed him, hardening in response to the memory of her touch. Unable to wake, he'd suffered in silence.

Nay, not suffered. He'd relished the beauty in her hands. He'd reached for her in his dreams. Comfort. Kindness. An angel.

He cursed again.

She was no angel. More likely, she was Satan come to tempt him, to torture him yet again. He'd learned his lessons well, tutored by the demon's darkest minion. He would not succumb to the temptation again.

Meghan Douglas, with her soft eyes and fiery hair, would see him defeated. The spawn of his enemy, of hell itself, she would weave her magic around him, killing him as surely as an arrow to the heart.

He opened his eyes, scanning the chamber for anything he might use to aid his escape. She could not keep him bound to the bed forever.

When he was free, he sneered, Meghan Douglas had best prepare herself for his wrath.

CHAPTER FIVE

"He's verra comely, is he no'?"

Mattie pulled the brush through Meghan's hair with practiced strokes before she replaced it on the table.

"Aye, that he is," Mattie replied, separating Meghan's hair into three thick strands and plaiting them down her back.

"And my heart simply breaks for him. He is a verra bitter man."

"Well, milady, he did wake to find himself bound and held for ransom."

"Ow!" Meghan's head snapped back.

"Sorry, milady."

"Of course, I ken he would be upset by it, Mattie. But I suspect 'twas more to his violence than he would have us believe. He was . . . frightened."

"Och. Great, fierce knights are afraid o' nothin'." Mattie pulled one last time and then secured the bottom of Meghan's plait with a small leather loop.

Meghan's brow knotted as she considered the words. " 'Tis what troubles me. He was so very threatened, he could no' hide it. He expressed himself with anger, though I still noticed the fear."

"Do ye ken it has aught to do with the scars on his back?"

Meghan pushed the curtains out of her way and climbed into the large bed. "I suppose a beating like that would put scars on yer soul as well as yer flesh, Mattie."

"Ye fancy him, do ye, milady?" Mattie's lips parted in a knowing smile.

Meghan's mouth came open. "Nay, Mattie. He is an enemy of this house. I am but curious."

Mattie laughed. "I do no' believe ye, milady. No' one whit."

On a sigh, Meghan answered, " 'Tis no matter how I feel. His loyalty lies with Ravenstone. 'Tis obvious for a garden stone to see."

"He's a man. A comely smile or two, an' he'll warm up to ye."

Meghan gasped. "Mattie!"

Mattie laughed again and then placed Meghan's gown into the trunk at the foot of the bed. "Ye ken 'tis true. Do no' be actin' so surprised with me."

Meghan's expression fell. She did know it to be true with most men. She snuggled lower under the fur throw. It seemed less than fair she should find a man

THE JEWEL AND THE SWORD

her heart reached for, only to have him spurn her very existence.

Heavy bootsteps echoed in the hall outside her chamber door. Her skin crawled as she recognized the prowling cadence.

Ian.

The steps slowed by her door and then stopped. Meghan tensed, her flesh turning cold. *What does he want?* But she knew the answer. He wanted her. Would this be the night he took what he wanted, her wishes be damned? Panic rose in her throat, cutting off her air as cleanly as if Ian's own rough hands pressed the passage closed.

The steps resumed, moving faster as they faded into the silence of the night. She closed her eyes in a silent prayer of thanksgiving to whatever angel had saved her.

"Are ye well, milady?" Mattie's hand on Meghan's shoulder startled her.

"Aye," she stated with a confidence she did not feel. She sat on her hands to hide their trembling.

"Ian will no' be kept at bay overlong. Especially with yer Da away."

"I ken yer right, but my father will come back soon. Fear no'."

"Do ye ken Lord Ravenstone will trade yer bonny knight for him?"

"Oh, he has to." A tremble of panic tore through Meghan's joints. "Why would he no'?"

Mattie shrugged. " 'Tis beyond my simple mind, milady."

85

Meghan fell silent, pulling the bedclothes to her throat as she lay back against her down pillow. She watched Mattie tend the hearth before climbing onto her pallet by the fire.

She'd never known a life other than this one. How quickly everything could change. Her father, always strong, had protected her. Now, 'twas her responsibility to protect his home and people.

Did she do the right thing?

Would her uncle release Morven in exchange for the unknown knight?

"Are ye going to discover what he's sore afraid of, milady?"

"What?" Meghan's voice caught in her throat.

"Yer knight? Are ye going to find out why he's sore afraid?"

Closing her eyes as sleep approached, she whispered, "I'm going to try, Mattie. I'm going to try."

† † †

Ian kicked the hound lounging before the fire. The animal yelped and then ran toward the opposite brazier. He leaned his hands on the mantle, his muscles coiled and tense. He'd nearly ruined everything.

Taking Meghan before his plan was complete would not gain him praise in the eyes of his clansmen. His body pulsed and throbbed with wanting. But he would take her soon.

As his wife.

Lachann approached from the scullery, his expression serious. "My lord, the dispatch has been sent as ye ordered."

"Good."

"Ye made a very good case for yerself, Ian. Henry would have to be mad no' to grant yer requests."

Ian snorted. He needed no praise from Lachann. His captain but made to assure himself a continued place at Ian's side. If he continued to serve him well, he would keep it. So his flattery served no purpose.

"And what of Lady Meghan's messenger?"

"He has been . . . er . . . detained." Lachann grinned.

"Very well."

Ian allowed the comfort of his coming success to ease his knotted muscles. He left Lachann and retired to his chamber in the north tower.

He struck a flint and lit several candles placed around the room. He moved to the farthest wall, where he opened the crude trunk hidden in the shadows.

Desire and greed flowed through him as he pulled the jeweled sword from its hiding place and held it in both hands, like a babe. He pulled the blade from its sheath. The gems winked at him in the candlelight.

"Ye and I will rule this place, will we no'? And with Ravenstone and the Douglas gone, no one will dare question us."

† † †

Devlin pretended to sleep, but he knew the moment

someone entered the chamber. By the time the presence reached his bedside, he knew who claimed his company.

Meghan Douglas.

She hummed a soothing lullaby. The scent of roses reached him as she bent to remove the bandage from his side. He inhaled, silently, deeply, against his own mind. Damn him, but he could not resist.

Then she touched him, and he nearly came undone. Her hands, warm and soft as a kitten, sent traces of fire through him, settling in his loins. The inability to shift his weight heightened the sensation, until he thought he might burst.

The bandage removed, she applied a poultice to his wound. Since the day before, the throbbing had lessened and the pain was nearly gone. Whatever the sweet smelling mixture, it healed him.

"There we are, my sweet knight." Her voice, like a songbird in spring, shattered him. His heart raced in his chest.

She tucked the bandage beneath him, using the same strips of muslin to tie it securely in place. " 'Tis healing well, Sir Knight," she mused with a sigh.

The sound pained even his armored heart, so full of longing was it.

Nay.

He would not fall into the same vile pit of deceit. Allyson had been kind and innocent too. At least on the surface. He had but to scratch that pristine covering to find the truth of her–a festering wound of immorality and hate. Months of interrogations in London had brought him the truth. Never faithful to him, even in the time before their marriage, she had spread her traitorous wings in more than a few bedchambers to gain the information she needed to continue her father's schemes.

The bitterness had lessened over the years, or so he'd thought. Meghan brought the same stirring in his blood that Allyson had. But this time, he prepared himself to withstand that part of him that answered to lust. He would not be subjected to the will of a woman again. They all played their games of seduction for the purpose of gaining what they wanted. They took without giving anything in return, and he would not fall for such lies. He wished his flesh felt the same.

" 'Twill make yer journey home possible, my lord. If no' for my father, I would wound ye again." His body stiffened at the threat. He hoped she didn't notice the slight twitch of his jaw.

"Then ye would no' leave me. Ye'd be forced to stay, so mayhap whatever demons hound ye could no' find ye."

Her warm hand trailed fire over his chest. When he felt her soft lips press against his own, he could no longer control the trembling she wrought through him. She removed her lips with a surprised gasp. Her breath touched his face, and he knew she hovered only a scant distance above him. Apparently convinced he still slept, she kissed him again. His arms screamed to hold her. His body ached to have her. He swallowed a moan.

She left him spinning in the words she'd whispered and the torment of her kiss.

A part of him threatened to call after her. As desperately as he wished to hate the woman, he recognized the longing in himself as well. He pushed down the traitorous thoughts. He but needed a woman to bed. Once free of this vile house, he would find one and quell the betrayal of his body.

† † †

"Are ye going to give me yer name today, my lord?"

"Nay."

Meghan walked into the chamber with a bowl and towel in her hands. Her mind raced with images from her dreams, and her heart fluttered in her chest, like a bird with a broken wing. His image had tormented her throughout the long night, and she realized, with a sigh, he meant to continue the foul treatment this morning. She was determined, however, not to sway in her mission of mercy.

She steadied her hands through sheer force of will, spreading her lips in what she hoped was a cheerful smile. "Never mind then. I have sent a letter to Lord Ravenstone, just the same. I'm sure with the description I provided him, he'll know ye. He can no' have so many braw men in his camp."

The man didn't answer. Instead, his gaze seemed to follow her every movement. Try as she might, she could no longer keep her hands from trembling once again.

"Ye know, Sir Knight. I'm no' so wicked as ye might think."

A grunt. *Well, 'twas something.*

"I can no' go about calling ye 'Sir Knight' either. So if ye will no' give me yer name, I shall name ye myself."

She thought she caught the slightest twitch of his eyebrow. Untying the muslin that held his bandage in place, she made an exaggerated show of thinking aloud. "Let's see now. Aigneas? Nay, there is very little 'holy' about ye." She could feel the muscles in his torso thicken as they slid beneath her fingers.

"Mordag? I can see ye upon the sea." She shrugged, moving to the table to mix more yalluc poultice for his healing wound. She said nothing aloud, but she was well pleased with his progress. The stitches were ready to come out, and the torn flesh would be healed completely within a few days.

She bit her lip at his continued silence. His ripped heart might take a bit longer.

She turned her gaze in his direction, watching him all but pout amongst the bedclothes. His chest rose and fell in a regular, deep rhythm, ever increasing in speed the longer she toyed with him.

She snapped her fingers. "I have it!" she squealed. "Oighrig. 'Tis perfect. 'Tis Celtic . . . it means . . ."

"I don't care what it means," he screamed.

She stifled a grin. "Why, whatever is amiss? Ye have said ye will no' provide me with yer name, and I meant only–"

"Those are women's names," he growled.

She schooled her features to reflect amazement where none existed. "Are they now?"

"You know very well."

His full lips twitched as his pride seemed to suffer overmuch from her game. She knew he barely controlled his temper and wondered why he would do so, based upon his behavior just yestereve.

Eno' games.

"Very well . . ." She applied a fresh bandage, salved with newly mixed poultice. "I shall call ye Brandubh."

She didn't know why the old name suddenly appeared in her mind's eye. Mayhap she thought too much upon her uncle and her knight's association with him. Mayhap his dark hair and sun-kissed flesh, when put into company with his brooding nature, made her think of it. Either way, *black raven* fit him well, and Brandubh would have to do.

Devlin grimaced as his loins ached. He'd remained hard for days, as thoughts of Meghan invaded even his dreams.

"Greetings, Brandubh," she called to him from the door. "How fare ye this morning?"

Tied to a bed with a sword gash in my side and a fire in my trews.

Still, her smile almost soothed him. He frowned in

response, hoping his scowl would warn her from the chamber.

It did not.

She placed a hand upon her curved hip and tilted her head. Radiant curls fell across her shoulder, teasing one breast as they trailed a blaze of fire to her waist. "What face is this? 'Tis a beautiful day, my lord."

He couldn't stop the grunt from escaping. Did she forget his humiliation each time she tended him? He twisted his hands into fists, noticing the softness of the saffron she'd placed over the chafes on his wrists.

Nay. She remembered. He'd awakened two mornings past to find someone had fastened the comforting strips around not only his wrists, but his ankles as well. The lingering scent of roses upon the bedclothes told him it was she. He cursed at the direction of his thoughts, renewing his defenses against her. His scowl deepened.

She hummed the same lullaby he'd heard her employ previously.

"Stop that."

"Oh my, the fierce warrior has found his tongue."

Her use of the word "tongue" made lustful images course through him, awakening every part of him. He knew exactly where his tongue could be found, and where to place it to make a woman scream his name. He wanted to taste her sweet nectar as she writhed in passionate abandon and . . .

He closed his eyes against the images she'd created and cursed as his body throbbed against his will.

She is the enemy.

"I can't help it, Brandubh. 'Tis one of my favorite tunes. My mother used to sing to me—"

"Don't call me that. 'Tis not my name. Must you speak at all?"

"Of course, Brandubh. 'Tis the only way to make one's wishes known."

"Then I speak. Loose me."

He stiffened as she kneeled next to the bed and unwrapped his bandage.

She sighed, her shoulders moving slightly. He closed his eyes, unable to withstand the twinges shooting through him by her mere presence.

"Leave."

"Nay. I must remove the stitches. The wound is nearly healed."

"I would have you leave it be and release me, my lady. I care naught if the wound heals."

Her even, white teeth bit into her lower lip as she concentrated on her task. With eyes narrowed against the tiny threads, she used the tip of a knife to cut them away. She ignored him, and he realized suddenly how much that fact irritated him. Worse, she kneaded the flesh of his side with her soft fingers, which did far more intimate things to him than irritate. He liked the feel of her hands on his body, and he hated himself for it.

"Do not think to ignore me, woman," he growled, raising his head and neck from the pillow and straining to see where she worked her fingers over him.

"Be still, please, lest I make a mistake and drive this blade into yer side." A raised eyebrow indicated the level of her determination.

Like a child chastised by a parent, he felt her glare rake over him. What was it about this slip of a woman that made him feel like an untried boy? He narrowed his brow, indignant in the fact that she spoke the truth. Did he not relax and leave her to her task, he might very well cause himself further injury. He put his head back upon the pillow and heaved a sigh.

"Fine. Complete the act and leave me be."

"Only a few moments more, my lord," she smiled. "Now lie still, like a good little knight."

Good little knight?

He but needed one night of her naked body stretched easily beneath the weight of his manhood, and he would show her exactly how inadequate a description she'd just delivered. He gritted his teeth against the thought.

Nay. He'd be better served to put such thoughts out of his mind and remember instead the center of her loyalties. Born of Morven Douglas, her heart no doubt harbored the same black seeds of hate as her father's. Allyson had proved this to him; hate was hereditary. He needed no more lessons.

Still, when she had removed the final stitch and applied a freshly salved bandage, and he knew she would touch him no more, something inside of him missed her contact. He missed the tendrils of her hair falling over him as she worked. He inhaled deeply the scent of roses enveloping him like a caress.

He closed his eyes.

Go. Leave me in peace.

† † †

Meghan ignored the surliness of his manner as she pulled a chair from the hearth and placed it by the bed. His eyes came open and his brow knotted as she did so.

"What are you doing?" he asked, as if she held a pot of boiling oil above his head.

"I am moving this chair so I may sit with ye." She placed herself in the newly positioned chair to punctuate the remark, placing her palms flat upon her thighs.

His eyes widened and he scowled. "Whatever for?"

"I thought ye were mayhap lonely. 'Tis unfortunate ye are so far from yer home and family. Would ye like to talk about it?"

"Nay." He turned his face away. But not before she caught a glimpse of what could only be horror cross his firmly set features.

Men. Her father was ever reluctant to discuss his feelings, or anything that might lead him to admit he felt anything at all.

Apparently, this stranger shared the trait and would guard his heart as well. The very mention of a meaningful conversation terrified him. Mayhap another tactic would lead her through the postern gate of his heart.

"Why do ye take this arrangement so personally? Yer well fed. We have saved yer life, with every intention of returning ye to yer people." She hoped the cracking in her voice wasn't as obvious to him as it was to her at the mention of his leaving. "I had hoped ye would no' take this personally."

He faced her again, his scowl creasing his forehead ever deeper. "You hold me prisoner. You torture me with incessant chatter. You are a veritable pest at best, my sworn enemy at worst, and you ask 'why' I take this to heart?"

Her lower lip quivered. Standing, she turned away, hoping he hadn't seen his effect on her. Pretending to tend the fire, she stirred the peat, even as a new flame caught, sending its soothing warmth over her breast.

"I do what I must."

"I'm certain of that. All women are selfish by nature. Certainly, you are no different."

She swallowed. The comment stung. *A woman had hurt him, though that hardly explained the marks on his back.* Whoever she was, Meghan was not she and deserved none of his rancor.

"I am no' selfish, Brandubh." She ignored the huff of breath he released at the use of her name for him. "I do this for my clan. Yer Lord Ravenstone is a vile man. He holds my father prisoner, for naught that was his fault. 'Tis one of the clansmen who made my father attack Ravenstone Castle. I would but try to set all to right."

"Then your laird deserves not the title."

"He is a good man," she retorted, stamping her foot.

His gaze turned ever darker. "You are a fool. I

know Morven Douglas, better than most. He is a murderer and a thief."

"Nay. He is kind and good, but misguided. I fear for our clan should he no' be returned to us."

"He will not be returned."

How could he be so certain? Could it be possible he was not close enough to her uncle for Lord Ravenstone to be swayed into releasing her father? In the days since Ravenstone's attack, she'd been so preoccupied with thoughts of her comely knight, healing him in both mind and spirit, that she'd never thought of the possibility he might not be worth the price of her father's freedom.

" 'Tis unacceptable." She puffed up her chest. "Ye do no' understand the consequences. If I do no' get Laird Douglas back soon, Ian will claim the clan for himself. If ye had even the slightest heart inside yer miserable skin, ye'd help me . . . write to yer lord and make him accept the trade."

"Is that why you've been so 'kind' to me? Let's forget I remain tied to this bed, your prisoner, these many days. I'm not daft. I know why you saved my life. You will receive no gratitude for it. But to try and ply me with kind words and tender touches?"

Her heart fell at the insinuation in his roughened voice, even as she remembered the taste of his lips.

"Nay. I but tried to make ye comfortable."

He scoffed. "You but tried to make yourself comfortable. You tried to confuse me with your soft hands and the scent of roses. I am stronger than you are, woman. Your tactics are lost on me."

She wanted to throw something. "Yer as black-hearted as ye appear, my lord. If my uncle refuses to trade ye for my father, if my father is no' returned to me . . ."

"What? Speak. What will you do?"

He challenged her. She could see it in his eyes. He dared her to say the words.

Clenching her fists, she refused to succumb to the blackness surrounding this man. She had thought to relieve whatever demons fought for his soul, but he was beyond saving.

She would not bend to his darkness.

Without speaking another word, she turned and strode quietly from the chamber.

† † †

Ian paced through the feasting hall, one large fist pounding into the other. As the clansmen filed into the chamber, he stilled and faced them squarely. From her position on the tower stairs, neither Ian nor any of the others knew Meghan watched in secret.

She recognized many of the men as simple farmers from the village. But most of the faces were new to her, or at least she'd only seen them for the first time since the raid. They were Ian's men, brought to back him in his bid for the clan.

When the room filled to bursting, Ian stepped in front of her father's chair.

"Laird Douglas is dead," he cried, bringing immediate silence to his audience.

"Nay," a man from the village shouted. "We have no proof of that."

"If he is no' buried on Ravenstone land now, he soon will be."

"How do ye ken that, Ian?" another man shouted.

'Twas only two opposing him thus far, but 'twas something.

"The man above stairs, the one Lady Meghan would save to trade for our laird will no' serve that purpose. I saw the Douglas fall with mortal wounds. Make me yer laird, now. Before King Henry decides yer fate for ye."

This bold claim brought a chorus of dismayed shouts from the men.

"What has Lady Meghan to say of it?"

She stepped from the shadows and approached her father's chair. A tense silence followed her through the room, until even the crackling of the fire seemed louder than thunder.

"She says no," she called. "The knight above stairs heals well. He will suit my purpose, and I will bring yer laird home. We've received no notice of my father's death. Until we do, we must assume he lives and breathes. Ian would lead ye to the depths of hell for his own purposes."

Under her breath, she added to Ian, "Do ye want war this night, Ian? Get ye gone from my house, or I will set the entire clan upon ye."

He growled low in his throat, sending a cold fear down her spine. He would try nothing here. Not in front of the clan. He needed them on his side.

"This is no' over, Meghan. Ye'll see."

Her clansmen, loyal to her father, ushered Ian from the hall and his followers with him. Afraid her knees would buckle, she sat in her father's chair.

"Do ye really think yer father lives, Meggie?" the baker called from the head of the celebrating mob.

"Aye, Peter. I do," she answered him.

I must.

† † †

"Och, milady. He's in a foul temper this mornin'." Mattie returned to the hall, her soiled apron and disheveled appearance evidence of the knight's mood. Since Meghan's last encounter with the brooding, incorrigible man, she'd allowed Mattie to tend to him. At this moment, she looked as if she'd forced the oatmeal down his throat, only to have him spit it back at her.

Meghan put down the tally stick she'd been using to check over the accounts with Malcolm and glared at Mattie. "When is he no' in a foul temper, Mattie?" She took a bite of her biscuit and honey, chewing more harshly than she needed to in her frustration.

"Well, this mornin' he's worse than he's been yet. He bid me tell ye he no' appreciates yer kind and gentle nature. He says ye would starve him."

Offended by the very idea, Meghan's mouth opened in disbelief. "I am no' trying to starve him."

Mattie chuckled. "Try tellin' him that. He says yer a witch, sent to torture him and keep him weak. He says when he gets loose, he's comin' for ye an' no other."

"Oh, does he now? Well, we'll just put a stop to this. Right now."

Meghan left her ledgers open on the table, picked up her skirts, and marched toward the staircase. She felt her cheeks flame as her temper rose. The man was impossible. She had tried explaining to him that, if he would but rein his temper, she would release his bonds. But he ever insisted, should she do so, he would do violence unto this house like she'd never before witnessed.

But treating Mattie as if Mattie were some demon sent to kill him was taking matters too far. Far from starving, the man had eaten much of what she'd provided for him. He preferred richer fare, certainly, but he still recovered from his illness. She would not see him made ill again from too much food, too soon.

Before she reached the door to her father's chamber, his vile threats reached her ears. He never ceased to amaze her. And what damage could he possibly do tied to his bed? Shaking her head, she pushed open the door and entered the room.

"Will ye please cease this bellowing?" The words died on her lips as she froze to the floor, her mouth immediately dry.

The bed was empty, and the blankets lay in a disorderly heap upon the floor.

"You." The growl came from behind her. She turned toward the feral sound, instinctively shrinking from the controlled violence of her escaped prisoner.

He emerged from the shadows, his powerful chest heaving with each breath. He stood with his feet set apart, his slightly bent arms to his sides. In one of his massive, callused hands he held the guard's dagger, in his other, the sword. As threatening as he appeared to her, she gasped for one reason, and one reason alone. Her *Sir Knight* stood before her, on the verge of madness. As naked as the day he was born.

She should close her eyes.

Instead, she allowed her gaze to roam over him. Standing proud and tall, seemingly unaffected by his recent illness or injury, he epitomized raw power and vehemence. Taut muscles encased by deeply bronzed flesh screamed for her touch.

Yer a fool, Meghan lass.

The man wanted her head. The last thing she should consider now was the taste of his lips. Her eyes settled upon that small space of his neck, just below his ear, throbbing with his fury. She shook herself.

How had he escaped?

She spun toward the entry, only to watch the heavy wood door slam shut where he'd kicked it. She backed away, and for each step she took, his threatening pace moved with her until her legs met the bed frame. She swallowed against the lump forming in her throat. Barely able to breathe, she doubted she could scream. Then she realized no guard stood outside the door.

As if reading her mind, he whispered through a sinister smile, "Scream if you will. There is no one to hear."

"Wh . . . Where is the guard?" she asked, hating the sound of weakness in her voice.

"There." He tilted his head, causing a lock of hair to fall devilishly upon his forehead.

At first mesmerized by the coy image, she shook off the feeling upon looking again at his eyes. Oh, aye, she shivered. 'Twas hatred she read in the blue depths. Vile. Strong. Wicked. Finally breaking the hold her fear had placed over her, she looked in the direction he'd indicated. Moan lay motionless in the corner of the chamber. Meghan shifted her eyes back to the knight's hands.

Knees suddenly weak, nausea threatened the pit of her stomach.

"Mother of Mercy."

"Prayers will do little for you, witch."

She blanched at the wintry tone of his voice.

He was going to kill her.

CHAPTER SIX

Consumed by rage, Devlin wanted to strangle someone, anyone. His fists clenched around the hilts of his stolen weapons, slick with sweat.

His attention fell on the one closest to him. Meghan. Devlin noticed the pulse in her neck fluttering erratically. Her normally creamy complexion lost any trace of color as she paled visibly. She feared him.

Good. Well she should.

Aye, she had saved his life, but only to suit her own purpose. Did he owe her thanks? Probably. Loyalty? Never. And he refused to allow the remembered softness of her lips past the walls of his heart.

"Aye. I could kill you. But I won't. Instead, you will lead me from this evil place."

She nodded. "H-hadn't ye better put something on?"

Put something on?

He glanced down and cursed. He supposed his clothes weren't a necessity, but at the very least a pair of trews would make riding his horse a bit more comfortable.

"Where are my trews?"

He kept his eyes fastened on Meghan as she skirted around the edge of the bed, never turning her back on him for a second.

When she reached a small trunk, she pushed it over to him. "In there."

He sighed. "A fine attempt at distraction, my lady. You open it."

She did so, picking up his breeches and boots. "I'm sorry. Yer tunic is ruined. This is all that remains."

"Get on the bed," he ordered.

"I will no'!" she squared her shoulders. The color of her cheeks revealed her displeasure. "I am a lady, and ye will treat me as a lady. I care no' the circumstances."

He closed the short distance between them, nearly amused by her reaction. She craned her neck, the blue of her eyes piercing him.

No fear. Or very little.

One simple request from him, and she had gone from trembling kitten to ferocious lioness.

"I'm not going to ravish you, if that's what you think."

"Oh," she replied. She narrowed her brow, his words obviously spinning through her mind. "Why no'?"

Why not? He nearly laughed.

Why not? He had never forced himself on any woman. He hadn't even been with a woman in nearly four years. His shaft twitched. He'd like nothing more than to sample what so tempted him, to taste again the sweet softness of her lips. The heat from her closeness seared the flesh of his naked chest and legs, as well as his other parts. He wondered, would she be bold in his bed? He shook his head clear of the erotic image devouring his control.

He lowered his shoulders. Her breasts grazed his naked chest, and for a moment he seriously considered taking her. He smiled as he imagined her chaste indignation when she'd only assumed he would. How would she react if he kissed her now?

Reaching an arm around her, he placed the sword on the bed, but kept hold of his stolen dagger. The expression on her lovely face, at first curious, now bordered on panic. He tilted his head as he approached her mouth. Presumably against her will, the pink lips parted on a sweet breath. Using the tip of one finger, he traced a path from her shoulder, down her arm, until he brought her arm behind her, his mouth hovering so close to her parted lips that their breath mingled. The sweet fragrance of honey mixed with her usual rose scent. He wondered what parts of her would taste of honey?

Her slight size fell beneath his shadow, and his fingers completely engulfed her wrist and hand. He pushed against her with his nakedness, causing her to lose her balance. As he'd hoped, she caught herself with her free hand, placing it behind her on the mattress. Her ragged, shallow breaths taunted him. He wanted to taste her. Damn him, he *wanted* to ravish her. The very thought of losing himself in her sweet embrace wreaked havoc in his gut, twisting him away from the man he thought he'd become. Blood pounded through his loins, crying for release with insistent pain. He tried to ignore the craving, but he could not deny it.

He wanted her.

She does not fight.

He could have her.

For barely a moment, he considered it. She had yet to even try pushing him away. He was no longer armed. She knew it, yet she still did not resist him. He shuttered his expression.

Nay. He still held his honor. 'Twas all he had left.

"I haven't the time," he whispered against her lips.

Twisting her in his grasp, he threw her onto the bed before she could change her mind and fight him. He fastened her hands behind her back with the same leather strips she'd used to bind him to the bed.

She squealed and then growled. Raising an eyebrow he leaned over her prostrate form, intensely aware of his lack of clothing as he did so. The position conjured any number of lustful possibilities as his body reacted with anticipation. His mind reeled from her closeness. He had but to lift her skirts . . .

He gritted his teeth against the temptation she presented.

"Hush, my lady. 'Tis no more than you deserve."

THE JEWEL AND THE SWORD

"Oooh," she grunted, kicking her feet. As he forced himself away from the bed, he barely escaped personal injury of the sort he would prefer to avoid.

"Not a very nice feeling is it, my lady? Held against your will?"

"Yer a fiend. A monster."

"Aye. And if you remember that, we'll get along just fine," he answered, fastening his trews.

He sat facing her, on the trunk, and pulled on one boot. "So, what is the quickest route from the castle?"

"I will no' tell ye. Why do ye no' get directions from the castle guard."

He chuckled. "You'd like that, wouldn't you? To see me set upon by your men?"

"Aye. Very much so. Ye can no' escape."

† † †

Meghan hated feeling frustrated. She shifted her position on the mattress. How could she have been so stupid? For a few moments, she had forgotten where she was, who she was. Most importantly, she'd forgotten she stood in a room with her escaped prisoner. So overcome by his raw, masculine sensuality she had allowed him to mesmerize her. She kicked the mattress again, struggling against the bonds. She growled when the bonds failed to part.

"I've escaped from more sinister beings than you," he muttered, pulling on his second boot and stamping the floor as he stood.

He crossed the floor with a tempered gracefulness so rarely found in a man of his size. She watched the muscles of his legs bunch and release under the skin-hugging fabric. Her gaze traveled up the length of them, until they rested on his backside, taut and firm. He knelt beside the fallen guard, pulling the man's sword belt from around his waist. The scars on his back caught her attention. She winced anew at the pain he must have suffered.

She understood his anger toward her. He'd obviously been held captive in the past. The treatment he'd received by whomever had done so had marked him with such fury she doubted he could see the difference between their treatment of him and hers. She'd no intention of torturing him, having him beaten, or even withholding food in exchange for the information she sought. But someone else had, and she realized her mistake in thinking him a willing participant in his own captivity.

When he turned, his expression hardened once more into the scowl he normally wore. With short, angry movements, he put on the belt.

He took up the sword and dagger. Sheathing the sword in his belt, he held tight to the dagger. With his free hand he pulled Meghan to her feet. "Now. You and I are going to take a little walk."

He opened the door, leaning out slightly before pushing her across the threshold. He seemed to know instinctively which way to turn as he dragged her along with him through the upper floor.

The Jewel and the Sword

"What is around this corner?" he demanded as they reached the end of the hall. He pressed his naked back against the brick wall, holding her flush against his chest.

" 'Tis the stairs to the feasting hall."

"Is there another passage?"

She thought immediately of the many secret passages riddling the old keep. She'd spent hours losing herself in them as a child. From the passages she could easily lead him through the garden to a forgotten gate.

"Nay."

He cursed.

"I told ye. Ye can no' get out of here. The guards will stop ye, for certain."

"But will they chance it whilst I hold their lady? The blade of my dagger pressed to her throat?"

Would they? She doubted it, knowing they would fear for her life. Malcolm would attempt to negotiate with him for her freedom. She could already hear him, pleading for her safe release the moment the knight passed the portcullis.

"Aye. They will kill ye."

"I'm not so easy to kill."

His hot breath carried to her ear, sending tendrils of fire through her. Wanton desire ached everywhere their bodies touched. Her knees weakened as he held her ever more tightly against him. She could feel the evidence of his arousal against the small of her back. Closing her eyes, she tried to quell the trembling in her limbs.

He could not be allowed to escape.

Bootsteps echoed in the stairwell below them. Meghan felt the muscles in his chest seize as he held his breath for the briefest of seconds. Then he cursed.

"Who is it?"

She rolled her eyes. "How am I supposed to know that? Am I a witch who can see through solid walls?"

He tightened his hold.

" 'Tis probably the change of guard," she squealed.

"Tell him to come no further," he whispered in her ear, pressing the tip of the dagger against her neck.

She considered calling for help, for she believed he would kill her. The only boon in her favor now lay in the knowledge that without her, he would surely die. She closed her eyes against the sudden pain brought to her fickle heart by the mere possibility of his death.

"Who comes there?" she called down the winding passage.

" 'Tis Ailean, milady."

She held her breath against the recognition of the name.

"Ye must no' harm him," she pleaded as Ailean's bootsteps continued up the stairs. "I have known him the whole of my life. Please, do no' kill him."

† † †

Devlin hated the shiver of sympathy her pleas sent through him. He would do what he must to escape.

Damn.

The fact Meghan Douglas begged for this man's life should mean naught. But deep inside himself, her pleas touched a part of him he'd thought long dead. He steeled himself against his own heart, as her wavering voice crashed upon him. He would leave this place, leave her, and be done with this whole affair, he swore.

"Tell him to go away."

The tip of the dagger moved slightly as she swallowed against the blade. Without knowing why, he removed the tip from her flesh.

"Ailean, do not come above stairs."

"I'm sure Maon would prefer it if I relieved him, milady. 'Tis my watch."

The voice was to the top of the stairs.

Jesu, he did not want to fight this man. He knew he would defeat the lad, but to what extent? Willing to take a life in the course of gaining his freedom was one thing, but to be forced into that end was quite another. He preferred the idea of gaining his freedom without being the instrument of another senseless death. Enough men had been slaughtered in the two battles already.

Cursing, he pushed Meghan free of his grasp and positioned himself in the center of the hall. He waited until the young man turned the corner and then pulled his sword from its casing.

"Ailean, do not fight him." Meghan's breathless plea came from behind him.

Why would she tell her man not to fight? The question nagged in the back of his mind and then disappeared as Ailean drew his own weapon.

"Are ye hurt, milady?" her man asked, his frightened eyes trained on Devlin.

"I am fine, but ye must no' fight him. Let us pass."

"Are ye releasing him then, Meggie? Because, it appears to me as if he's overpowered a helpless female and seeks to escape."

"Very good, Scot," Devlin sneered as he carefully studied his new opponent.

Ailean was no older than Meghan, by the look of him. Her previous pleas for Ailean's life echoed through his mind. They'd grown up together. As he had with Henry and Will.

He couldn't help but hear her breathing behind him, ragged and on the verge of tears. He pictured her as she'd been just moments before, hot with wanting. He couldn't erase the image from his mind. Could he replace it with another? Would he be able to stomach seeing her heart broken by the death of her friend?

"I'll save ye, Meggie. Do no' be frightened."

"Well, aren't you just the hero," Devlin commented as he engaged the boy.

The guard fought well, but lacked both the skill and training needed to defeat a seasoned warrior. He would easily best the boy in a matter of strokes, if he could but concentrate. Each thrust, however, was punctuated by the sound of Meghan's pleas.

He should be finished with this, he cursed silently as he spun away from the guard's descending blade.

It took a few talented maneuvers longer than it should have, but Ailean's weapon lay on the cold stone floor and the man himself sat on his rump, his back pressed against the wall with the tip of Devlin's sword to his throat.

"Hold! Please, do no' do this!"

Meghan's sobs reached his ears just as he should have pushed the blade home. At that moment, his world consisted of nothing but the sound of his own heartbeat and the sweet torment of her voice. He looked at her, huddled helplessly against the wall, her arms held awkwardly behind her by the cursed leather straps. She slid to her knees, her cheeks shining with tears. She looked as if she would die should he complete this one act.

"I have every right," he bellowed toward her.

"Please, do no'," she whimpered. More tears traced her reddened cheeks.

Deep, loud voices made their way into the corners of his mind, followed by the heavy thud of bootsteps. Reinforcements. They must have heard the fight below stairs. He looked at Ailean, read the terror in the boy's eyes.

A word spun though his mind. Freedom.

"Bloody hell!"

Devlin closed his eyes. Removing the blade from the boy's throat, he tossed it away. The piercing echo of the steel as it met the stone floor reverberated through his soul.

He met Meghan's eyes fully, disgust for his own weakness surrounding him in a blanket of misery. But he'd been unable to complete the act that would brand him a monster in her eyes. For his life, he didn't know why he cared.

115

Before he realized they'd even reached him, two sets of hands were grasping his arms and pulling him toward the stairwell. He turned his head in Meghan's direction, to find her bonds had been cut and her arms were wrapped around her stomach. She leaned against the wall, her face raised in prayer toward the heavens.

He felt ten times the fool.

† † †

Meghan had never been inside this part of her father's keep. She'd had no reason to visit anyone held here. She wished she had no reason to come here now, but her father's men had taken her knight away after his attempted escape. She'd argued with Malcolm until she could scarcely form a complete thought to have the man returned above stairs. He'd refused.

Two days had passed since the man she called Brandubh had nearly killed her friend. Nearly, she reminded herself, and anyone else who would listen. But her knight had slaughtered no one, though he'd had the opportunity. By his very nature and lifestyle, he possessed the ability. Yet he'd spared Ailean's life to the forfeit of his own freedom. And even Moan had received little injury, besides a lingering ache in his head and a loosened tooth as a result of the day's activity.

In truth, he seemed far less a threat to them than Ian. Yet Ian walked freely among them while their prisoner languished in bondage.

She took little comfort in the fact Ian had not

The Jewel and the Sword

entered the keep in the several days since she'd forced him to leave. Instead, he'd focused his attention on convincing the clansmen to side with him. Several of the maids brought her reports of his activities. Ian had visited each of their menfolk, plied them with ale, and filled their heads with his own traitorous ideas. His power grew daily and more of the clansmen seemed to come to his way of thinking. Even Mattie's father had told her that perhaps Ian as laird would be better than no laird at all.

Making a face as she placed one hand on the wall to feel her way through the darkness, she hissed. The slimy moisture upon the walls reeked of mold. She wiped her hand upon her dress and forced herself forward. Following the direction of several dim torches, she finally took one from its sconce and held it before her. She stepped in a puddle, the cold water seeping into her slipper.

Och. 'Tis not fit for a beastie here.

She heard the sound of a chain clanking against stone and stopped.

Nay. No' chains.

She strained her eyes in the dim light. There, a stone's throw away, sat her knight. Locked in a cage, his face bruised and his leg shackled, he leaned against the weeping walls.

Unable to stop herself, she rushed forward. He heard her and raised his head. The cold glare spoke volumes of his hatred for her, and it stole her breath. She skidded to a halt before she reached his cell. By the expression on his battered face she suspected, had he not been shackled as far away from her as possible, he would have thrown himself to the furthest edge of his leash and strangled her.

What happened to the man who'd teased her body into waking dreams of desire? The man who sparked fire inside her with naught but the whisper of his breath upon her cheek?

Timidly, she placed one hand on the flat bars.

"Go away," he stated.

She swallowed against the lump in her throat. "Nay, I can no'. I brought ye–"

"I don't care." He sounded more than angry. He sounded . . . furious.

Solitary drops of water, dripping into some unseen pool nearby, punctuated the steady cadence of his words. Meghan shifted nervously, gripping the iron closing him away from her. Her heart broke for him. This was not what she intended when she thought to keep him. She expected he would cooperate with her. Though now that she knew him, she realized such a thought was preposterous. He would never help her defy his lord. He was too proud. She bore witness to it each time he deigned to level even a glare in her direction.

"Why did ye fight with Ailean? Had ye killed him swiftly, ye might have escaped before an alarm was raised."

"He fought well. I was not able to kill him swiftly. By the time I had my chance, the cause was already lost. Why take his life?"

She scoffed. "Come now, Brandubh. I witnessed the battle, ye remember? Ye could have killed him with one thrust and made yer way through the keep. I'm not saying ye would have gained yer freedom, but 'twould have been more of a chance."

He remained dismally silent, though she could see from the uncomfortable manner in which he shifted his position, he heard her clearly enough.

"So, ye're back to no' talking with me, is that it?"

Still nothing. He didn't even turn his head to acknowledge her presence.

"Very well then," she sighed as she made her way carefully over the uneven floor to his side of the cell. "I brought ye meat and cheese, and ale."

"I want nothing from you, woman, save my freedom."

The bitter words stung. Meghan bit her lip to keep from crying. She rarely cried, yet she'd cried more since this whole foolish adventure began than in her entire life. She would not let him see her weep again. Were he to discover the cause of her tears while he and Ailean had fought, he would scorn her for it.

May the saints preserve her, she had not cried for her friend. All she feared was Brandubh's death. The very thought of his injury, or worse, caused her skin to shiver with icy dread. She had spent most of last night trying to convince herself that her concern lay with her father. By the time the sun's rays peeked into her chamber, she had been forced by her own conscience to admit the truth. She *cared* for the soulful, mysterious man. More than concern, she mourned for him. Her father's confinement inside the walls of Ravenstone Castle only served her now as an excuse to keep him.

So she was tempted to give in to his demand for freedom. She'd known, before she'd begun this game, it would be distasteful. But she had no idea how he would play upon her body and soul. She certainly never dreamed he would be confined in such a dreary, ill-conceived place as this. A thought struck her, even as she hated the logic of it. If she did release him, would he tell his lord of her mercy and might her father be released as well?

"Where would ye go, if I were to manage yer release?" she asked him.

"Home."

"Have ye a wife there, mayhap even now worried for yer safe return?" She prayed he would say he did not.

A dim light entered his eyes. He appeared sad for a moment before the heat of anger returned, snuffing the pain as quickly as if he'd been doused with water. He turned his gaze on her, and she could feel the heat of his fury upon her cheeks.

"Nay. No wife."

She hoped the relief rushing through her did not reveal itself in her expression.

"Ye speak as if ye've lost someone, my lord."

"What do you know of loss?" he growled.

She felt like a child under the heady gaze of one wiser than she could ever hope to become. "I lost my mother," she answered.

He fell quiet, and she guessed he reined his temper and his heart.

Finally, after several tense moments where only the echoes of her own breathing filled her ears, he replied, "I do not wish to speak of it. She's been dead these ten years. 'Tis all that matters."

She? Whoever she was, he must have loved her very much to still feel such pain after so long a time. "I'm sorry," she whispered.

"Don't be. My *wife* was an evil woman, as most women are. She deserved to die."

Shock made her pulse race. His own wife had been the source of his anguish? "Evil?" Certainty that she'd heard him wrong edged her voice with curiosity.

He looked away, examining the moisture collecting in the crevice of the bricks on the opposite wall. "Aye," he answered, his voice rough. "In her veins flowed the blackness of hate and treachery."

"And ye claim 'all women' are of the same mind?" Meghan felt her ire growing at his callous attitude.

He turned back to her, his blue eyes piercing through her with heated lances. His gaze trailed over her. Lord, but he stole her breath when he looked at her with such obvious wanting. Her hands shook, and she gripped them tightly to still the telltale sign of her insecurity.

Finally, he pinned her eyes with a deadly glare.

"Aye. All women are cut from the same bolt, my lady. In answer to your question, should you release me, I will go home. Alone. And just so we're not mistaking each other's motives, I will kill anyone who gets in my way."

CHAPTER SEVEN

"What made ye so heartless?" Meghan looked at her hands clenched in her lap. "Losing yer wife?"

The quiver of Meghan's bottom lip rocked Devlin's soul with pain more torturous than any sword. She took the full, rosy lip between her teeth to still its trembling. He stifled a groan of regret. What was it about her that made him lose control so readily?

"Why do you care?" He finally admitted to himself he needed to know. For days, he'd been trying to figure out why he'd sacrificed himself merely to spare her feelings. And now he'd threatened her.

Again.

Still, she had come to him offering comfort, undaunted by his nature. Most women, and many men, fled from his slightest growl. Yet she remained steadfast in her desire to save him.

From what, he could not imagine.

"Are ye no' one of God's children?"

His head snapped up at this. He'd been called many things over the course of the past ten years, but never a child of God. How should a man react to something like that? Since Allyson's betrayal, he'd given little consideration to God, and he doubted if God had given him any thought in return.

"Am I?" He cleared his throat when he realized his voice had gone hoarse.

"Of course ye are," she replied with a smile as she seated herself on the ground next to him. She sat close enough for him to touch. Even the rose scent she used in her hair made its way through the iron grid to reach him.

What are you doing? You're encouraging her to stay?

"We are all God's children. I believe yer a good man, my lord. Sometimes, bad things happen to good people, and we suffer for it."

He could listen to the sound of her voice for hours, so sweet was the melody of it.

Nay. Tell her to leave.

As she continued to speak, his heart softened and his loins hardened in response. He steeled himself against the assault.

Meghan, by her very gender, but played with him. She offered comfort for a price. He would not pay it. He didn't need anyone, least of all some prattling female, to make his life complete. His life ended ten years before, with the betrayal by his wife and the death of his unborn child. He closed his eyes against the memory.

"Take my father, for instance–"

"What?" he snapped. His mood, already foul, was made more so by the mention of Morven Douglas.

"He is a verra good man, who did a verra bad thing. My uncle, yer benefactor, holds him prisoner for something little more than a misunderstanding."

"It is more than a misunderstanding. People were killed."

Silence surrounded them before she finally graced him again with her voice. " 'Tis unfortunate, I know. And restitution should be made, but does this excuse the taking of more lives? Innocent lives? Lord Ravenstone attacked my home, as well. People were killed. Ye yerself nearly died."

"Your home was attacked in retribution."

"There, see? Retribution has been made."

She bit her lip again. Her head tilted to one side as if she thought of something powerful. He could see the intelligence in her eyes. Even the intellect of this woman drew him to her, and he hated himself for it. Still, he thought he would burst with wanting.

After a moment's silence, she continued, "Although there is the matter of the sword."

"Aye, there is that."

"Ye know of the sword?" Her crystalline eyes widened.

"Aye. Everyone knows of it." He didn't lie. The story of his father's trophy graced the minds of all his people.

"Well, I do no' ken where 'tis." She sighed. "If I did, I would return it to Lord Ravenstone upon his agreement to exchange . . . ye for my father."

She cast her eyes downward. He believed her, and for the life of him, he could not fathom how Morven had raised such a woman. How had a man so hateful have had any hand in creating such a divine creature as this?

"Milady," the hushed voice of her maid slid through the passages. "Where are ye? I can no' see a blasted thing."

Meghan stood quickly, as if she felt guilty for visiting him. "I have to leave now. I'll return soon."

In an instant, she disappeared into the hollow blackness. Tossing his head backward he relished the pain of impact with the wall.

Twenty times the fool.

He never learned. For years, he'd managed to keep every woman at arm's length. Quite a task, especially in London, where so many ladies threw themselves at him, hoping to marry the richest man in England. He ignored them all, preferring to slack his masculine needs in the company of one who would not assume too much. The very thought of visiting a whore now repulsed him. His mind might tell him to ignore Meghan, to forget her unique, fey beauty, but his body could not.

If he was to leave this place alive, his wounded pride screamed, he needed to listen to his head. And not the one between his legs.

† † †

Meghan stooped beside the well and picked up three-year old Aigneas. Her blond hair hung limply around her shoulders, and her pudgy cheeks were smeared with dirt, except where her tears had washed away the grime.

"There now, do no' cry, sweetling. 'Tis only a scrape," she clucked.

Aigneas sniffed, wiped her nose with the back of her small hand, and then pointed. "Who be dat mon?"

Meghan followed the direction of her chubby fingers to see her knight coming from the scullery door. He squinted against the sunlight, and her conscience roared in protest, even though she'd tried many times in the last few days to have him brought back into the keep.

"That man is an English knight, Aigneas. I do no' ken his true name, but ye may call him Bran, if ye've a mind to speak with him."

"Bwan," she repeated. "Does he bite?"

Meghan laughed. "I should think no'."

"My bwrover bites me, milady."

"Well, I shall have to speak to him about that. But I think Sir Bran is safe eno'."

She looked toward him again, to find his gaze narrowed on her. What was it about his eyes that made her heart skip a beat and her hands shake? She could not read his shuttered expression, which only heightened her sudden nervousness.

Aigneas struggled against her, and she placed the child on the ground. Never shy, the little one waddled toward the knight.

Meghan giggled at the uncomfortable expression appearing on his normally dark features. Aigneas all but climbed his legs, until her persistence rewarded itself, and he lifted her in his arms.

Meghan could not hear them, but based upon Aigneas's rubbing of his jaw, and his sudden smile, she assumed the little girl had made some comment about his beard. She'd been unable to shave him since he'd been moved to the dungeon, and several days' growth obscured his jaw. The memory of his smooth, warm flesh beneath her fingers swirled through her mind. Her stomach clenched, chasing her breath away. She closed her eyes and dispelled the image as quickly as she could. How could just the thought of his unshaven face make her so weak inside? As if her whole body were ablaze, melting into a pool where her feet should have been. 'Twas disturbing, and yet delightful, the feelings he caused in her. She leaned against the low wall and rested her eyes on the knight again.

Raibeart escorted him as he walked the length of the fence and back. She watched Aigneas's face, as the little lass smiled and then laughed.

Such a fierce man, his manner surprised her. She'd

suspected goodness in him, but his treatment of the child confirmed it.

Malcolm joined her, lifting the bucket from the well. "I thought he might enjoy a breath of spring air, Lady Meghan. 'Tis a beautiful day, is it not? I thought also ye might approve of it?"

"Aye, Malcolm," she replied. Though sudden storms each afternoon had left the ground muddy, the air held a crisp chill in the morning, and even now as the sun reached toward the highest part of the sky, the day proved a pleasant one indeed.

Eyes trained on her captive, she studied his face as he still squinted against the sun's rays. Prior to his rebellion, she'd noticed a healthy color in his complexion. Only a few days in her father's prison, and he already looked sallow and pale. Another few days and she would fear for his health. "Will he be returned to the dungeon?"

"Aye. I only allowed him to come above upon his word he would no' try to escape."

"And ye trust him?"

"Aye. For now. I ken ye want him placed back in yer father's chamber, but we can no' risk it."

Meghan knelt as Aigneas ran toward her, and she scooped the young girl back into her arms.

"He is a bonny knight, milady, and he pwromised to kill a dwagon fer me."

"Did he now?" Meghan encouraged the child's fantasy with a surprised expression. "And what else did he say?"

"That ye awe a bonny lass, and he should vewy much like to kiss ye."

Meghan snapped her head in his direction just as Raibeart led him through the scullery door.

'Twas nonsense. She frowned. He but entertained the child. Didn't he?

† † †

"Milady!" Mattie collided with Meghan where she stood in the far corner of the bailey dipping candles. Meghan lost her grip on the wick.

"Och," she exclaimed. "Now I've dropped the candle into the vat."

"I'm sorry, milady, but ye must no' concern yerself with such things now. Oh dear, 'tis too foul to even think of, milady."

Frustrated and overheated from her chore, Meghan wiped her forehead with the sleeve of her gown before she turned toward Mattie. "What? What is too foul?"

"One of the clansmen says he heard Ian planning to attack the keep." Mattie appeared on the verge of tears.

This was very bad. Ian had become ever more dangerous since the night of the meeting. Could he have been planning to take over the clan by force so quickly? "Who heard him, Mattie?"

" 'Twas Donnan, the butcher's son."

Donnan would not lie about such a thing. If he said he'd overheard plans, she believed him.

"What will we do, milady?"

The Jewel and the Sword

"We will leave the keep before he gets here, Mattie. And plead with my uncle for the return of my father. We must go to England."

Meghan gathered her wicks and the finished candles and walked toward the feasting hall. Mattie followed, her panic rising even higher, if the squeak in her voice was any means to judge.

"Nay," Mattie cried. "Ravenstone's a monster, milady. We can no' do such a foolish thing."

Meghan rolled her eyes. "What choice have we, Mattie. I'll no' sit here and wait for whatever Ian has planned for us." Or me, she added silently. Her stomach turned.

"We can no' go to England alone, two lasses." Mattie snorted. "We'd be better off facing Ian down with a large stick."

"Yer right, Mattie. We'll need an escort," Meghan stated the obvious, as she balanced the candles in one arm and threw open the hall door. She held it open for Mattie, who narrowed her eyes at Meghan as she passed.

Meghan ignored the suspicion in her friend's expression and turned away.

"Ye've got that impish look about ye, milady. What are ye thinking now?"

"Nothing, save we have an escort already. One who should be more than happy to take us away from here."

Mattie stopped in mid-stride, turned, and stood directly in Meghan's path. Her arms akimbo, she declared, "Nay. Ye can no' be thinking of the knight, milady. He's yer father's sworn enemy."

"Of course I speak of the knight, Mattie. He wants to go to England, and so do we. 'Tis simple as that."

"And why should he be willin' to help the likes of ye."

Unwilling to allow Mattie any suspicion she harbored her own doubts, Meghan skirted Mattie's firmly planted feet. Calling over her shoulder as she hurried toward Malcolm's counting room, Meghan replied, "For his freedom, Mattie."

† † †

Devlin found sleep impossible in the dank space. Water dripped incessantly from the walls of the old keep, setting his bones to chattering shivers.

How many days had it been since he'd attempted escape, only to foolishly throw it away to keep Meghan's eyes from crying? Had his mother received the ransom letter yet? Would he be released soon?

More questions than he had answers for flew about his mind, like honeybees searching for precious nectar.

The door at the end of the long passage opened. Instantly alert, Devlin sat straighter against the wall. A few minutes passed before Malcolm, in the company of two cloaked figures, stopped in front of his cell.

" 'Tis a bit late for visitors, is it not?" Devlin asked, hiding his curiosity behind a mask of indifference.

Malcolm withdrew a key from his gipser and inserted it in the lock.

The smallest of the figures removed her hood. He could barely make her out in the dim light from the single torch, but her familiar scent filled his nostrils the moment she released her hair from the thick fabric. He closed his eyes briefly.

Did she sleep upon a bed of roses?

Meghan glanced at him with large, doe eyes, ringed with worry.

What was happening? He trusted the wary slice of suspicion wiggling in his gut far more than he trusted her. Something very wrong slithered amongst the walls of Douglas Keep, and he wanted no part of it.

The door to his cell swung open. Meghan took the key from Malcolm and rushed inside. She knelt in front of him. He inhaled a deep breath and savored her clean, fresh scent, suddenly aware of his own filth. She fumbled with the lock on the shackle encasing one ankle.

"We must hurry. There is no time to explain."

He gained his feet instantly, taking her by the shoulders and pushing her back against the rough wall. "What are you doing here?"

She squealed. "I'm releasing ye, Brandubh."

He narrowed his eyes. "Why?" He growled.

She had the decency to look away. Just as he suspected. She schemed some nefarious plot. He ignored the heart-breaking stab of pain in his chest at the confirmation of her true nature.

"I need yer help," she whispered, and raised her eyes to meet his full on. "And ye need mine. Will ye listen to reason, or no'?"

Taken aback, he gentled his hold on her. "Speak."

"Ian Douglas is planning to attack the keep this very night. He could be well on his way here this minute. If he succeeds, and I'm quite certain he will, he will kill ye."

"Why would he do that? Without me, he stands little chance to reclaim his laird."

"He does no' want Morven returned," Malcolm admitted. "Please, my lord, believe her. Put these clothes on and be quick. Ye must leave now if ye want to save yerself."

The third person offered him a sack. He didn't take it, but he did release his hold on Meghan. He pushed back his hair with both hands.

"Who is this Ian? Why does he not want Morven returned?"

"There is little time to debate the issue. Meghan can tell ye all ye need to know once yer away."

Had he heard the man correctly? "You want that I should take Meghan with me?"

"Aye. And her maid. 'Tis no' safe for them here."

He raked his gaze over her. The folds of her heavy cloak shook with her trembling. Her creamy complexion paled in the wavering light. She looked not only frightened, but as if she tried to hide the fear behind a pretense of courage.

His gut clenched at the obvious fear she held of the man named Ian. No matter whose blood ran in her veins, she did not deserve this. In that moment, he knew he could not let her suffer at the hands of this Ian, whatever designs the man had for her.

He took the sack. Grumbling to himself, he sifted through it. It contained a fresh tunic, trews and a cloak, not unlike the one Meghan wore.

"Where is my sword?"

Malcolm's eyes fell upon his lady. Devlin followed the gaze and watched, as she seemed to consider the full import of what she did.

" 'Tis all right, Malcolm. Give it to him," Meghan whispered without conviction.

Did she trust him so little? And if so, why would she even ask this of him?

To get her father back alive.

"Here, my lord." The old man withdrew the sword and scabbard, handing them to Devlin.

"And the other sword?" He took his weapon from Malcolm, but made no move toward escape.

"I've already told ye, my lord. I do no' ken where 'tis. We've no time to search for it now."

He ran a hand through his hair. She knew the right of it, and the knowledge he'd lost the sword, mayhap forever, disappointed him. But lives meant more. Even hers.

"I can't believe I've agreed to this." He sighed, removing his tunic and pulling the fresh one over his head. "Which way?"

Devlin followed Malcolm through the dank passages. He could sense Meghan, hovering so close behind him he could feel the heat of her body upon his back. He could almost feel her breath. A part of him wished she would touch him.

Within a few moments, they reached a long-forgotten door. The hinges had rusted in the dampness, and the wood was split down the center as if weary of its duty to defend.

"Child." Malcolm sighed.

Meghan pushed past him. Her body slid against him in the tight confines of the corridor, and he sucked in his breath. Devlin ached to hold her, his long-standing vow be damned.

"Malcolm." Devlin could hear the sadness in Meghan's voice as she addressed her friend. "Am I doing the right thing, Malcolm?"

"Aye, child. Ye've no choice. All will be well in the end, ye'll see."

The hair on the back of Devlin's neck awakened. What was that sound? Horses. Lots of them. Devlin grimaced. So that part of her story rang true.

The attack begins.

"Hurry." Malcolm pushed open the door. "God be with ye."

Meghan gave the old man one final hug and crept outside. Devlin peered at the man, who clapped him upon the shoulder. "I love that child as if she were my own. I ken ye are a knight and noble. Do I err to trust ye with her life?"

"Nay, Malcolm. She'll be safe with me." Devlin didn't know why he felt obligated to assure this stranger of Meghan's safety. Except he recognized the love between them as something rare and kind. Many years had passed since Devlin had been involved in protecting something so . . .

Special.

Once outside the cracked door, Devlin found Meghan waiting for him with three horses. Midnight recognized him and called out a whinnied greeting. His heart lurched at the unexpected reunion. He'd given up hope of ever meeting his trusted companion again. Scanning the immediate area for threats and finding none, he hurried to where Meghan waited.

Without words, he lifted her into her saddle. She felt weightless in his hands. His fingers burned where he'd touched her, even through the thick wool encasing her entire form. He didn't need to see her to know how perfectly she would fit with him. He'd pictured it many times already.

Devlin took the two remaining sacks from Mattie and fastened all three to the back of his saddle. After helping her to mount a chestnut palfrey, he leapt onto Midnight's back and pulled the reins sharply around.

"Do you both ride?"

"I do," Meghan answered. "But Mattie is no' as experienced as I am."

"We need to go that way, to avoid your Ian." Devlin used his reins to point toward a craggy path leading further into Scotland. " 'Tis the wrong direction, but I don't know of any other way to escape the area. We'll have to circle around later. Mattie? Can you ride there?"

"Aye, milord. I shall try."

He kicked Midnight's ribs, and the horse leapt

forward to a gallop. How did he end up in this position? At what point should he simply spur his horse over the crag and disappear?

He couldn't do that. He wouldn't do it.

As he led them along the narrow path, one word echoed through his mind.

Honor.

Bloody Hell.

"Secure the women in the solar." Ian stamped inside the feasting hall of Douglas Keep and barked the order to his men. "Except Lady Meghan. Bring her to me."

Taking the keep had been a simple task. Malcolm had barely put up a fight, nearly inviting Ian to establish his forces inside the keep's defenses.

He surveyed the hall in which he'd been forced to bow, scraping and sniveling, before each laird. 'Twas finally his. He dared anyone in the Lowlands to try to take it from him. His sword itched to cut out their hearts.

"Lord Ian." Malcolm approached him, scurrying like a frightened pup.

Ian sneered. He would enjoy making this man suffer. Malcolm had ever discouraged Morven from considering Ian as a candidate for Meghan's hand.

"I have no time fer ye, old man." Ian growled.

"Ye'll want to hear this."

THE JEWEL AND THE SWORD

Ian narrowed his eyes, leveling a glare upon Malcolm capable of sending seasoned warriors screaming into the night. But Malcolm didn't move. Instead, he seemed to be rooted to the rush-covered floor.

Ian grunted.

Malcolm's lips curled into a knowing grin. "I surmise yer looking for Lady Meghan?"

"Aye." Ian stepped closer to the steward. "What do ye know of it?"

"I know she's no' here."

"Ye lie. Ye've hidden her. Tell me where now, and I'll tell my men to kill ye quick."

There. Now the old man licked his lips. Small beads of sweat appeared on his forehead.

"I do no' lie, Lord Ian. She and her maid escaped more than two hours ago."

"Why do ye tell me this, Malcolm? I have swift horses and trained men to find her. Why would ye betray yer lady?"

"I do no' betray her. She is well away and yer men will no' overtake her. I tell ye in hopes to spare the lives of those left behind. In yer effort to find her, were she still here, I do no' want ye to harm these people."

Ian turned away. Could this be a trick? Malcolm had said she 'escaped.' How would Meghan have known to leave? If Malcolm had previous knowledge of Ian's raid, 'twould explain the ease with which the keep had fallen. Unwilling to accept the information at face value, he sneered and turned toward the stairs.

Malcolm followed.

Taking the steps two at a time, he stalked toward Meghan's bedchamber. If he failed to find her here or in the village, the steward would greatly suffer for it.

The door crashed against the wall of her chamber, quivering on its hinges. Ian marched into the room, his fists clenched, his breathing ragged.

Empty.

By God, he would have her head for this treason.

He left the room, nearly leveling Malcolm in the process. Finding three soldiers near the top of the stairs shuffling the last of the women into the solar, he stopped the nearest soldier. He took hold of the man's tunic in his gauntlet and twisted until the fabric threatened to cut off the flow of blood to the soldier's head.

"Take four men and find Meghan Douglas."

The man's eyes widened. "Where has she gone, my lord?"

Ian pushed his soldier against the wall, lifting him several precarious inches from the floor with one hand. "I do no' ken. Yer goin' to find her and bring her back."

"Aye, my lord." The man trembled.

Ian released him. After instructing the remaining guards to bring several women to prepare a meal, he stormed in the direction of the hall.

Chapter Eight

Devlin maintained a slow pace to ensure the women would have little trouble navigating the rocky outcroppings as they made their way north. Another half day in this direction would see any pursuers lost, and he would turn them west before making his solitary journey south.

To England.

Meghan rode her horse like a seasoned warrior. Not only did she ride astride, but the many times he checked her progress, he saw her jaw set in a determined line and her eyes like that of a hawk upon the trail.

He glanced back at her now, and he ached for her. He'd never wanted to be a saddle so much in his life.

What made her so fierce yet so timid at the same time?

She had faced him with strength and pride the day he'd nearly escaped. Though terrified, she'd refused to back down. He reluctantly admitted he admired her for it.

He also admired her stamina. They'd ridden for hours now, and yet she complained naught. Many women would fear the blackness of the night, worried over the sprites and witches of the dark. But she braved whatever fears she had in stoic silence.

He ran a hand through his hair and grunted as he tried to push any soft thoughts of her away. He didn't want to admire her. He wanted only to get away from her as quickly as he could. He turned to satisfy himself they still followed and saw her straighten in her saddle.

† † †

Meghan's back screamed in protest as her mount stumbled upon a jagged rock. She refused to moan aloud, biting her lip instead. If Brandubh could keep this gruesome pace, so could she. The fact remained she'd escaped Ian, and her knight lived. She would ride to the end of the earth and back to see that it remained so.

Her knight rode with a confidence born of experience and strength. As she looked upon his straight back, her heart danced. Strong in body, if not in spirit, she wanted nothing more than to help him find peace.

Her expression fell. That would never happen.

"We'll camp here," he said finally.

THE JEWEL AND THE SWORD

He had not spoken since leaving the keep. She missed hearing his voice.

He dismounted and reached up first for Mattie and then Meghan. Once she and her maid were down, he returned to his horse and removed the three sacks. He reached into the sack containing a bow and a full quiver of arrows and pulled them free.

"Should we gather firewood, milady?" Mattie asked, as she fell into a heap beside a large rock.

"Nay." Brandubh's voice was stern, but not unkind.

Still, Meghan saw no harm in a fire for warmth, and for heating the bits of venison Mattie had packed for them. "Why no'? Surely, we'll freeze if we do no' have a fire."

Meghan felt the hard set of his gaze crawl over her, his expression one which should brook no argument. She placed fisted hands on her hips and waited for his answer.

He clutched one of the arrows he'd pulled from the quiver as he crossed his arms over his broad chest, his head cocked to one side, studying her. Heat raced to her cheeks, but she refused to lower her own glare. He wasn't as harsh as he appeared. He'd already proved he had a decent heart, or he would have left them at the keep to fend for themselves.

"This Ian of yours," he began. "What danger does he pose to you? I understand why he wants me out of the way, but what of you?"

The way his eyes roamed over her told her he knew well what Ian's designs upon her were. Still, Meghan's knees swayed as if they were made of sackcloth. She swallowed as her palms broke into a sweat. She removed them from her hips and wiped their slickness on her skirt.

"Lord Ian fancies Meghan, milord. But she wants no part of him." Mattie sighed as if she couldn't understand Ian's reasoning or motives.

Meghan understood them. More than she wanted to. Ian didn't love her, but love had little to do with lust. And power. She saw that same knowledge reflected in Brandubh's eyes as well.

"Eno' Mattie," she scolded. To her knight, she asked, "Do ye ken we've been followed, my lord? 'Twould be difficult, would it no'? Ye changed our direction many times."

He answered her with a reassuring tone in his voice. "We crossed the same streams two, sometimes three times, but 'tis possible. Your Ian's guard may be within earshot right now. Do you still have need for a fire?"

What if, right at this moment, Ian's guard, led by that wretched man, Lachann, stared into the night for some clue to her direction? A sliver of fear made its way through her limbs, and she scanned the trees for any sign of pursuit. She swallowed again before speaking. "Nay. No fire this night."

Her knight moved behind the trees, and she already missed him.

Meghan crept closer to Mattie, sitting beside her on the ground. Uncomfortable, she wished her knight would return.

As if she'd conjured him up, he stood before her. He'd changed into the trews and under-tunic she'd *borrowed* from one of the men-at-arms. She forced her eyes away from the striking picture he made, the moonlight falling over his shoulders like some ancient god.

He seemed more comfortable now. Though, from the tense set of his massive shoulders and the keen manner in which his eyes scanned the darkened landscape, he still did not lower his guard.

Was he always so protective? Did he ever take a moment to relax and enjoy himself? She supposed he might with his family. She'd seen him only in tense situations. She imagined him in another place, where the world did not crash in upon him, taking the joy from his life. She had only seen him smile once. She sighed. 'Twas a very nice smile.

"Are ye hungry?" she asked.

"Aye." He leaned against the rock with one foot propped against it.

"We packed venison and some cheese. Eno' for several days, at least."

He raised an eyebrow. "Where are we going?"

"I hope ye like it." She prepared a few morsels for him. Placing them into a square of linen, she handed him the inadequate feast. He crossed the three strides separating them. From her position on the forest floor, her eyes fell almost immediately to his thighs, and higher. She blushed suddenly as the recalled image of his naked body surfaced unbidden.

"My thanks." He squatted gracefully in front of her

as he took the offered repast. "Now, answer the question. I've freed you from your Ian and his threats, and I have done so at risk to my own life, without question. Just where is it you think I will take you?" He took a mouthful of spiced meat and chewed lazily.

† † †

Devlin watched the indecision play across Meghan's features, turning her creamy complexion a pasty white. He knew exactly where she thought he would take her.

Ravenstone Castle.

Never. His home would be the last place he'd ever take Morven's daughter, or any woman for that matter. He didn't trust her any more now than he had before she helped him escape. In fact, he trusted her less. If it weren't for the fact he had heard the charge with his own ears, he wouldn't even believe the keep had been attacked.

"So, my lady?"

She lifted her quivering chin. Her large, moist eyes raked over him. He felt the power of her emotion like a fist in the gut.

Damn.

What was it about him that made him such a fool for a woman's tears? He'd never been able to withstand such an assault. Not even with Allyson. The bitter taste of betrayal turned his meal to ashes.

Aye.

So much has this weakness cost you.

He spat the soured meat onto the ground. He would not listen to her tearful pleas. He would take her safely away, but that was all he could offer her. The sooner he deposited the temptress upon the doorstep of her nearest neighbor, the better.

"Nay, I will not take you to Devlin Barnett's home," he growled, rising to his full height as he stared down at her.

"But I must speak with him." Her voice quivered. "He must release my father, or Ian Douglas will destroy everything and everyone."

Devlin snorted. "Morven Douglas seems no match for this Ian. Mayhap your clan is better off with a real leader."

He regretted the words the moment they left him. Her shining eyes, so kind when they weren't ablaze with any number of passions, grew dark and sad.

"Ye have no right to say such things," she spat.

He knew her father better than she did, he'd wager. But he couldn't tell her that. Free or not, he kept his identity a secret. Until he set foot again on his beloved English soil, safety remained an illusion.

"Go to sleep," he demanded. "We have only until daybreak to rest. Mayhap two hours." He walked away from her, away from the anguish in her eyes and the defeated set of her shoulders.

Behind him, he sensed her lie down on the hard earth. He could hear the soft breath escaping her chest, as she tried to remain silent in her tears.

He'd never felt so cold in his life.

† † †

Once back in the hall, Ian took his place in the laird's chair. "Bring me ale," he ordered one of the soldiers, who complied without question.

Meghan's disappearance darkened his mood considerably. But not completely. He still had time. His men would find her and bring her back. There, in front of all his people, he would handfast with her. And by the next moonrise, she would belong to him.

Body.

Mind.

Soul.

Lachann stalked toward him, his helm tucked beneath his massive arm. "What do ye want we should do with the castle guard, Lord Ian?"

Lachann put his helmet on a trestle table, then leaned his backside against it and rubbed a hand over his face. 'Twas late. His men tired.

"Kill them," Ian responded.

"Kill them, my lord?"

"Aye. Slaughter them like pigs as a warning to the clan. Whosoever runs afoul of my good graces, dies."

"Aye, my lord." Lachann took up his helm and left the room, his bearing proud.

'Twas time Clan Douglas learned of a powerful leader. Under Ian's command and leadership, this clan would become the most feared in all Scotland. Too long had they been forced to endure the mealy weakness of Morven Douglas.

Ian remembered well the day Morven had come to Douglas Keep. The angry young man had seemed a threat to Ian then. Even though Morven's mother had been common-born, the training he had received made him a valuable tool to the Douglas. He'd trained the men of the clan to be soldiers, capable of fighting against the English who would hunt them. The men responded exceptionally well, each of them dedicated to learning the craft of war.

But in the end, it had been Morven's upbringing and his noble half that had allowed him to court and marry the laird's daughter. For this, Ian hated Morven.

Elspeth had been a beauty, strong of heart and delicate of form. As much as it was possible for a heart full of hate to love, Ian had loved her. She died of fever when Meghan had been only seven years of age. Elspeth's death had killed her father as surely as if she had pierced his heart with an arrow. On the laird's deathbed the old man named Morven his heir.

It still stung. If Morven had not arrived when he did, the old laird had agreed to allow Ian to court Elspeth. Eventually, he could have won her heart. But once Morven made his pursuit known, Ian became ever more inferior in her eyes.

He finished his ale and poured another cup. First Morven stole the only woman Ian had ever loved. Then he'd taken the Clan Douglas as well. And now, in the same traitorous vein, Meghan had managed to elude his grasp. He gritted his teeth, tasting blood on his tongue.

He grimaced as the taste fed his bitterness. Aye, he would have her back.

✝ ✝ ✝

"I have no' had time to thank ye, Sir Knight, for helping us." Meghan pushed her palfrey to catch up with Devlin's large, black warhorse. They'd risen after only a few hours rest and were again making a steady pace northward.

"No thanks are needed, my lady. I have no intention of taking you to England," he replied. He suspected she attempted to find his good graces. She should know by now that he had none.

"But ye did no' have to take us with ye at all, and ye did. Why?"

He slid his gaze in her direction. She looked frightful; her hair mussed beneath her coif, her kirtle smeared with the damp earth upon which she'd slept. If anyone came upon them along the forest trails they now rode, each of them could easily pass for a peasant or gipsy.

Still, Meghan shone like the sun. Her eyes danced in the early morning light, her skin gleamed like cream, begging him to sample just one taste of her full lips. He shifted in his saddle to release the tightness of his trews.

He cleared his throat. "I couldn't very well leave you there."

"Why no'?" She tilted her head in such a way the

dappled shadows of the trees played in her eyes, enhancing her fey beauty.

"Excuse me?"

"Why could ye no' leave us there? It seems to me, ye could have left us behind if ye chose to. Certainly, Malcolm posed no threat to ye once ye had back yer arms."

He hated that she could read him so easily. And why hadn't he left her there? Jesu, he should have. Just listening to her voice did things to him he'd never thought possible.

"I should have," he grumbled, before he'd even realized his intention to speak.

Damn. He didn't have to turn his head to see the quiver in her lip the second before she pulled it between her teeth. Why was it each time he felt strong enough to keep her at bay, he felt guilty the moment he did so?

Guilt where this woman was concerned was wasted, he soon discovered, as she began prattling again.

"I think 'tis yer honor which guides ye, Sir Knight, more so than ye'd have us believe."

"Is it possible for you to be silent for any length of time at all?"

She rode silently beside him for several moments. He harbored no illusions, however, concerning her ability to remain so.

"Ye have my thanks, just the same." She turned her horse, circling back to ride once more with Mattie.

He missed her. Before she'd been gone more than

a heart's beat, he felt her absence. Pain settled over him. Nay, not pain.

Loneliness.

† † †

Meghan watched her knight's strong back, ever erect in his saddle despite the grueling pace he set, his recent illness, and the four days spent locked in the hell of her father's dungeon.

Did he never tire? Not just tire in body, but did his soul not cry out for comfort of any sort? Hers did.

She hadn't known true sorrow before he had happened into her life. Before his arrival, her responsibilities around the keep kept her busy. She'd believed her life as near to complete as possible. She patiently waited for her father to select her husband from the men of the clan. She tended her mother's herb garden. Every so often, she ventured to the village, as her mother had done for years, to see to the needs of the clansmen and their families.

None of those activities seemed worthwhile anymore. The thought of her father choosing her husband appalled her now. None of her clansmen made her heart soar from a mere glance. She doubted any of them would gaze upon her body with open, fierce longing, as did her knight.

Except for Ian. She shook as a deliberate queasiness clutched her stomach. The very thought of his huge, rough hands pawing her made her ill. Ever insistent in his pursuit, she'd made a strong effort never to be alone with him. Had she not convinced her knight to take her away from the keep, she hesitated to think what might have befallen her last night.

She turned her attention back to her knight. When he slid a heated gaze over her body, she could all but feel his hands upon her. The warmth of unfamiliar sensation wrought by those looks refreshed itself even now. She sighed. And yet, he seemed ever unwilling to pursue his wants and desires if, in fact, they did exist.

She smiled. According to young Aigneas they did. But she held little hope for romance based upon the chattering of a bairn. And he was ever in a foul mood when she saw him anyway.

Perhaps his surly demeanor resulted from his weariness. He hadn't slept last night. She hadn't slept either. She'd listened to his tense breathing as he kept watch over them. Of course, he watched for his own benefit, but she rather liked believing his concern lay with her as well.

He must be exhausted.

"Mattie, are ye tired? I'm so weary, I can barely keep my seat." She spoke louder than necessary.

"Ye need no' shout, milady. I'm—"

"Are ye no' needing' a rest?"

Meghan raised her eyebrows and tilted her head in the direction of the quiet man leading them.

Mattie smiled as she replied, "Och. Aye, milady. I do no' think I can ride much longer. My back aches so."

"My lord?" Meghan called, when he failed to

respond to their charade. "Would a rest be in order soon?"

"Nay."

She eyed Mattie with growing impatience.

Mattie whispered, "If he does no' rest soon, he could very easily become ill again."

"Well I know it, Mattie. We'll simply have to keep needling him."

It took more than an hour of complaining, but he finally reined his mount into a copse of trees.

"We'll camp here."

He climbed from his horse in one swift movement. Meghan smiled as he approached. " 'Tis a lovely spot ye've selected, Sir Knight."

And it was. Surrounded by trees, a river's thundering roar made its way to them through the forest. A clearing thick with new grass for the horses to graze sat to the east, while the ground boasted soft cover for sleeping.

He reached up for her, and Meghan allowed him to help her to the ground. He winced as he did so, causing a frown to replace his usual scowl.

"Are ye hurtin', Brandubh?"

He stepped away from her as if she'd struck him. "Nay."

He helped Mattie from her palfrey and turned away. "I'm going hunting. Gather wood for a fire. 'Tis safe enough now."

Meghan sighed as Mattie approached her. "If he refuses to rest, Mattie, I fear he will injure himself."

"Aye. But should he refuse to hunt, milady, we

shall all of us starve," Mattie mused at his departing back.

† † †

Devlin cursed silently as he strode from the clearing. Leave it to a woman to praise the beauty of a place and never consider the ease with which one could defend it.

And her constant feigned discomfort... He cursed again. She worried over him, and well he knew it. He did not want or need her concern or her comfort. Even when he'd been unable to contain the boyish reaction to touching her upon lifting her from her mount, she'd thought him weak.

A fallen log rested across the narrow trail. He stepped over it, running a hand through his hair. As he lowered his arm, he noticed again the welts now healing on his wrist. She'd wrapped both wrists, intent upon giving him whatever relief she could manage.

How long had it been since he'd felt the burning of a lady's touch? His mind raced through the women he'd seduced; they were only wenches intent on satisfying his manly urges in exchange for the right to boast they'd had him. He'd been well into his cups on each occasion and doubted he even recalled them all.

But a lady's touch? The gentleness only found in the arms of someone who truly cared for him?

Ten long years.

Nay.

Allyson had never truly loved him, that much was

obvious to everyone. After her death, he'd been consumed with discovering the extent of her treason. He'd prayed she betrayed only her King, but his discoveries proved otherwise. Yet, he'd allowed himself to be duped by her beauty and her false words of love.

She had been so beautiful and innocent, he thought at the time. The first time he saw her, she sat alone in a corridor of Henry's castle. She seemed so sad and alone then that he'd been drawn to her. Her father, Lord Reginald, had been put to death for treason. It was the last time he'd allowed sympathy to effect his judgment.

Until Meghan.

Bloody hell, but he was a fool.

He positioned himself in a small glade, sitting motionless in the waning daylight.

Waiting.

For what?

For Meghan to come meandering down this same path? For another chance? The foolish dreams danced in his mind. If only he could trust again. But could he afford the risk?

† † †

Meghan found the flint Malcolm had packed in one of the bundles and lit the dry heather beneath several stacked sticks. The fire sparked. She leaned in to blow gently on the burgeoning flame.

Night approached quickly, and nervousness rooted itself in her stomach.

"Mattie, get ye to the stream for water before 'tis too dark to see," she called over her shoulder between breaths.

"Mattie? Are ye about?" she asked again when she received no answer.

The fire caught in earnest then. Meghan straightened her back and turned toward where she'd last seen her friend. Not finding her in the clearing, she ignored the prick of dread making the hair on her nape stand up. She'd likely as not already gone to fetch the water.

The late afternoon sunlight vanished as the golden rays fell behind the trees. The clearing darkened to a twilight of eerie shadows. She wished her knight would return soon. She shivered as she set about slicing hard bread with her eating dagger.

"Where's Mattie?"

"Och, that hurt," she replied at the unexpected sound of Brandubh's voice.

"What?"

"Ye startled me. Now, I've cut myself," she answered around the end of her finger. She removed the finger from her mouth and examined the tip. She bit her lip against the sting.

"Here, let me see it."

He took her hand in his own. Heat shot through her, climbing up her arm and settling with a tingle in her breasts.

"Does it hurt?"

"Aye. A bit," she whispered, not really thinking of

her finger at all, but of the nervous excitement throbbing in her blood.

"You should be more careful," he insisted, releasing her hand so quickly a blanket of ice fell around her.

She knew she scowled, but she didn't care. "Ye should make more noise."

Amazingly, he offered her a lopsided smile. 'Twas catching, that smile. Mayhap 'twas a good thing he did it so rarely, or the whole of Scotland would walk about the countryside grinning like fools.

"Where's Mattie?" He repeated his original question, and she narrowed her brow.

Mattie had been gone a long time. Longer than would be required to fetch water anyway.

Meghan stood. "I assumed she went to the stream, but she's no' returned. Ye do no' suppose something's happened to her?"

"With my luck? Aye. She's been taken by a dragon, and you'll ask me to fight it to get her back."

Meghan laughed then. So, he did possess some sense of humor.

But he didn't smile at his own jest. His serious expression told her he truly believed whatever delayed Mattie's return would interfere with his freedom in some way.

"Come. I'll not have you wandering off while I search for her. We go together."

He didn't wait for her, but marched into the thicket without a backward glance.

She had half a mind to wait there, just to spite him.

Then she remembered the eeriness of this place while she'd been alone, in the dark. She lifted the hem of her gown and followed his straight back into the trees.

"Mattie," his voice called loudly. "Are you there, lass? Answer me if you can hear me."

After what seemed like an eternity, Meghan squinted through the trees. She could see very little since darkness had settled over the forest. "Something terrible has happened. I ken it."

"I'm sure she's fine. No one has followed us."

She hadn't thought of that, and she frowned. What if one of Ian's men had found them and at this very moment held Mattie, just hoping Meghan would search for her?

"I promise. No one has found us, Meghan. Think you I would shout so loudly for her if the enemy lurked in the shadows?"

She bit her lip. "Nay, I suppose yer right."

Just then, Mattie's anguished cries trickled through the limbs of the trees. Meghan's ears perked as she strained to determine the direction from which the sound came.

"Over there." He pointed, taking Meghan by the elbow and leading her toward the cry for help.

Even with the threat of whatever had befallen Mattie, the jolt of sensation at his contact with her dizzied her steps.

"Milady?" came another of Mattie's cries. "Over here, milady."

Meghan stepped out of the trees onto the rocky shore, a mile downstream from their camp. Mattie lay against a rock, soaked to the skin, her lips blue from the cold water.

"Mattie!" she gasped, kneeling at the side of her friend. "What has happened? Are ye well, Mattie?"

Her knight stepped behind her. She didn't need to see him to know the expression on his hard features. He radiated irritation.

"My leg be broken, milady." Mattie sniffed. "I fell into the water and was carried this far before being pushed aside by deadfall. 'Twas then, meetin' with these rocks here, I felt the bone snap."

"Does it hurt? Ye poor thing." Meghan stroked Mattie's wet hair from her face.

"Nay, milady. The water be cold eno' to keep the pain away now."

Meghan looked at her knight's face. He would know what to do. Wouldn't he?

"Move," he stated.

She did as he asked, backing out of his way.

He took her place, kneeling beside Mattie's shivering body. Desire and trust hovered above her as she listened to his voice.

"Mattie," he began, the rich tenor of his voice soothing, even though he'd barely spoken a word. "This is not going to be pleasant for you, no matter what. I'm going to find something here with which to tend the break. Then I will try to keep your leg as still as possible while I move you back to camp. But first we must remove you from the water, ere you freeze. Do you trust me?"

Meghan listened to the gentle words coming from her fierce knight. Minus his normal scowl, his features softened. He still looked as if he could fight a wolf and win with little effort, but a new quality played across his face as well.

Tenderness.

Meghan caught Mattie's searching glance and nodded. Aye. Mattie could well trust this man to do everything in his power to save her pain.

But could she?

Chapter Nine

Devlin stepped into the frigid water and examined Mattie's leg. The lower portion of her left leg bent at an odd, inhuman angle. When the chill of the water wore off, she would feel pain like none she'd ever experienced. Even the agony of the initial break, thankfully, had probably been dimmed by the icy stream. He hated the thought of moving her at all, but there was no avoiding it. Left in the water, she would catch her death.

Her leg remained wedged between two large rocks. If he moved one, the other would shift, causing Mattie even more pain. He studied the angles of the rocks, the angle of her leg, and then decided to make the move as quickly as possible. Perhaps, if he moved with enough speed, he could at least lessen the length of the torture.

"Are you ready, my lady?" He smiled at the frightened

expression on Mattie's face, and the slight blush staining her cheeks at his use of the title reserved for others.

"Aye, my lord. As ready as I'll ever be."

He ignored Meghan's curious perusal of him. She looked at him as if he'd lost all sense. Did she believe him so heartless he could not offer comfort to anyone?

"Up we go then."

In one swift movement, at least he hoped it swift, he shoved the larger of the rocks away and reached into the water to scoop her into his arms. His breath caught. The stream, fed by the melting snow from the recently past winter, bit into his flesh like tiny knives. Placing one arm behind Mattie's back and the other beneath her knees, he bore her weight to the shore. The broken leg swung freely from his forearm. To her credit, Mattie did not scream. Neither did she fight him. Instead, she clung to him with enough force to choke the air from his lungs.

He moved her only three or four steps from the shore's edge and set her gently upon the moist earth.

Meghan rushed to her side. "Oh, Mattie, ye had us so worried. How ever did ye fall into the water?"

"I do no' ken, milady. I'm sorry for causing ye to worry. But I'll be fine," Mattie smiled.

"I wasn't worried. I don't even like either one of you," Devlin couldn't resist adding with a straight face.

He didn't fool Mattie apparently, as her sharp wit returned. " 'Tis no' true, my lord. I ken ye like me verra well, indeed."

He didn't miss Meghan's sharp intake of breath and

the stiffening of her limbs. Was it jealousy he sensed coming from her now? Did she not approve of his bantering with her maid? He snorted to himself. She had nothing to fear. He would do his best to keep clear of them both. Especially Meghan.

He left the two women at the edge of the stream and went in search of a strong, straight branch to use as a splint.

When he returned, having found a very good piece of wood for the purpose, Meghan had removed her cloak and covered Mattie's shivering, wet form with it. Devlin knelt again by Mattie's side and moved the span of wool covering the injured leg.

"Meghan? You'll need to hold her down now."

"Pardon me?" Meghan sputtered. She'd heard him correctly, though he imagined she wished she had not.

"Hold her down," he emphasized. "I'm going to set the bone. 'Twill hurt. Badly."

"Oh, dear," Meghan whispered as she knelt at Mattie's head. "I'm sorry, Mattie."

Mattie's tears etched small red trails down her cheeks, and Devlin's heart went out to the young girl. Having experienced first hand the setting of a broken limb, he knew well how much pain would be inflicted the moment he touched her.

"I ken I'm going to be sick, milady," Mattie cried, placing her hand over her mouth.

" 'Tis the pain, Mattie. But all will be well. We're going to do this quickly, and you must be brave."

"I'll try, my lord," she whimpered.

"Hold her well, Meghan."

He waited until Meghan leaned all of her weight on Mattie's shoulders then he straddled Mattie's undamaged leg. He grasped the broken leg and immediately pulled. Mattie released a sound from the depths of her soul. Only the soul could form a scream of such blatant anguish. After what seemed an eternity, he released the injury. The leg, though badly bruised and bright red from the cold water, held the proper shape.

Without waiting for the pain to ease, he reached toward Meghan's gown, ripped a long piece from the bottom and used it to tightly secure the branches he'd cut to Mattie's leg.

He'd completed the task before Meghan had time to berate him for tearing her dress. She did so now. In earnest.

"Was it truly necessary to destroy my gown?"

She stood over him now, her eyes flaming and her hands upon her hips.

"Aye." He rose to tower over her, using his height to intimidate.

It didn't work.

"Mayhap next time ye feel the urge to rip my clothing from me, ye'll have the decency to provide warning first."

The images conjured by those words attacked him with a heated vengeance. He wanted nothing more than to tear every stitch from her body, to finally feast his hungry eyes on the charms that lay hidden beneath the finery.

She did not blush. In her innocence, she apparently hadn't even realized what she'd said, or the sensual connotation of the statement. He stood rooted to the ground as if he were one of the trees surrounding them.

He should kiss her. He remembered the taste of her lips, regardless of the fever-induced delirium he'd suffered at the time. She'd tasted of honey, and ale, and woman. What would she taste of now?

"Oh, milady," Mattie winced. " 'Tis only more trouble I've caused fer ye now, and well I know it. And now, because of me, ye've ruined yer lovely gown."

Devlin ran a hand through his hair, his body frustrated and hard.

"Nay, Mattie. 'Tis lord 'Have-my-own-way' who ruined my gown."

"My own way?" he bellowed. "If I were to have my own way, my lady, you and your maid would be settled rather nicely in your own keep, instead of dragging my arse halfway through this cursed country in the opposite direction of my own."

Damn the woman for getting inside him like this. At least now, he had an excuse to be rid of her. The first manor, clan, home, or kirk they passed, he would drop these two on the steps and hie himself back to England.

"Oh! My lord, I am so sorry for rescuing ye from certain death for the simple request that ye escort us to safety. How dare we presume to intrude on yer good graces," Meghan railed back at him.

In shock, he could only look at her. The color rose high in her cheeks, turning them a pink several shades darker than he'd ever seen them before. Finding his tongue, he answered, " 'Tis you who held me prisoner to begin with, my lady. Had you not done so, no 'rescuing' would have been in order."

"Mayhap I should have left ye on the feasting hall steps then, my lord, where I'm certain any number of wee beasties could have fed for a month!"

His reply to her vehemence perched on the edge of his lips when Mattie's wounded cry cut him off.

Jesu, that woman could make Saint Joseph rue the day he'd been born. He glared at her one last time, before turning his attention back to Mattie. Unfortunately, she did the same.

Meghan knelt beside him, her arm brushing against his as she ran her slender fingers over Mattie's brow. The inevitable regret for his comments burned through him as fiercely as her touch.

His level of amazement at her ability to soothe Mattie's fears and pain grew with each movement of her hands. Mattie's breathing evened, and her color showed hints of normal through her icy flesh.

"I did not mean to ruin your gown," he whispered before he even knew he had formed the thought.

Meghan's hand stilled, but she did not look at him.

" 'Tis of no import, my lord. Ye did what ye had to. I simply would have preferred some warning."

"I felt arguing with you would waste valuable time. The sooner I bound her leg, the sooner the pain would lessen."

Now she turned her narrowed eyes on him. The

intensity of her gaze heated him. "Why would I argue? Do ye ken I love this dress more so than my friend?"

"I don't know. Many women would refuse to use their garments for such a purpose." He suddenly realized this description did not fit Meghan at all.

"My lord," she replied with tight lips. "I hope someday ye will come to understand I am very little like 'many women.'"

† † †

Meghan rolled to her back. The moon cast a hesitant glow through ghostly clouds, but much of the sky remained clear, twinkling with thousands of winking lights. Her back ached and her body grew wearier by the day, but something inside her told her she had done the right thing. Would her father agree? She couldn't help but wonder if she would make him proud when she arrived at Ravenstone Keep to champion him. He was a very proud man, and the possibility that he might not appreciate her current sacrifices loomed over her.

Posh. Men seldom knew what was good for them.

The fire crackled as the embers died, drawing her attention, followed by a quiet moan from Mattie's pallet.

Meghan rose from her pallet and stirred the flames, sending a rich amber light over her maid, who lay only an arm's length away.

"Does it pain ye overmuch, Mattie?" Meghan wished she'd thought to bring her herbs with her when they'd escaped the keep. She could easily brew

THE JEWEL AND THE SWORD

something to ease whatever pain Mattie experienced.

"Nay, milady. Yer knight was ever so gentle."

Pulling the wool cover to Mattie's neck, Meghan satisfied herself that her friend experienced little of the chill in the air before returning to her pallet.

Her knight.

He would never be hers. She'd finally admitted to herself, the moment he'd stooped in front of Mattie's soaked form in the stream, that she wanted him in a way she'd yet to fathom. She'd known how badly her body craved his, how desperately she wished he would soothe the fires pounding through her at his touch. But more than this, she wished for his love.

The words he'd spoken were firm, the directions precise, brooking no argument from either of them. But kind and filled with warmth.

'Twas then she'd known gentleness flowed through him.

She hadn't really been upset by his use of her gown to fasten the sticks to Mattie's leg. Only the shock of having him tear it so suddenly caused her reaction. And when he had whispered his apology? She'd thought her heart would leap from her chest. The caress of his whispers still hummed through her veins.

"He has a kind nature beneath that wicked shield, I'd wager," Mattie said, gritting her teeth as she rolled over, making her words sound pinched.

"Aye," Meghan replied, after giving the matter thought.

" 'Twas with the very arms of an angel he carried me back here."

"Aye." The arms of an angel. Meghan sighed as she allowed sleep to creep through her limbs. An angel who offered kindness to bairns and maids.

But not her.

† † †

The next morning Meghan awakened to find herself and Mattie alone in the small camp. Mattie still slept at her side, so she crept away as quietly as she could. The longer Mattie slept, the more time she would have free of the pain.

Leaving the clearing to attend to personal matters, she scanned the forest for Brandubh. He doubtless had taken the bow and arrows to hunt for something with which to break their fast.

Upon returning, she found him at the edge of the clearing stripping small leaves from several long branches.

"Brandubh," she offered, ever uncertain of his mood.

He lifted his head and frowned. Her question answered, she said nothing, but sat down next to him on the soft earth. She picked up a branch and helped him strip the leaves.

"What are you doing?" he asked without looking at her.

"I'm helping ye, my lord. 'Tis a great many branches, here."

"I can see that. Why are you doing it? Do you not

fear to mar your delicate hands?"

"I do no'." She sighed. "What are we doing, by the way?"

She thought she heard him chuckle and looked at him to see if he smiled.

He did.

His entire countenance changed. Gone were the lines in his brow and the dismal glow of his eyes. Instead, he radiated happiness.

"We are making a litter to carry yon maiden. She could barely ride before she broke her leg. I reckon she would much prefer not to ride now."

Meghan couldn't speak for a full minute. "Ye have a very nice face, my lord, when ye do no' frown." The husky quality of her voice startled her, along with the words she spoke. She lowered her eyes to the branch in her lap, but still felt the heat of his gaze.

He cleared his throat, but said nothing.

"I ken ye no want our company forced on ye, but mayhap we could set aside our differences for the remains of our travels, my lord?"

She raised her face to his to find his smile vanished and one eyebrow quirked at her in question.

" 'Tis only that we have many miles left," she continued, "and I find the company of yer smile–"

"A truce then," he interrupted.

She could read nothing in his expression, as he seemed to mull over her suggestion.

"Aye. A truce."

He stripped the leaves from the last of the branches

before he answered with a smile. "Very well then, my lady. I shall endeavor to heed your desires."

Heed your desires.

'Twas too much to hope for.

† † †

A gentle breeze swept across her cheeks, and she raised her hand to smooth away the loose tendrils tickling her cheeks. "Will ye tell me yer name?"

He laughed again. "Nay, my lady."

"Why no'? 'Tisn't as if I still hold ye prisoner."

Devlin's humor left him at her comment. Nay, she did not hold him prisoner, but he would not allow her to capture his heart. His heart argued the fact as she pulled another loose curl away from her lips and tucked it behind her ear. "You have no need for my name," he replied, more curtly than he'd intended.

Though she only sighed in response, he could feel the quiet moment slipping away. He should let it go. But he couldn't. He liked being with her like this. The warmth of her offered friendship swept over him with heated breath.

"Tell me about where ye grew up, my lord. I have heard so very little of life in England. Is it much different than in Scotland?"

He felt his brow narrowing at her question, and as she looked at him, his concern mirrored itself in her expression.

"I'm sorry," she added quickly, putting aside her

The Jewel and the Sword

branches. " 'Tis none of my concern. I shall leave ye to yer work."

She gained her feet and brushed the leaves from her gown. His stomach knotted.

Bloody hell. He'd offended her again. By the time she'd taken two steps from him, he already missed her.

"I was fostered under Lord Harold Hamilton, with my cousin and King Henry." He spoke into the branches he sorted by length and breadth at his feet.

He did not look up, but sensed her stop and turn back to him. Her eyes resting on him filled him completely, and he could feel her bewilderment at his confession.

"So, 'tis normal for young men to leave their homes in England as well?"

She returned to his side, but instead of sitting on the ground, she leaned against the trunk of a tree, her hands flat behind her full rump. He turned away and closed his eyes against the wish it were his own hands touching her there.

"Aye."

"And what of the rest of yer family? They missed ye, certainly. Do ye have brothers or sisters?"

"Why do you want to know these things?" He set down the last of the sticks, having formed a ladder of sorts on the ground. He stretched his back and placed his hands on his hips.

She shrugged in response, causing a thick curl to fall from her shoulder across her breast. Absently, she pushed it back over her shoulder. "I am but curious, my lord. I never had any brothers or sisters. My mother was no' a strong woman, physically. She nearly died bearing me, and my father forbid her from having any more children."

Devlin released a quiet snort, hoping she could not hear him. 'Twas very much like Morven to presume to dictate to God Himself who should and should not conceive. "I have no brothers either."

"Sisters?"

"Nay," he answered.

"But ye had the benefit of fostering," she sighed.

"Aye," he answered. Despite his conscious desire to keep her at a distance, he found himself curious about her as well. "Was it lonely for you? Growing up with no one to play with?"

She smiled and glanced toward camp. "Nay, my lord. Mattie was my playmate, long before she became my maid. I often pretended she was my sister, and she did the same, I ken."

He remembered the few times Mattie had spoken to Meghan with less than due respect, and laughed. "That explains a lot, my lady."

He removed his tunic and laid it on the rock beside her. A moment later, he took off his undertunic and reached in his belt for the dagger he'd found in the bundle Malcolm had provided for him.

"What are ye doing?" Meghan's gasp surprised him. When he looked at her, her eyes were wide and her cheeks pinked.

"I'm going to make strips from this garment to finish

building the litter for Mattie." What was wrong with her? She looked as if she would swoon as her eyes roamed over his chest, sending spirals of heat through him. It had been a long time since a woman's appreciation of him had had any effect on his own control. His throat tightened. "Why? Would you prefer to use your gown?"

She cleared her throat as she pushed herself off the tree. "Nay," she mumbled.

It was on the tip of his tongue to call to her, take her in his arms, and kiss the blush from her cheeks. Her earlier comment concerning his ripping her clothes from her still burned through his blood, but as he watched her stiff back disappear into the trees, he knew he couldn't do it. As tempting as her full, pink lips beckoned, he would keep his distance. He had to.

Lord, how he sometimes hated his honor.

† † †

Meghan's words still echoed from the walls of Devlin's mind as he led his charges toward the gate of an old kirk. Two nuns worked in a garden next to the structure. He'd never been so thankful to see a member of the Church in his life. He could leave the women here and be well on his way before the sun crossed its zenith.

Ever since Meghan incited his blood with the comments concerning her clothing, and a certain method for removing them, he'd been burdened by his body's pubescent reactions. Two sleepless nights and the better part of two days later, and he still ached for her.

"We're nearly there, Mattie."

Meghan drew her mount to the side of his charger.

He felt her eyes rest on him. He liked it when she looked at him. He shifted in his saddle and added this as yet another reason to leave her behind as quickly as possible.

"How long do ye suppose we'll stay here?" she asked.

How long? We?

He concentrated his attention on the kirk, trying to ignore the scent of roses reaching to him from beneath the aroma of earth and woman. "You may stay for as long as you please, my lady."

"But I'm sure ye'll be wanting to continue to England as soon as possible. I'll need only a few minutes to settle Mattie with—"

"You are staying here," he interrupted.

He gripped the reins more tightly in his hand. What was it about this woman that set his blood to flames? She talked too much, and she ordered him about as if he were some servant. She had scolded him on more than one occasion and more often than not, when forced to endure her ceaseless chatter, his head hurt. Yet a simple glance or the scent of roses in her hair made his knees tremble and his heart race.

'Twas unnerving.

"I am no' staying here when my father is in England. If I must, I will journey to London and bring the matter before the King himself!"

He gritted his teeth. King Henry's involvement in this game of irony boded ill for all concerned. He could feel it. Henry had a desire to solve most problems with a sword, or a marriage. Neither one appealed to Devlin.

"Henry will be of no help to you," he said, fighting the urge to glance at her.

"That remains to be seen. If ye take me to my father, I will no' have to even ask it of him."

He ran a hand through his hair again, his jaw clenched unto breaking. He would not be baited once more into this conversation. "I'll not discuss it further."

He pulled Midnight to a stop in front of the kirk just as an old priest came from the front door.

"Hail, strangers," the priest called with cheer in his rough voice.

Devlin nodded as he dismounted.

"Father." Meghan smiled, as she nodded in the old priest's direction.

Her smile sent tremors through Devlin. Was he making a mistake, not taking her with him to England? He dismissed the thought. She still didn't even know his name, and when she learned it, never again would he be witness to the light of her smile. At least, not directed toward him.

"I am Father Monroe, and 'tis pleased I am to welcome ye to St. Benedict Abbey."

Devlin lifted Meghan from her saddle, doing his best to ignore the soft curve of her waist beneath his hands. Still, he released her as soon as her small feet touched the ground. She stepped away from him to speak more with the priest, while he circled behind Mattie's palfrey.

"Will ye be staying for the night then? We have little to offer, but what we have is yers." Father Monroe followed him around his horse and apparently noticed Mattie for the first time. "What's this?"

"She's broken her leg, Father." Meghan tsked. "I'm afraid her travels must end here, at least for a while."

Devlin's ears pricked at Meghan's use of the word "her" regarding who would be ending their travels.

"Nay, woman. You will both remain here," he growled.

Meghan stared at him, her eyes shining. He glared back, determined she read him clearly. The ensuing silence hovered in the air for nearly a minute, during which time he never once removed his eyes from hers.

If the priest found the tense conversation odd, he didn't find it necessary to discuss it. Instead, he clapped his hands, and smiled. "Well, if ye'll see to bringing the lass inside, yer lady and I will make a place of comfort for her whilst she heals." He then took Meghan's arm and led her away.

Devlin fastened his gaze on the sway of Meghan's hips teasing the fabric of her cloak. Her bearing, ever proud, annoyed him and called to him at once. He needed to get away. Now. Before it was too late.

"Ye ken she'll no' let ye leave her here," said Mattie.

THE JEWEL AND THE SWORD

He shook his head and looked down at Mattie, still lying helpless on the litter. A knowing light shone in her eyes.

"She has no choice in the matter, Mattie." He grimaced at the rueful laugh he received in response. "Are you ready?"

Without waiting for an answer, he picked her up and followed the path to the living quarters behind the old church.

Once inside, he found Meghan and the priest had turned aside the sheets on a small, wood-framed bed set into the corner of the room. Also in the room were a table and five chairs, a larger bed, and a cabinet arranged with religious artifacts and linens. He placed Mattie on the bed and pulled the coarse blankets over her legs.

"Does this suit you, my lady?" he asked.

"Aye. Very well, milord," she answered with a seemingly genuine smile, even though the short trek from the horse to the bed must have pained her.

"Good. You'll recover well here, with the priest, the sisters, and Lady Meghan to tend you. I'll see to it you have gold to help you on your way once you've healed."

Why had he said that? He owed them nothing. He cringed inwardly. Nay. He owed them his life. He owed Meghan his life. The least he could do was help them make their way somewhere safe. He didn't explain further, but turned and marched toward the door.

"Where do ye go, my lord?"

"Elsewhere."

Halfway to the horses, he heard the door open and close behind him.

Bloody hell.

"We must discuss this, my lord," Meghan called.

"Nay." He did not slow his pace, though he turned to find her racing toward him. Within a few seconds she appeared at his side, forced to take two steps to his every one.

"Why no'?"

He reached Mattie's palfrey and untied the straps holding the litter to the saddle. He repeated the task on the far side and the branches fell to the ground. "Because there is naught to discuss."

She huffed to herself then and placed her fisted hands upon her full hips. "Why is it when a man wishes to discuss something, 'tis the most important speech upon the earth. Yet when a woman has something to say, a man may refuse to converse upon his own whim?"

"Luck."

He threw the saddle over his shoulder and stomped toward the stable where the priest housed his own mount. She would follow him, he had no doubt. She would be heard, no matter what he said.

Her voice behind him confirmed his suspicions.

"Do no' walk away from me, my lord. We're no' finished here."

He placed the saddle on the floor of the stable,

THE JEWEL AND THE SWORD

turned and collided with her as she stood in the doorway. Instinctively, he grabbed her shoulders to keep her from falling. She pulled away from him as if he'd slapped her, but remained in his way. A challenge resided in her eyes.

"Now ye will listen, my lord?"

Did she think he could not leave? He stepped closer to her in the dim light of the stable. Her chin quivered. She still met his eyes, though her head tilted back due to his height.

"Get out of my way, woman," he whispered. "Think you I will not move you from my path?"

"Ye would no' dare," she retorted with such indignation in her voice that Devlin acted upon it immediately.

He took both of her shoulders into his hands. Meghan's mouth dropped open. He lifted her from the ground, took two long strides forward, and set her gently down. She appeared small and delicate when compared with his large frame. The thought of how easily she could be hurt by someone of his size needled its way into his conscience.

His gaze locked with hers. The color in her cheeks rose to a fiery red. Her eyes blazed.

Then she kicked him in the leg.

"What was that for?" Frustration surged through him. He should have seen it coming.

"Because ye will no' listen to reason," she spat at him, pulling her leg back for a second attack.

Though he felt no pain from it, the fact she had the gall to do it annoyed him. The fact she'd impressed him as well irritated him even more so.

Unwilling to risk further assault, he stepped around her toward the horses. He still needed to tend to her mount before he could depart this place. And depart he would, regardless of her desires.

By the time he removed the saddle from her horse and turned, she was gone. He'd expected to see her standing on the path, eyes blazing, breath ragged. He refused to scan the church grounds for her. He cared not where she had hied herself off to, so long as she wasn't around him. So long as he did not have to see her stubborn chin, her dainty ears peeking from beneath her brat, her slim waist and full breasts . . .

His body, ever hard since he'd known her, tightened further at the soft images. He cursed. He'd thought to stay long enough to eat a true meal, but changed his mind. He had to leave now.

† † †

Meghan paced inside the small rectory. Trying to convince him to take her to England had been a waste of time. She would do well not to confuse his gentleness in given circumstances with weakness of nature. Such a strong man would never agree to her demands simply because she asked it of him. And she would not beg.

"Milady? What are ye thinking of now? Ye've got that look again. The one that says ye'll be up to yer neck in trouble afore long."

The Jewel and the Sword

"I'm no' thinking anything, Mattie. I'm just waiting for his lordship to finish tending my horse ere we depart for England."

Mattie's voice scoffed, "Do ye really ken he'll take ye all the way to yer uncle's manor, milady?"

"He'll have to. I'm no' giving him a choice."

Mattie laughed causing Meghan to turn from her position by the window. She placed her hands akimbo and glared at her maid. "And what, pray tell, is so funny?"

"Naught, milady. Except he said that very thing about you."

CHAPTER TEN

By late afternoon, Devlin rode steadily toward his homeland. A day filled with haunting visions and hard riding, he'd been unable to outrun the images of Meghan's face or the taste of her lips. He traveled slowly now, granting respite to his worn horse, his progress made ever slower as the rain pelted him and made the road slick with deep mud. In familiar territory, he had only three more days of travel to reach his home.

What would he do when he arrived there? He didn't know for certain, other than release Morven. As much as the thought of freeing the man sickened Devlin, Morven needed to care for his daughter. Left alone, he shuddered to think what might happen to her.

Then why did you leave her?

He ignored the voice inside his head.

The Jewel and the Sword

The air around him sizzled as a bolt of lightning sliced the sky. Thunder crashed over his head with enough force to make him duck. A scream followed the storm's fury and ripped through him.

He turned Midnight toward the sound and spurred him forward. Within a few moments he found the source. In a puddle to her knees, just off the road, her horse stamping impatiently a few feet way, stood Meghan Douglas.

"What the bloody hell are you doing here?" he shouted above the storm.

"I followed ye, obviously," she yelled back, looking not at all contrite and more than a little annoyed.

She was annoyed? Devlin fought against the heat flooding his veins as he gazed down at the soaking wet cloak outlining each of her curves. He leapt from Midnight's back and stalked over to her.

"You could have been killed. Are you daft, woman?"

"Nay. I but want to see my father. Ye go to Ravenstone Castle. 'Tis only common sense if I followed ye, I would find him."

Her logic astounded him. Her bravery amazed him.

"And what did you think to do when you arrived? 'Excuse me, Lord Ravenstone, but I'd like my father returned to me, please.' Do you really think a 'monster' would even allow you to see your father?"

She bit her lip. Blood rushed to his loins forcing him to turn his back on her. He ran a hand through his wet hair, suddenly realizing the rain had stopped.

"I do no' ken. But I will try."

A wave of compassion settled over him. He didn't know where it came from, and he tried to shake it off. He didn't want to feel sorry for her. But he couldn't deny the way her forced confidence made his arms ache to hold her. He turned back to her and winced.

"Don't you do it," he warned.

"What?"

"Cry."

"I'm no' going to cry," she squeaked, puffing her chest out. "I never cry."

She looked like a wet rooster trying to crow when, in fact, she had little voice left at all. Against his own wishes, his heart lurched. She continued to train her eyes on his face. She blinked twice, her long black lashes spiky and wet. He guessed they weren't wet from the rainstorm, but from the unshed tears which even now threatened to escape.

He sighed.

Aye. A hundred times the fool.

"Don't look at me like that."

"Like what?" she hiccuped.

"Like you trust me."

"But I do trust ye, my lord."

Words escaped him as he narrowed his eyes at her. She trusted him now, but what of later, when she learned who he was? She would hate him.

Suddenly, the ruse he'd been playing seemed less like self-preservation and more like . . .

Lies.

The Jewel and the Sword

"You shouldn't trust me, my lady."

She stepped closer to him.

"I've seen yer kindness, my lord. Ye can no' be so mean as ye pretend."

"You think not?"

If she took even one step closer, he'd prove to her the extent of his wickedness.

"Nay. And even if ye are no' trustworthy, and ye've said as much, then why should I trust what ye've said, even about yerself?"

The sound of her voice, prattling on about such nonsense drew him to her. His eyes narrowed.

"Now, why are ye looking at me like that?"

He took a step toward her, unbidden. He was helpless to stop himself.

He didn't answer her. Not with words, anyway. Taking her in his arms, he pressed his mouth to hers before she had a chance to back away. She tasted of honey again. Sweet, intoxicating honey. She molded herself to him, giving him license to increase his wanton attentions. His body encompassed her smaller frame.

What harm could come from a kiss?

She did not resist, but instinctively opened her mouth to his unspoken command to do so. A woman full-grown, 'twas her right to push him away, yet she did not.

Nay, no harm in the honesty of a simple embrace.

She doesn't know who you are.

The thought struck him like a gauntlet.

His blood beat a battle cadence in his temples, and he pushed her away. She frowned silently, her lips swollen from his attention.

"What's wrong?" she panted.

It wasn't her fault. He forced a smile. Where she was concerned, he had no fight left. Not now, anyway. "Nothing."

He could see she didn't believe him.

"You win, my lady. I'll take you to your father," he grumbled against his better judgment.

She sniffed. "Ye will?"

He splashed through the mud and took up the reins to her horse. "Are you able to ride?"

"Aye. The puddle broke my fall." She turned her brilliant smile on him. The skies seemed brighter, and the sun peeked from behind a storm cloud sending white light streaming over her shoulders.

He laughed as he lifted her into her saddle.

"You know," he began, climbing onto Midnight's back, "I should be very cross with you. Anything could have happened. Ian's men might have found you. Or brigands, criminals, even traveling soldiers could have easily mistaken you for a peasant maid." He choked back the direction of his thoughts. Had anyone taken liberties with her, he would have killed them. The sobering thought made him frown.

Meghan's mind and body still reeled from his kiss.

At this moment, she'd more likely be mistaken for a queen, so heady did she feel. She glanced at his expression.

Did he feel it too? The spark of connection she experienced whenever he turned his crystal eyes on her? She dared not hope, if the frown marring his features was an indication. She sighed inwardly. Hoping for his love seemed increasingly far-fetched. But she would remember his kiss and maybe make him smile again.

"Ye have the most uncanny way of switching yer mood, my lord." She shook her head piteously at him. "A mere moment ago, yer whole face beamed happiness, and yet now ye frown again."

She caught the hint of that endearing lopsided grin he shared so seldom. "Why should I be happy? I'm once again forced to endure your company."

The words held no sting. Just sharing his company brought her a joy she couldn't explain or understand. Although she'd meant only to follow him, hoping he would lead her to Ravenstone's manor, traveling beside him proved both safer and more pleasant. If only he would continue to offer her the occasional smile.

"Tell me about yer lord," she asked, attempting to keep the easy flow of conversation they rarely shared.

He hesitated before answering, as if he wished not to speak of it. He must have decided no harm could come from her question as he replied, "What do you want to know?"

"Is he as ferocious as we've been led to believe?"

"Oh, aye. There is no more wicked man in all of Christendom. He dines upon the lifeless bodies of small children each full moon's eve, and when angered, fangs grow bloody from his jaws."

Meghan couldn't stop herself from laughing. Of course, his description of his liege matched all she'd been led to believe of the man, but hearing it spoken aloud with the hint of wit in his voice made her fears seem preposterous. "I doubt that, my lord. 'Tis a man we speak of, is it no'?"

"Aye. Lord Ravenstone is mortal," he whispered.

"Is there kindness in him, as well? I mean, when he's no' breaking his fast upon wee bairns?"

"There used to be."

The serious tone in his voice sent a shiver over her. "But no longer?"

"Nay. He is a good leader. But ever lonely."

"Mayhap 'tis his loneliness which makes him unkind." Meghan could see well how her knight and his lord could be friends. She recognized the man he described in him. He shifted in his saddle as she studied him and then cleared his throat loudly.

"How is it you managed to follow? Did not the priest, Father–"

"Monroe," she finished for him. She continued to examine him, unsure whether he truly did not remember the priest's name. Very little passed without his knowing, so she doubted it. "Aye, he forbade me from coming. 'Tis why I waited until all were ensconced in their prayers."

"You did what?"

His shoulders squared as he directed those beautiful

blue eyes on her. The ice-tempered glare froze her next words in her throat. She swallowed against them.

"You followed, even knowing I would be out of your sight?"

She nodded slowly.

He heaved a sigh, sounding as if it came from the very depths of his soul.

"I'm sorry, my lord. I ken I should no' have left alone."

"Then why did you?" he barked at her, freezing the blood further in her veins. He growled under his breath and looked straight ahead.

"I will get to my father and plead with Lord Ravenstone for his release, and his help, whether or no' ye take me there." She paused, unsure how he would accept her next words. "But ye have my thanks for escorting me. I simply could no' abide staying in the kirk indefinitely."

"I had planned to send a garrison to escort you to a relative's home," he responded.

"Och, well, then why did ye no' tell me? I would have appreciated that. Being taken even further from my course with strangers, no less. Armed to the teeth, I'm sure." She hoped the wit in her tone lay thickly upon her tongue. "And where, pray tell, would this garrison have come from?"

"There." He pointed to his left.

Meghan followed the direction he indicated and gasped. Sitting among several low hills rose a keep the size of which she'd never seen. With four towers and too many windows to count, the castle loomed massive on the horizon. "What is this place?"

"Dunburough. The home of my . . . friend."

She eyed him with suspicion. He withheld something in that statement. She could sense it. She wanted to learn as much about her knight as possible, before she would never see him again. So against her better judgment, she pressed him. "I did no' ken English knights had Scottish friends."

"They don't."

"Yet ye say this fine Scottish castle belongs to a friend."

"This is a fine English Castle. It is the northernmost defense."

"Ye mean . . ." She turned in her saddle to look behind her.

"Aye. We've been in England for nearly five whole minutes."

"I have never been so far from home," she whispered. She was in England. From this moment on, she would tread on enemy soil. The full impact of her thoughts sent shivers down her spine.

The jingling of harnesses brought her attention to several men riding to meet them.

"Wait here," he told her. Tempted to argue with him, she refrained based solely upon the set of his shoulders. She would do well to obey this time.

He rode to meet them, and her breath caught in her chest at the magnificent image. Sitting straight and tall, his dark hair flew behind him like a banner.

Confidence poured from him. She wet her lips, suddenly dry, and realized her mouth watered.

Swallowing hard, she pulled her mount to a stop and watched him meet with the castle guard. In the center, the apparent lord of this large manor smiled in her direction. His broad shoulders and strong build easily matched that of her knight. His open, pleasant expression spoke of a friendly nature. It did not surprise her that this light-hearted man would befriend such a man as her escort. His lightness played well against her knight's dark, brooding nature.

After several minutes, he rode back to her with a grim expression. Of course, his expression seldom revealed anything else. He might be in a very fine mood.

"We've been invited to stay," he remarked. "I would advise you not to speak."

"And why is that?" Meghan asked, her hand instinctively settling on her hip.

"Because while we've been riding north and circling around to avoid your Ian, he has sent word to King Henry of your father's capture by Ravenstone, the raid, for which he laid blame squarely upon Morven's shoulders, and your disappearance. Henry's messenger rested here less than a day past, on his way to Douglas Castle to deliver the King's reply."

She could feel the color drain from her face. "What does that all mean?"

"Ian has requested the leadership of Clan Douglas be passed to him. And there's more."

"What?" she gripped the reins until the leather bit into her palms.

"He's requested you for his wife."

† † †

"Here we are." Meghan's hostess brought a shimmering white gown from a trunk at the foot of the large bed in her chamber. "I think this should do it."

Meghan's eyes widened at the expensive material and golden threads which made up the gown. "Oh, nay, I could no' possibly borrow such a fine garment as this, Lady Lydia."

She already liked the young woman. Though she appeared several years older than Meghan, she possessed a child-like friendliness that belied her age. And her position as chatelaine of Dunburough Castle. 'Twas her brother who had smiled at Meghan so sweetly upon their arrival. Lydia's husband, she learned, had died in battle two years ago.

"Posh. Of course you can," she replied with a sigh, placing a hand on her slim belly. "I'm afraid I shall never wear it again, since the birth of my Rebecca these three years past."

As if hearing her name, a small girl rushed into the room. Lydia put the gown on the bed and picked up the squirming child with a firm grip.

"And what have you been about, my sweet? Bothering his lordship yet again?"

"Aye, mummy," she giggled.

"I am occupied with Lady Meghan at the moment, so why don't you go bother his lordship just a while longer," she replied, setting the child back on the floor.

Meghan laughed after Rebecca, as she sped away to do that very thing if the mischievous glint in her eyes was any indication.

"She is a beautiful little lass, my lady."

"Aye, but a pest more often than not, I'm afraid. Come. Let us get you dressed."

Fully aware she would not dissuade her new friend from loaning her the gown, she allowed Lydia to help her put it on. The fabric kissed her skin and made her feel beautiful.

" 'Tis lovelier upon you than it ever was on me," Lydia offered.

Meghan's cheeks burned with the compliment. She dipped her head slightly, hoping Lydia would not see.

"I think his lordship will find you most pleasing. And not my brother." Lydia winked. "His *other* lordship."

"Oh, I do no' think so," Meghan answered. Though, even the thought of him finding her so made small tremors in her belly.

"I've known him many years, my lady. And even an old woman like me can still see the way he looks at you."

She felt like denying Lydia's words, but she, too, had seen the heated gazes with which he studied her. And the heat of his kiss had seared through her as well.

Nay. 'Twas lust he felt for her. Nothing more.

"Be that as it may, Lady Lydia, I fear he but looks without any intention of making his desires known. No' to me, anyway."

But how she wished he could love her.

† † †

"Now, you want to tell me what all that nonsense upon your arrival was about?" Will sat across the trestle table from Devlin, his own cup of ale nearly drained for the third time.

Devlin turned on the bench and scanned Dunborough's large feasting hall.

"She's not here, Dev. She's above stairs with Lydia. Bathing, I should think."

The thought didn't help Devlin's condition. What he wouldn't give to attend to her bath. He gave himself a mental shake.

"I appreciate you helping me. She has no idea who I am, and I prefer to keep it that way."

"I don't pretend to understand why, but your thanks aren't needed. This is your castle, in case you've forgotten. I but live here."

"And manage it, you and your sister. And very well, I might add."

" 'Tis of little import. I want to know where you've been since the attack on Douglas Keep. Your mother believes you dead."

Devlin winced at that. "Did you not receive a ransom letter?"

Will shook his head. "Nay, not that I'm aware. And I've only returned to Dunburough three days past."

"Meghan said she'd sent a missive requesting her father's release in exchange for mine."

"If she did, it never arrived."

Devlin's next comment never left his lips as his attention fell on Meghan's descent from the tower stairs. Her visage stole his breath, making speech something of a challenge.

Will turned on his bench and released a low whistle, then stated, "As I said. Bathing."

The white gown she'd apparently borrowed from his cousin, Lydia, fit her well. Trimmed in gold that just matched the strands of her hair in the firelight of several torches, the raiment paled in comparison with the flush of her cheeks when she caught his gaze. She smiled. His heart hammered in his chest.

"Dev?"

Devlin's attention snapped back to Will. He cleared his throat and repositioned himself on the bench. "What?"

"She is Morven's daughter. What are you thinking?"

"I'm not thinking anything," he replied, too quickly.

He hated the scrutiny with which his cousin often viewed him. Of all his family, even his King, Will's opinion of him mattered foremost in his mind, and he'd never been able to hide his own emotions from his very good friend.

"I think you're taken with her."

He could feel the blood rush from his face. "Nay.

'Tis but a passing illness."

Named Meghan.

"You cannot merely dally with Morven Douglas's daughter, my lord."

If Will used the formal title as a twisting knife, to indicate Devlin's responsibility to his villeins, it worked.

"Although taken seriously, it would make for peace between you and Morven."

"Your speech is wasted, Will. Whoever Ian is, I'm certain once Henry grants him Meghan's hand, Morven will be less my problem and more his. Now leave off," he growled, unwilling to continue the topic of conversation. What he felt, or did not feel, for the daughter of his foster brother concerned no one but himself. "And remember. You're the only person who knows who she is. I expect it to remain so."

"Why? You seem perfectly willing to return her to this Ian soon enough."

"Not until I have my sword," Devlin lied. He truly did not want Ian to have Meghan, any more than she wanted to go back. But his feelings were moot when taken into consideration with Henry's wishes. With a petition before him, and no dissent upon the matter, Henry would grant the request without a second thought.

"Devlin," Will groaned. "You must . . ."

Meghan's whisper screamed over the din of the noisy hall. "Yer name is Devlin?"

Devlin released a growl in Will's direction.

† † †

"My lady." Will stood and offered his place at table to Meghan, seemingly ignoring the ferocious sounds emanating from Devlin's throat.

Devlin.

She finally knew his name. She liked the sound of it, and it fit him well. She repeated it to herself several times. 'Twas a very nice name. She still didn't understand why he'd been so secretive about it.

"My thanks." She smiled at her host as she took the offered seat. "As well for revealing Sir Knight's true name. 'Twas becoming tedious addressing him with diminutives. Why 'twas such a secret, I shall never know."

Devlin continued to glare at his friend. She thought she recognized a hint of warning in his icy blue eyes. Some unknown communication passed between them. She sensed it within the tension suddenly surrounding her. As if he knew her curiosity threatened to get the better of her, Will offered her a tray of meat and cheese.

"I'm no' hungry, Will," she replied.

"We have traveled far this day. You must have some hunger." Devlin's threatening countenance softened, as a concerned inflection entered his tone.

"Are ye worried for me, my lord?"

"Aye, Dev. Do you worry for her?" Will chimed in. When Meghan turned to look at him, his full mouth spread into a knowing smile.

She looked at Devlin again. His cheeks paled visibly for only a moment before he ran his strong hand through his hair. He stood, kicked the bench away from him, and left the feasting hall without another word.

Will took his place across the table from her then.

"You must pardon him, my lady. He's not such a bad sort, once you get to know him."

"Aye, I suppose," Meghan answered while Will placed several pieces of cheese on her trencher.

He refilled his cup with ale and offered it to her. "Truly. I've not seen him so taken with anyone in a very long time."

She detected a hint of sadness in his voice. Odd, since he seemed ever cheerful since their unexpected arrival upon his doorstep. "Why is that, my lord?"

"Did you know he was married once?"

She nodded her head, hoping he would take it as a sign to continue. He did.

"Aye. His wife possessed a beauty so rich and powerful men would kill to claim her," he scoffed. "Men did kill to claim her. Such betrayal leaves many scars on a man."

"I saw them," she whispered.

At first she thought Will did not understand her, but then he nodded. "On his back, you mean? Aye, 'twas the result of Allyson's treachery. But more deeply rooted are the scars on his heart."

"What happened to him?" Meghan's own heart broke, and her spine stiffened for whatever words she might hear.

" 'Tis a very long and complicated story, my lady."

"I have nowhere to go."

Will sighed and refilled the cup. Meghan suddenly felt as if she were intruding in some secret place. A place only the two friends shared. She bit her lip to keep from telling Will she had no right to pry.

"Allyson's father was loyal to the rebel barons who would have seen King Henry removed from power before he even had the chance to prove his worth. Devlin believes himself weak because Allyson convinced him she had no part in her father's treachery."

"I find nothing weak about Devlin," Meghan smiled.

"I have to agree with you there. But it took him many months to recover from his injuries, and in that time he convinced himself his own weaknesses had endangered everything he held dear. Including his King. Allyson not only knew of her father's political leanings, but also helped him achieve them. Devlin, to her, proved to be little more than a willing, if unknowing, fellow in the duplicity."

Meghan's eyes followed the path Devlin had taken out of the hall. He must punish himself greatly to still bear the guilt for such things. "But he didn't know what she was about."

"Aye, true enough."

"Has the King forgiven him?"

"Aye." Will took a sip of ale and offered the cup to her again.

She took it and drank, but found it difficult.

"But he has never forgiven himself, and he's never trusted a woman since," said Will.

"In that case, my lord, I believe yer quite mistaken. Why would he be 'taken' with me, as ye say?"

"I'm afraid only Devlin can answer that question. 'Tis not my place to say."

Will departed then, leaving her alone at the trestle table. She bit her lip as she considered whether she had the courage to ask Devlin about it. If it was true, what Will had said about Devlin being "taken" with her, then she owed it to both of them not to give up. She pushed her trencher away and traced the route Devlin had taken from the hall.

She found him in the tiltyard, leaning against a curved stone wall. The heady scent of flowers and herbs filled the air. He turned toward her.

"Go away," he growled.

"Nay. I rather enjoy the night air." She stepped next to him along the wall. Where he leaned his elbows on the rough stone surface, she raised her arms and placed her chin on her hands. She studied his form in the moonlight. So very tall, she wondered how often he bruised himself from the simple act of entering a room without remembering to duck. The thought brought a smile to her lips. Handsome, strong, educated. All the parts of him came together to create the man she saw before her.

And another part, as well. His wounded heart. In order to help him, she needed to fully understand why and how his heart had been so damaged.

"What happened to yer back, Devlin?" She steeled herself for his reaction.

He stiffened beside her, and she watched as the knuckles of his laced fingers whitened. Yet he remained silent.

"Did your wife's betrayal have something to do with it?"

He cursed. "Will told you about Allyson?"

Meghan's heart lurched at the thickness in his voice. "Aye, but no' everything. Only that ye were married and she betrayed ye."

He stood to his full height. "Aye. There is nothing more to tell."

"I do no' believe ye," she sighed. "Ye fail to explain the marks on yer back. Ye must have experienced more pain with those lashings than any one man could take. Yet ye survived. 'Tis a testament to yer strength."

"Why do you do this, Meghan?" If he continued to run his hands through his hair so frequently, she doubted he'd have any left.

"Do what, Devlin?"

"Torment me."

She stepped closer to him, drawn to his heat as if she would freeze did he not hold her. Instead, he clenched his fists. "I do no' mean to torment ye, Devlin. I but mean to know ye."

To love ye.

† † †

"You don't want to know me, Meghan."

Why didn't she just leave him be? Devlin watched the moonlight dance in her eyes. Her lips parted slightly as her head tilted back to look at him. Her mouth begged to be kissed. Well. And often.

When she raised one hand and placed it tenderly on his chest, he groaned. "I do want to know ye, Devlin."

'Twas all it took. He gathered her shoulders in his hands and pulled her against him, half expecting her to push him away. Instead she raised her other hand and fisted his tunic in her slender fingers. He dipped his head, and she readily accepted his kiss. She fit him so well, it frightened him. Fire pumped through him, sending blood to his loins. Afraid she would fear his arousal, he moved his hips back. But she followed him, pressing her body against his. Then she opened her mouth to his searching tongue, allowing him free access to explore her sweetness.

Light and beauty. Kindness and grace. All of the things he'd missed in his life came from within her, filling him. He ran his hands over her back, forming her to him. She did not struggle, but moved provocatively against his shaft. Searing heat rushed through his body.

Nay. She would consume him if he but let her.

Never again.

He pushed her away, stumbling back several steps as he stared at her perplexed expression.

"Devlin?" Her voice filled his soul.

"Nay, Meghan. Nay," he stammered.

THE JEWEL AND THE SWORD

Don't let her cry.

But he knew she would. Thankfully, before she released the unshed tears from behind her sparkling eyes, she turned and fled the bailey.

Heartless bastard.

Aye. That he was.

CHAPTER ELEVEN

Ian sat at high table, making his way through a pitcher of ale. Many of his clansmen lounged with him in the feasting hall. His personal guards returned from their search for Meghan and approached him with measured steps. They had searched for days, and again they apparently returned to him with nothing.

"Tell me," he growled.

"No sign of her, Laird Ian," Lachann reported.

He slammed his fist on the table with such force the nearly empty pitcher tipped on its side. The contents spilled across the table and dripped to the floor. "He's taken her to England."

" 'Tis possible, my lord."

"Laird Ian? A messenger from King Henry requests an audience." Malcolm approached him. He

The Jewel and the Sword

sneered at the old man. It had taken only two beatings before Malcolm had decided to serve his new liege.

"Bring him to me."

The messenger appeared haggard, his face dirty and his breath short. He offered a tired bow before handing Ian a satchel.

Ian ripped it from the man's hands. "Go. Eat. Ye may sleep here this night and return to England in the morning with my reply."

Paying no more attention to the man, he tore open the seal on Henry's fine parchment.

He read the words carefully, unable to hide the smile forming upon his lips.

"Ye were well received by His Majesty?" asked Lachann.

"Aye. Oh, aye."

A serving maid placed a new pitcher of ale beside him, and he poured a fresh cup, congratulating himself on his cunning. Sending the letter to the King immediately upon Ravenstone's capture had been brilliant. Intercepting the messenger carrying the ransom letter even more so. A few nicely worded phrases and he had duped the King of England into championing his cause. He laughed aloud, ignoring the puzzled look on the faces of his men.

"What does it say then?" Lachann inquired without impatience.

"It says I am Laird of Clan Douglas, Lachann. And the wench is mine."

Lachann shook his head, apparently bewildered. "I

admit it, *Laird* Ian," he stressed, "I had no faith ye would succeed in this madness."

"And why would ye doubt me when ye've seen first hand the measure of my resolve?"

"Aye, and the measure of yer failures." Lachann laughed aloud at his own wit.

Lachann's comment would have brought swift pain to the speaker if the words had come from any other. But Ian and his most trusted ally had experienced the bitterness of defeat together. He'd earned the right to jest.

Ian laughed with him. Confident now that he would not be thwarted, he relished the relaxation filling his limbs. " 'Tis nearly done, Lachann, all which we have fought for these many years."

"Aye, Ian. When do we ride?"

"Soon. Let them think they have seen the last of us." Ian smirked. "Then I will take what is rightfully mine."

Aye, soon.

Very soon he would assemble a garrison of soldiers and make his way to Ravenstone Keep.

To claim his bride.

† † †

Devlin's neck ached when he woke the next morning. He'd spent most of the evening in his cups, dicing with several of the garrison housed at Dunburough. The coin in his gipser pinched, and he assumed he'd won more than his share. Looking around in the filtered light of the dawn, he groaned. He'd slept in the stable. But then, he'd slept in worse places. Midnight nudged his shoulder. He'd slept with worse bedmates as well.

He pushed the horse's snout away and stood. Pieces of straw fell from his trews, but he ignored them. He needed a cup of ale. Quickly.

Once outside the stable, the full impact of the rising sun blinded him. He narrowed his eyes against the bright light, shading his face with one hand.

The soldiers had begun their daily training exercises. The clang of steel reverberated inside his pounding head, threatening to send him to his knees.

"Here. Drink this, my lord."

Meghan's voice caught him off guard. He spun in the direction of the sweet sound to find her handing him a cup. His stomach clenched, and he steadied himself against the wave of dizziness brought by the sudden movement.

He took the cup and sniffed it. "What is it?"

" 'Twill make ye feel better. Honestly, why do ye men do such things to yerselves. Ye can no' tell me 'tis the first time ye fell into a barrel of ale. So why do I have pity on ye, now, when the punishment so verily fits yer crime?"

Her chatter did little to quell the ache in his head. Once she'd finished her scolding, he repeated his question. "What is it?"

" 'Tis a brew to ease the pain in yer head and putrid stomach. Drink it. It will no' kill ye, though it tastes much like it will."

"When did you make this?" He sucked in his breath as the sun's rays reflected from a sword blade and into his eyes.

She placed her hands on her hips and, in the process, pulled the front of her gown tight over her breasts. The outline of her chemise showed through the lightweight material. He groaned aloud. Temptation to tell her exactly why he'd drunk himself into oblivion last eve soared to the front of his mind.

Why did he drink? Why did he suffer so in the aftermath of too much ale? Because of her. He'd spent the night gaming with his men, drinking her out of his mind, else he would have climbed the tower stairs to her chamber and finished what he'd started.

"Last night. When I went in search of ye, and found ye in the stable, dicing and carousing like some common-born . . ."

She didn't finish her sentence, but by the color in her cheeks, he knew her temper flared.

"Like some common-born . . . what?" he prompted.

"Scoundrel," she spat.

Aye. Mayhap he'd finally found a way to be rid of her. All he had to do was drink himself into the next level of existence on a daily basis. Then she'd have no desire to be near him.

A horse whinnied too close to his head, shattering his thoughts with the power of a smith's forge. He pinched the bridge of his nose between two fingers and closed his eyes tightly against the pain.

Nay. Such self-abuse would solve little.

The Jewel and the Sword

He eyed the cup. "Must I drink all of it?" He didn't know why he trusted her, but since the alternative to her treatment included the possibility of cleaving off his own head, he felt no harm could be done.

"Aye." She sighed. "Every drop."

He inhaled deeply and put the cup to his mouth.

"Jesu," he cried after one gulp. "What is in this witch's brew?"

"Many things, my lord. Including one raw egg."

Raw egg? Did she wish to make him ill?

"I will no' drink this," he said, handing the cup back to her.

" 'Tis yer choice." She took the cup back. "If yer unable to brave a simple tonic . . ."

She baited him. He knew it by the glint in her eye. The same shimmering sparkle that had appeared when she'd tried to pry his name from him.

Several men shouted in the tiltyard behind him and another horse screamed. A cacophony of noises surrounded him, each one a hammer inside his skull. Meghan stood in front of him still, the cup held loosely in her fingers.

He took it from her, put it to his mouth for the second time, and swallowed the mixture in three large gulps.

He knew his face must appear ridiculous as he forced himself to swallow what he assumed to be the egg.

"Very good, my lord. See, that was no' so bad, was it?"

"Argh," he growled in response. He handed her the cup and turned. Then he called over his shoulder, "If you still wish to see your father, be ready to depart in one hour, my lady."

† † †

They traveled in silence for nearly half a day before Devlin led them from the road and into a copse of trees. Shaded by the branches surrounding it, a clearing in the center offered enough space for Meghan to lay out the meal prepared by Dunborough's cook and the horses to graze on the sweet grass nearby. A stream flowed somewhere near as well, evidenced by the trickle of running water.

He dismounted and then reached for her. She allowed him to help her only because she feared she would fall if she did not. While at Dunburough, Devlin had seen fit to trade her reliable palfrey for a mare several hands taller than suited her. Once on the ground, however, she moved quickly away from him.

She took a blanket from the pack attached to the back of her saddle and spread it on the soft ground. From the third horse she unpacked a basket of food. At least they were better prepared for a journey, having packed bedding, food, and a change of clothes before leaving Dunburough. What Lord Will assumed regarding her hasty abandonment of her own home, she did not know. But he'd been kind enough when she requested provisions and promised to pay him when she could. In fact, he'd smiled broadly and told her to take whatever she liked.

She noticed Devlin making his way through the trees away from her.

"Do no' hie yerself away too long, my lord," she called after him.

His only response came in the form of an impatient wave.

Anxiety riddled her now that they were close to Ravenstone Keep. According to the man-at-arms with whom she'd spoken, she and Devlin would need to camp only one night before arriving at the keep.

She could manage one more night. Couldn't she?

On the morrow, he would deliver her to Lord Ravenstone. She didn't know if he lived within Ravenstone Keep, but his bearing told her otherwise. His natural ability to command indicated he was himself noble and a lord of some standing. A part of her hoped he would leave her and continue to his own home. Another part of her screamed in protest.

The knowledge Devlin did not want her had devastated her. As he'd held her last night, and her body pooled in his arms, she'd hoped, nay, prayed he would claim her. And not because he could then help her father. Shame needled the edge of her heart even now. She had pushed all thoughts of her father aside during the heat of that kiss.

But he did not want her. He'd made that perfectly clear.

She'd come to the conclusion, after a sleepless

night, to arrange for the release of her father and go to London to petition the King for his assistance in reclaiming the clan. Perhaps her father could arrange for a decent match for her there. Since Ian had petitioned for her hand, only her father could sway Henry from granting such a request. While she assumed the King would care naught for her happiness, the knowledge of Ian's violence and hatred of the English would help her cause. She hoped.

She finished preparing their meal and scanned the trees for any sign of Devlin. He'd been gone long enough to attend to any personal needs. She thought about starting without him, but her level of impatience was such she did not want to finish before him and have to wait. She stood, gathered her skirts, and followed the direction he'd taken into the forest.

The sounds of running water drew nearer until she finally saw his outline against the opposite shore. He had removed his tunic and was kneeling beside the water's edge.

The sounds of the forest faded away until she heard only her beating heart. He dipped his hands into the water, cupped a certain amount, and poured it over his head. Droplets glistened from the spiky strands, darkened unto black by the moisture. He shook his head, sending a misty spray in all directions. He cupped more water and splashed his face.

The muscles of his arms and shoulders bunched with quiet elegance at his movements. Even the scars on his back could not hide his raw, sensual power. Her fingers curled as she imagined the feel of him beneath them. The thought of stroking his warm flesh created an empty place somewhere in the region of her belly. A place that burned as if on fire.

He does no' want ye.

She turned away, the void in her body suddenly filled with bitter despair. She stepped on a twig, and a loud crack rent the silence. Fearful he would discover her watching him, she raced back to the clearing, refusing to give audience to her persistent tears.

† † †

Devlin sensed her presence even before the snap of a twig revealed her location among the trees. He felt her eyes on him as distinctly as if she touched him. They heated him despite the cold water he'd hoped would quell the passion in his loins.

Bloody hell.

He resumed scratching his neck and cheeks with the blade of his dagger.

He'd sworn never to allow another woman to claim his heart. How had this happened? That, after years of blissful peace, a woman had managed to break through his defenses? And what woman is she? The daughter of his most bitter enemy.

A bonny lass with fire in her hair and her eyes, and a temper to match.

He didn't need her in his life to complicate his existence. He'd found peace after Allyson and needed no reminder of what women were capable of.

Still, every time he looked in Meghan's direction, his blood fired. His pulse raced and his loins pained him unto madness.

He scooped one last handful of water, threw it over his back and shoulders, and rinsed away the last of his beard. He rose, donned his tunic and laced his trews.

For the next day and a half he could continue his charade. What would happen when they reached his home and his true identity revealed itself? The thought of avoiding the situation all together reared its head. He could leave her with the Sisters of the Redemption and then, when he reached his home, send Morven to her. He'd not have to deal with either of them ever again.

The sisters lived not far from here. He could be rid of her before dinner. If he knew Mother Elizabeth, Meghan would not sneak away this time. A sardonic grin split his face, as even now his knuckles ached from the old nun's censure.

Nay. He sighed. He would not subject Meghan to such a woman. But he knew the real reason he would not deliver her into the sister's care. He wanted one more day in her company before she learned to hate him all over again.

† † †

A cold wind blew across Devlin's shoulders. He peered into the sky to see heavy black clouds collecting on the western horizon. A bolt of lightning ripped through the clouds, followed by a distant rumbling of thunder.

He glanced at Meghan, who shivered visibly.

"Are you cold?"

"Aye." Her teeth chattered as she spoke.

He pulled a cloak from behind his saddle and offered it to her. She accepted silently, fitting it above her head and pulling up the hood.

"Will the rain delay our arrival at Ravenstone Castle, my lord?" she asked, her disembodied voice sounding sad from beneath the woolen confines of her hood.

If only it would.

"Nay," he answered, "though we may wish to make camp sooner than we planned. We should be able to travel another few hours before we're set upon by the storm."

"Very well," she sighed.

Her melancholy bothered him. With each step they took closer to her father, she withdrew from him further. He'd expected her to thrum with excitement, prattle his ears off, and beam with joy. Instead, she had spoken nary a word in the time since they'd stopped for the midday meal.

"I'm sorry I doubted you," he offered.

"What?" She turned her head toward him and blessed him with the view of her face.

"This morning. That mixture you made for me? 'Tis an amazing brew, indeed, to have chased away the pain so quickly."

"Oh," she replied. " 'Twas nothing, my lord. I can provide ye with the recipe for yer cook, if ye like."

If I keep you, I'll have no need for excessive drink.

He fell silent for another hour as the wind increased its intense howling around them. He checked the skies again and frowned, as the clouds approached much faster than he'd thought they would.

She seemed not at all concerned with the sudden change in the weather until a crash of thunder broke from the black sky. Her horse reared, screaming into the wind. Devlin immediately reached out and took the reins in his hand, effectively quieting the distraught animal. Sparks sizzled in the forest behind them where the lightning had struck the tallest of the trees.

"Be you well?" he yelled over the screeching wind.

"Aye," she answered, breathless. He knew better. One look into her wide eyes proved her terror.

Rain splattered on the road in a torrent, immediately soaking them both. The drops, whipped by the wind, sliced into his cheeks with stinging accuracy. On his own lands now, he knew exactly where to take them for shelter.

"Give me your reins, Meghan. I'll lead your mount."

He expected an argument, but apparently the severity of the storm stole her independent streak. She handed the reins to him and held to the saddle with white, trembling fingers.

"Where do we go?"

"A house in the forest. We'll wait until the storm passes before we move on."

Devlin left the road, guiding the horses into the wind. He lowered his head to keep the rain from blinding him, letting Midnight pick his way through the overgrown trail. He could barely hear Meghan's whimper over the sound of rain and thunder as they made slow but steady progress. But hear it, he did, and his heart wrenched.

After several long minutes of fighting wind-whipped branches and shivering temperatures, Midnight whinnied over the din. Devlin raised his head to see the small stone house in a distant clearing. It should be well stocked. He'd planned to come here upon his return from Scotland. He turned in his saddle to see Meghan huddled against the horse's neck. He frowned at the irony. He'd planned to come here alone.

As if she could read his thoughts, she lifted her head. The wind whipped her hood back to reveal her cheeks, swollen and red.

Why does she cry?

Fear, more likely than not. He quickened their pace until Midnight stopped of his own accord in front of the small house, seldom used other than as a staging point for the hunt. Inside lay fuel for a large fire, warm linens and stores for several large meals.

And one bed.

He leapt from the saddle and rushed to help Meghan to the ground. She shivered uncontrollably in his arms. Where he usually put her down as quickly as possible, this time he held her against his chest. She looked up into his eyes, and he hated the expression in them.

She looked . . . abandoned.

Cradling her in his arms, he carried her toward the door. He kicked it open with the heel of one boot and swept her inside.

"The owner of this house may have a problem with that." She tried to smile, but no joy reached her eyes.

"I am the owner. I don't mind."

Though he suspected it wouldn't last, a small spark of laughter shone through her cold exterior. He placed her on the chair before the fireplace and then set about striking the flint, which had been laid out for his use. The fuel caught almost immediately, despite the moisture hanging in the air. Within moments, a glowing light surrounded them with its accompanying warmth.

"All of the items you've packed will need to dry, my lady. However, you'll find some raiment in yonder trunk to keep you warm at least."

He turned to leave, but stopped when he felt her hand on his arm. How could a hand, so cold it shivered, leave such heat where it touched? The tremors caused by her fingers gripping his arm traveled immediately to his loins. He gritted his teeth against the familiar pleasure.

"Where do ye go?"

"To tend the horses. I'll stable them and return shortly."

"Oh, of course." She smiled weakly.

"I will give you adequate time to warm yourself," he stated and then left through the only door.

Once outside, he leaned against the exterior wall of the house. He closed his eyes and allowed the cooling rain to fall onto his upturned face. How could he possibly spend the night with her, here, in this tiny space, and not take her? 'Twas impossible. He eyed the stable. Mayhap he should have been born a horse, considering how often he slept in their company.

For two nights in a row he would sleep with his horse. He laughed. If Will ever found out about this, he would be tortured unto his last breath.

CHAPTER TWELVE

Meghan's heart sank to the pit of her stomach when she watched Devlin leave the small, cozy room. The change in his behavior in the last several hours warmed her. Though a part of her feared he'd been kind and giving to her only because they neared the end of their journey and he would soon be rid of her.

She stood and removed the wet cloak with a shiver and then inspected the room. The house, made from stone, had only the one room. Neatly appointed with an old table, four chairs, a bed, and three trunks, she could tell he lived here alone. She hung the cloak beside the fire to dry and then searched one of the trunks for something decent to wear. She found an undertunic made from soft, worn wool. Designed to cover Devlin to his knees, it would cover her completely. The laces on the neckline might pose a problem since, even fully bound, they would barely conceal her bosom. She supposed, paired with a blanket used as a shawl, she would be decent enough.

Sending a glance to the door to ensure he did not return, she pulled the wet gown over her head. Then she frowned. She needed help taking off her chemise. At least twenty ties held it in place in the back. She struggled to reach them, finally giving up and settling herself at the hearth. She took a throw from the bed and placed it at her feet. Sitting in her chemise to allow the linen to dry, she could easily cover herself when Devlin returned.

Tomorrow she would be free of this pain. After tomorrow, she would never see him again. She choked back the sob. Gaining her feet, she paced the room, rubbing her arms to warm her cold limbs.

Nay, 'twas useless. She would never be warm again without his embrace. A part of her she hadn't known existed until she'd found him, knew this for fact.

She might as well just go back to Scotland and give herself over to Ian. It mattered not with whom she would spend her miserable life, if not her knight.

And if such were the case, what harm could there be in a fond memory or two? She spied the bed tucked against the far wall. Heavy fur throws covered the down bedding and linen sheets. She nearly cried.

What did she think now? To give herself to a man who would use her and then leave her? A man who had stated plainly he did not want her, even though the hardness of his masculine parts pressed against her body told her otherwise?

She knew he wanted her. He just didn't want to keep her. Could she spend the rest of her life wondering what one night with him might have been like?

Nay.

She eyed the door again. Then bit her lip as she crossed to it and threw it open.

"Devlin?" she called into the raging storm. She didn't even know if he would hear her over the crashing thunder and racing wind.

He did.

She smiled.

He approached the doorway, soaked to the skin. His tunic lay pressed against every muscle of his chest and arms, revealing the hollows and planes of each solid curve.

"I'm nearly finished. Why have you not changed into dry raiment?"

His labored breath made his chest rise and fall, and she ached to touch him again.

" 'Tis why I summoned ye." She turned her back to him and looked over her shoulder. "Might ye loosen these ties for me?"

Devlin swallowed. Hard. When he didn't move, she reached back and took his hand, leading him inside the room.

"Close the door, Devlin. 'Tis cold."

† † †

Her essence enveloped him. He knew the seductive quality of a woman's voice, but the purring escaping her lips now fired his blood like none ever had. *What was her game?*

"Please, Devlin."

He didn't care. With trembling fingers, and not from the cold, he worked the ties loose one at a time. As he did so, the linen chemise exposed her back. His lips ached to touch her damp skin. His mouth watered at the remembered taste of her lips.

He needed to get back outside where the cold rain could begin to quench the fire raging inside of him.

The stable. He would sleep in the stable.

He groaned. Why must he sleep in the stable when her eyes held such invitation? His inner voice warred with his conscience. And with the opening of each tie, the inner voice scored a heady point.

Finally, the last knot lay separated at the small of her back. He could make out the dimples above her buttocks in the dim light offered by the fire.

"My thanks, Devlin," she whispered, stepping away from him as she held the front of her chemise close to her chest. She needed but to take her hands away to expose herself fully to him. Silently, he begged her to.

What am I thinking?

He started to speak, but swallowed the words. He'd imagined it. She but needed help disrobing. His fantasies of taking her, even keeping her for himself, had tainted his mind into hearing unspoken lust in her voice. 'Twas the only explanation.

As quickly as he'd appeared at her summons, he left the room. He left a half-naked temptress standing open-mouthed in the middle of a room with a bed. He *must* be mad.

Once outside the rain fell upon him again. This time, the frigid drops did nothing to soothe his blood, or the ache between his legs. Truth be told, he'd finished tending the horses before she'd even called to him. He had no reason, besides his own honor, to be standing in the rain. He moved under the eaves on the north side of the building for shelter.

But he couldn't very well stand there all night. He peered through the crack in the thick window covering and could just make out the firelight reflecting off Meghan's back.

He would wait until she dressed and then allow himself reprieve just long enough to warm himself. Then he'd sleep in the stable.

She still hugged the chemise as she stood staring at the door he'd just left. Her shoulders slumped as if she were . . .

Disappointed?

Could he be imagining her desire for him? He must be.

Feeling like the lowest of all rogues, he could not tear his eyes from the window. She turned to the fire and bent at the waist to stir the flames awake. His body hardened even more as his hands clenched to hold her hips and ease himself slowly inside her from behind. He closed his eyes as the image possessed him, body and mind. He opened them again only to continue the sweet torture.

Standing before the fire, its amber light illuminating every full curve of her, she allowed the chemise to fall away.

He averted his gaze and pressed his back against the wall next to the window. But not before he saw her breasts formed in taut peaks as she stared into the flames. He licked his lips longing to taste her salty sweet flesh.

Don't look again. 'Tis unseemly.

He ignored the voice, his own guilt already swelling along with his loins.

She reached toward his undertunic slung over the back of a chair. When she picked it up, he expected her to cover herself in its warmth. He should be beaten for this, but still he hated the idea of losing sight of her naked perfection.

She hesitated in her movements. He groaned as she took her bottom lip between her teeth, apparently in deep thought about something. She dropped the garment where she stood and walked to the bed. She crawled into it without the benefit of clothing and pulled the cover to her neck, granting him an exceptional view of her backside as she climbed into *his* bed.

He turned away from the window and stepped once more into the small yard, allowing the rain to beat upon him.

"Jesu," he whispered to himself, heavy raindrops splashing his upturned face. "Are you dead, man?"

Nay. Not anymore.

† † †

Meghan prayed Devlin would return to the house. He'd slept in the stable yestereve when perfectly good beds remained unoccupied inside Dunburough Keep, just to be rid of her. What made her think throwing herself at him would bring him inside his own home, which boasted only one bed? He didn't want her. 'Twas apparent.

The door latch lifted, and Devlin entered the room slowly. He closed the door behind him, but did not step further into the room.

He dripped water onto the floor, either unaware or uncaring he did so. His eyes riveted her own.

"Do you know what you do, Meghan?"

She swallowed. "Aye."

"If you do not, tell me to leave now. And I'll go."

"Nay. Do no' go."

He stepped closer to where she lay in the bed, one shoulder having escaped the fur cover.

"I can't promise you . . ."

"What? Tomorrow? Next week? I ken ye can no' make promises, Devlin."

I do no' care.

"I meant, I can't promise you I will stop if you ask it of me . . . later."

She felt the heat rush to her cheeks then and knew they turned pink with her blush. "I will no' ask it of ye."

"You are maiden."

It wasn't a question. He stated her status as an untried virgin plainly, so she could not accuse him of debauchery later. She knew of only one way to answer him. She sat up in the bed, releasing the covers to fall in a pool at her waist.

He groaned aloud. The sound vibrated through her, stroking to life the tempered blaze in her heart. She didn't care if she could have him only this night. She wanted him.

When he reached the edge of the bed, he placed one large, warm hand to her cheek. She leaned into the touch. He urged her upward, until his free hand cupped the other side of her face and she rested upright on her knees.

He smelled of fresh rain and leather. She breathed him in, letting the essence of his masculinity encompass her. He took her mouth in his, and she did not wait for him to prompt her to return his kiss. She opened for him as his tongue delved deeply inside, sweeping a trail of passion through her entire body. Her breasts felt heavy; her nipples ached for his touch. She arched into him, undeterred by the cold shock when her body connected with his wet tunic.

He pulled his mouth away from hers. She gasped at the loss of him, only to be rewarded by his mouth on her nipple. He laved the turgid peak with his tongue, then took her breast into his mouth. Finally, he scraped his teeth over the erect tip and she gasped aloud.

When she thought she could take no more of the torment, he pulled away. He tilted his head to stare the length of her, his eyes setting her limbs to quivering as easily as his mouth.

"What?" she smiled.

"I but admire you, Meghan. You are perfectly formed. Beautiful."

She felt herself blush again. His ragged breath upon her cheek warmed her still further. Then he laid her gently upon the downy softness of his bed. She pulled at his tunic, but he slowly removed her hands. He held them both in one of his, above her head, as he traced his tongue over her ribs, and then her navel. She squirmed beneath his attentions.

"What do ye do to me?" she whispered on a breath. She felt him groan against her stomach. Then, with his free hand, he found the pooling desire between her legs. When he stroked her there, she bit her lip, afraid of what he might think should she cry out.

"Do you like that, my Meghan? You can tell me if you do." She heard the passion in his voice.

"Aye, Devlin. Very much." She pressed against his hand like a wanton, unable to stop herself. 'Twas like each part of her body had a mind of its own, passionate and free.

He shifted her again, until one of her legs nearly fell from the bed. She opened her eyes to find him settling his mouth at the juncture of her thighs. Instead of his hand, he touched her with his tongue.

Any protest forming in her mind as she read his intention died upon her lips at his completion of the act. She tossed her head upon the pillow, moaning so he must think her mad.

She was mad. Mad with passion and desire.

And love.

When he finally released her and moved his hand to knead her breast, she thought she would scream. Then she felt the finger of his other hand enter her body. She tensed for barely a heartbeat, and then she did scream with joy.

"You enjoy this as well, my Meghan?" His teeth scraped against her as he spoke. She threaded her fingers in his still-wet hair, pressing herself against him shamelessly. She had heard stories of what men and women did together, and she knew some women even enjoyed the act. But never in her innocent mind had she ever suspected this.

Colors, rich and vivid, collected behind her tightly closed eyes. A trembling began in the pit of her stomach and moved lower until finally she exploded in a torrent of lightning flashes. She lost all concept of time and space as she floated softly, and ever so slowly, back to the bed.

"Meghan?" Devlin nuzzled her ear. "Are you all right?"

She inhaled her scent from his full lips. "Aye."

Devlin stood and removed his tunic before bending to unlace his boots. If he did not take her soon, he might explode. She'd responded to his touch in ways he'd never before experienced. Even Allyson had not felt the heat of his passion as Meghan had.

Wanton.

Passionate.

She still recovered from her peak. Her breathing had slowed some, but her eyes remained closed. He relished the small smile she wore and felt a twinge of pride that he had been the one to place it there.

He kicked his boots off and drew down his trews, climbing into the bed beside her. She turned toward him, stretching like a she-cat in the wild. She practically purred, and he couldn't stop the chuckle from escaping his throat.

"Are we finished?" she asked.

"Nay, love. We're far from finished."

"Good." She smiled seductively. "What do we do now?"

He laughed again. "Whatever you like, my lady."

"I should like very much to make ye happy, Devlin. As ye made me happy." She blushed, and he thought he would die.

The smile fell from his lips as he gazed upon her innocent eyes. She remained a virgin. If he left now, she would be less damaged. When she stroked her fingers over his nipples, he knew he would not release her. Not now.

Not ever.

The Jewel and the Sword

He took her fully into his embrace and rained kisses upon the hollow of her neck. Grasping her wrist gently, he guided her hand to his manhood and taught her how to stroke him. He could not withstand the intensity of her touch for long. He touched her, testing her readiness. She moaned as he prepared her. He could easily lose himself in her sweet embrace, and desperation to feel himself inside her body overwhelmed him.

He positioned himself above her and probed her tight entrance.

Her eyes flew open and he cringed.

"Do you wish me to leave?" He prayed she would not deny him, but knew he would withdraw if she did.

"Nay." She relaxed beneath him.

That was all it took. He plunged himself inside of her, holding her close as he felt her barrier break against him. He gave her a moment to adjust to his size, rocking against her only when her startled gasp faded to quiet breathing.

He lifted his head to gaze upon her face. Heightened pink appeared in her cheeks as her passion returned. He thrust against her then, feeling the sensation of her body move through his own. They moved together in an ancient dance of timelessness, until he felt her peak around him.

Then he thrust one final time, burying himself inside of her with his whole being.

Lost.

Lost forever.

† † †

The morning after she and Devlin made love, Meghan felt beside her for his hard form, only to find she lay alone in the bed. She cracked open one eye to confirm the discovery. Fully awake, she sat upright and scanned the small chamber.

Nothing.

The sound of early morning filtered through the windows. Several birds chirped, and Midnight's distinctive whinny sliced the dawn.

He tends the horses. She would wait for him within the folds of the downy bed. Smiling, she leaned back amongst the softness.

She'd lost count of how many times he'd loved her. Committed to memory were the endearments whispered upon the wings of passion. He'd said he would keep her forever in his heart. He'd loved her so thoroughly, even now her breasts tightened and her womb clenched.

The sun moved through the windows, and he had yet to return. She sighed and tossed the bedclothes aside. Taking her chemise and kirtle in hand, both thoroughly dry from their night beside the fire, she dressed as best she could without the benefit of her maid, or Devlin's strong hands.

Where did he go?

She put on her brat, shoved her hair away from her shoulders, and stepped outside. She found him in the stable, saddling her mount. Midnight stomped the ground, already prepared for the journey.

"Devlin." She smiled.

The curve of her lips fell the moment his eyes met hers. Anger burned fierce within his blue orbs, sending rivulets of disdain over her.

"Break your fast, my lady, and be quick about it. If you have any personal matters to attend, do so now as well. We will not stop again before we reach your father."

"Devlin, have I done something wrong?" She felt the stinging of tears behind her eyes, but blinked them back.

"Get yourself ready," he snapped. "We leave before the hour."

He stomped away from her, his strong back stiff and his fists clenched.

Her throat closed around the painful lump created by his surliness. She ran back to the small house, slamming the door behind her.

How could he ruin it? She'd given herself to him, and he'd cared nothing for her sacrifice. His words last night had been lies meant to sway her to his own pleasure. She would have preferred his silence. The more she thought of the sweet, passionate things he'd said to her whilst making love, the angrier she became. She wanted to break something.

She spied a shelf along the opposite wall, covered with trinkets and several books. Rushing to it, she pushed everything off the shelves with one full swipe of her trembling arms. Picking up a book, she tore the cover from it and threw both pieces to the bed. Then she retrieved another. She wanted to scream.

She'd never before experienced a temper tantrum. The freedom of it released her, and she felt like laughing. Her anger directed itself now toward not only Devlin, but also her father, Ian, Malcolm, and every man she knew who instructed the path of her life.

But mostly, Devlin.

He could take her for his own. No one could stop him, but himself. And yet, he would not. She knew it as certainly as she could find the location of the sun at dawn.

"Enough," he bellowed from the door.

Fury clouded her vision as he grasped her shoulders firmly in his strong hands. He shook her until she stopped fighting him.

"Stop this madness. Now, Meghan," his voice threatened.

She stared into his grimly set features and watched the curtain fall over his eyes. She could read nothing in his expression as he tossed her away from him.

"Get on your horse, my lady. We depart."

Chapter Thirteen

Devlin stomped out of the house, his own guilt chasing him like a demon from hell. He had no right to be angry with Meghan. His hatred should be directed only upon himself. He should have slept in the stable instead of discovering every tender plane of her body.

Awakening her desire even as he renewed his own.

He managed to convince himself upon waking this morning that she had been the one to blame. No man could withstand such seduction. But he knew better. She played with a fire she had not understood.

He should have been stronger.

He should have thought the matter through with his brain rather than his burning loins. By midday, she would know him for who he truly was. She would hate him then, so why should he wait for her wrath? 'Twas just as well she hated him now.

The door creaked open behind him. Shoving all thoughts of his own debauchery aside, he took the leads of all three horses and approached the angry woman standing in front of his house. Bright red fused in her cheeks. Her narrowed gaze burned a hole straight through his chest. He nearly gasped at the pain.

"Get on." He cleared his throat when his voice failed to respond. "Get on."

"I can no' 'get on,' and well ye know it." She spat fire with each word. Her loose hair tossed as she spoke, and he could almost feel the tendrils slip between his fingers.

"Damn."

" 'Tis no' my fault ye selected a horse too large for me, Devlin. Ye can no' be angry with me for that as well."

He gritted his teeth.

Vixen.

He dropped the reins. Picking her up from the waist, he carried her to her mare and tossed her unceremoniously into the saddle.

"Ooh," she squealed, catching the pummel to steady herself. Once settled, she glared at him. "My thanks."

"My pleasure," he replied.

Silence reigned for longer than it should have. Their eyes battled with unspoken taunts.

"Argh." He ran a hand through his hair and stepped away.

He climbed into his saddle, took up the reins for the third mount, and spurred Midnight toward the road.

He could not get them to Ravenstone Keep quickly enough.

† † †

"Do we no' stop for a meal, my lord?"

"Nay," he growled.

Meghan's backside throbbed between pain and no feeling at all. Traveling for so many hours without so much as a rest, much less a meal, worked her nerves and her aching limbs into a frenzy. Hours had passed since they'd left his house. She wanted this over with. She wanted to confront the wicked Lord Ravenstone and demand the release of her father. In her present mood, she dared him to deny her.

"How much further then, my lord?"

He did not answer her.

Damn his silence.

"Why are ye so bloody angry with me?" She pulled her mare to a stop in the middle of the road.

He carried on, apparently not realizing she'd stopped for several moments, or choosing to ignore it.

When he turned toward her, he shot her a glare meant to intimidate. Well, she would not be intimidated by him, or any other man, ever again.

"Get you moving, woman."

"Nay. No' until ye tell me what I've done to make ye so foul."

He growled and spun Midnight around to face her.

She continued, undeterred by his offensive gesture, "I did nothing ye did no' appreciate last eve, so why do ye fester so this morn?"

He brought Midnight's flanks next to her mare's head and stopped beside her.

"I should not have touched you, Meghan. You should not have tempted me," he whispered, refusing to look at her.

"Why?"

"Because you belong to another. Mayhap Ian. But you do not belong to me, and you never shall. We had no right."

"Ye may regret, Devlin. But I will no'. And I find yer desire to shut me out when we have so short a time left . . . deplorable."

He tilted his head as if to study her. Then, he drew his sword, which she thought rather odd.

"You will hate me rather soon, Meghan, I'll warrant. So what 'time we have left' matters naught."

He laid the flat of the blade against her mare's flank. The animal bolted forward, and she clung to the reins, her breath caught in her chest by the surprise.

The mare raced along the drying road, throwing mud behind them. Devlin moved in beside her, and then passed her. He did not slow down, so neither did she. The horses galloped, side by side, for several miles before she caught the tangy scent of the sea. Only when

THE JEWEL AND THE SWORD

confronted with an overturned cart in the road did they pull the lathered beasts to a halt.

"I do not care if ye thought I would stop. My load was heavy, and I could not navigate such a turn!" The angry words of the man who apparently owned the cart met her ears with unchecked ferocity.

"Well, you bloody well should have been looking where you were going, Charles. Mayhap had you kept your eyes upon the road . . ."

Both men stopped arguing when they lifted their faces and saw Devlin.

The man called Charles immediately removed his hat and bowed. "My lord," he stammered, his face quickly losing all traces of color. "We thought you dead."

The other man mimicked the respectful bow and eyed Devlin with suspicion bordering on fear. "Be you a ghost then, my Lord?"

Devlin grimaced. "Nay. As you can plainly see, I'm very much alive."

"Your Lady Mother has fretted much these past weeks. I spoke with her at the keep only yesterday, my lord, and she seemed ever distraught. Do you go home now?" Charles asked.

Meghan caught Devlin's wince from the corner of her eye. Home? We just left his home.

Devlin raised his hand to quiet the man, but apparently the second man did not see.

" 'Tis a happy day indeed when the dead Lord Devlin of Ravenstone returns to the living."

241

Lord Ravenstone!

Her heart hammered in her chest so severely she could no longer breathe. Her mouth fell open; her eyes burned. Desperate to catch her breath, she simply stared at the man who had spoken.

"What be the matter with your lady, my lord?"

"Bloody hell," Devlin cursed as he dismounted. He immediately crossed to Meghan and pulled her from the saddle.

She hadn't the strength to resist him and allowed him to set her on her feet. She couldn't think. Shock stole her heartbeat. The man she'd allowed herself to fall in love with could not be the man she'd been raised to loathe. Could he? She looked at him through new eyes.

The man she'd been raised to loathe.

"Y-ye . . . yer my uncle." She thought she would die.

"Nay," he shook his head. "You there." He pointed to Charles. "Tend these horses."

He led her several feet away, she suspected to a place in the forest where the villeins could not overhear them.

"I am not your uncle."

Slowly her shock subsided, and she felt the familiar tendrils of anger sweep through her.

"Ye are Lord Ravenstone!"

"Aye, but not your uncle. We share no blood, Meghan. Think you I would have made love to you if we did?"

"Ye are a beast and a liar. I put nothing so degrading past the likes of ye."

She pulled away from his grip on her arm. How dare he touch her!

"Morven and I only thought we were brothers. True, we were raised together, but we share no blood. You must believe me."

"I do no' understand," she screamed, her throat searing from the words. She couldn't help it. She swallowed the bitter tears trying to escape.

"Do not cry, my Meghan."

" 'Tis why ye said I would hate ye soon, is it no'?"

"Aye. I wanted to tell you. So many times. But I couldn't. Knowing how much you hated me."

So many feelings spun in her mind. Aye, hate lurked in the shadows, remnants of her childhood where Lord Ravenstone assumed the shape of a dragon with wicked, bloody teeth. But also love, confusion, pity, and shame. She ignored all of it and squared her shoulders.

"I should like to see my father now," she whispered through teeth clenched so tightly her jaw ached.

He reached to her face and brushed away a tear with the pad of his thumb.

"Very well, my lady. I'll take you to him."

† † †

The keep loomed before him, never looking so forbidding or lonely. Not even when he'd discovered the full vastness of Allyson's duplicity had his home seemed so empty.

He didn't know exactly what he'd feel when Meghan learned the truth, but he hadn't expected to feel so alone. He never should have allowed himself to feel at all.

The guard at the gate held the same fearful expression as Charles and Edward had when they saw Devlin approaching. The man crossed himself three times before he and Meghan even reached the gate. Then he crossed himself again, for good measure, Devlin supposed.

"You can stop that now, Bart. I'm no ghost."

"My lord," he stammered. "But where have you been these past weeks?"

"Detained. Kindly allow us to pass."

As if he only then realized he stood between his master and the bailey, Bart jumped aside and pulled the gate open.

Soldiers surrounded him immediately, some of them with expressions of awe, others just happy to see him. Before he was able to dismount, his mother raced from the main doors of the feasting hall and ran down the steps. He climbed out of the saddle, uncomfortable with the raucous greetings he received, and caught her in an embrace.

"They told me you were dead, but I did not believe it. In my heart, I knew you lived."

His mother's tears flowed like rain down her cheeks. His own throat choked back emotion. "I'm alive, Mother. 'Tis all that matters now."

THE JEWEL AND THE SWORD

"Aye. And tonight . . . we feast."

He scanned the crowd behind him for Meghan, but found only her mare, riderless. The sudden panic in his chest shocked him. He breathed only when he looked more closely and saw her standing to the side of the boisterous assembly. She worried the hem of her sleeve and looked frightfully pale.

"Aye, Mother, whatever you wish. But first, we have a guest. Please, return to the hall and have food brought. She hasn't broken her fast in nigh two days, and I worry over her."

"A lady?" His mother's curious expression followed his.

"I'll bring her inside, Mother. Please, 'tis a trying time for her. 'Tis Lady Meghan. Morven's daughter."

"You brought his daughter here?"

"I'll explain in a moment. Please, Mother, just go do as I bid."

His mother hugged him tightly again and then rushed up the steps.

"Meghan?" He walked over to where she stood, the new center of attention as the entire garrison's eyes followed him toward her. The moment she saw him, she dropped her sleeve and stood with the tense bearing of a soldier.

"Where is my father?"

Aye. She hated him for what he'd done, for who he was. She had every right.

"Inside. First, you must break your fast," he offered.

"Nay. I would see him now."

He reached for her arm to escort her inside, but she pulled away. She marched, back straight as an arrow, up the stone steps leading to the feasting hall. He ran a hand through his hair and debated the ramifications of climbing on Midnight and leaving the keep forever.

"Don't the woman like you?" called one of his soldiers, laughing.

He sighed. Moving swiftly up the steps behind Meghan, he answered under his breath, "You have no idea, Kildaire. You have no idea."

† † †

The feasting hall of Ravenstone Keep shone like a new gem. Whitewashed walls boasted tapestries depicting ancient lore, from dragons to pagan gods, to Greek Mythology in a riot of colored and gilded thread. Trestle tables lined the walls where maids had already started moving them into the center of the room.

They prepared for a feast to welcome their lord back from the dead.

Her heart sank. She wished he were still in the netherworld. If he were not brought back to life, she could still pretend he loved her. The knowledge of his true identity knifed through her soul, splitting her into two ragged, bloody pieces upon the rush-covered floor.

A woman she assumed to be Devlin's mother greeted her at the door. Her age proved impossible to judge, but Meghan assumed her younger than she appeared. The worry caused by the whole sordid affair had probably deepened the lines around her eyes and mouth.

Her eyes in the same shade of blue as her son's shone with happiness, however. Her regal bearing placed her easily as the lady of this house.

"Welcome, child, to my home," she offered. " 'Tis long I've wanted to meet you."

The mist forming in the woman's eyes spoke of love long awaited. She should be Meghan's grandmother? Nay, according to the stories she'd been raised with, Lady Ravenstone was but her father's stepmother. But who was her father then? If Morven and Devlin shared no blood, could it be her father wasn't even related to the old Lord Ravenstone? She shook her head, and confusion made it ache.

"You should like to see your father, now, I realize. But perhaps you would like to wash the dust of the road away first?"

Meghan looked down at her kirtle, covered in mud. She remembered her lack of help dressing this morning as well, and nodded to Lady Ravenstone. "Aye, my lady."

"Such a quiet girl," she tsked. "I hope the journey did not tire you too greatly."

"Nay." Not the journey.

"I want you to know, your father has been well cared for here. His wound healed without illness, and he resides in his own apartments. He is the son of my heart, you know. And I feel a kinship to you as well."

"My father is injured?" Meghan stopped in mid-step.

"Was. Was injured. He is well now. You'll see. Oh, child. How long I've waited for a chance to see you, the grandchild of my heart."

Meghan felt the sting of her blush as it rose in her cheeks. How could such a kind woman raise such a beast for a son?

"Morven does not know of your arrival. I'll inform him as soon as you're settled with a bath and some food to break your fast. Devlin mentioned you have not eaten well."

Meghan looked back and found Devlin leaning against the doorframe, watching her. Why would he say such a thing to his mother? What difference did it make if she never ate again?

Meghan ignored the wistful thoughts circling in her mind. Devlin cared nothing for her, and never would he. She followed Lady Ravenstone to a chamber rich with velvet and lace. Rose-colored curtains enclosed a large, downy bed and heavy, carved furniture lined the walls. A silver disk hung over a table set with a pitcher and bowl for washing. She approached the odd ornament and caught her reflection.

"What is this?" she asked Lady Ravenstone.

" 'Tis called a mirror. Devlin brought it from Italy many years ago . . . for his wife."

"This was his wife's chamber?"

"Aye. 'Tis seldom used now, but 'tis the only chamber suitable for a lady."

"He must have loved her very much." Meghan's

heart nearly stopped beating, and renewed pain shot though her tired limbs, making them ache.

"He did, once."

Meghan turned back to the mirror. Her hair hung limp, and dirt marred her cheeks. Except where her tears had left trails in the dust. Would she ever be happy again?

If he would but return her love.

A knock sounded on the heavy, oak door. Lady Ravenstone ushered in several men carrying a large copper tub. They placed it before the fire, and a string of maids emptied buckets of steaming water into it. The final maid dropped several handfuls of rose petals, some of them crushed, onto the surface of the water.

"What's this?" she asked the maid.

The girl, appearing much younger than Meghan, curtsied briefly. "My Lord Devlin said you preferred roses in your bath, milady."

"Aye." Meghan clenched her fists against an image of herself and Devlin, surrounded by the steaming water and floating petals.

Cease. 'Twill never happen in this lifetime.

Two of the maids remained to assist with her bath. Lady Ravenstone stopped at the door. "If you have need of anything, send one of the maids to me. I'm very glad you're here."

Then she hurried away. To make preparations for the feast, Meghan supposed.

She allowed the maids to help her undress and then slipped beneath the water. She bathed the dirt away with scented soap and a coarse cloth. The maid washed her hair. When she finished, since the water had turned cool, she stepped from the tub and allowed the maids to dress her. Her own raiment was tattered now, and too dirty to wear again, so she'd been provided with one of her ladyship's own gowns. The deep green dress set with gold trim fit only a little too loosely and would meet her needs well.

"You look lovely, my lady," the younger of the two maids offered as she put the finishing touches on Meghan's hair. Rather than a simple plait, the talented girl had swept her hair to the top of her head, allowing the riotous curls to flow in unkempt cascades down her back. On the top, she placed a gold circlet that enhanced the golden strands hidden amongst the red.

Meghan could see all of this as she studied her reflection in the strange mirror. She'd never seen herself before, outside of a still pond or a rain barrel. Before her stood a woman who was a far cry from the desperate bairn she'd seen reflected a few hours before.

"My thanks," Meghan answered the girl. "But 'tis no' my doing. 'Tis yer talent and care that makes for this comely package."

The girl giggled as she collected her things and dashed from the room.

"Would you like to see your father now, child?"

Lady Ravenstone appeared behind her in the mirror. Meghan turned.

"Aye. Very much, my lady."

Lady Ravenstone entwined her left arm with Meghan's right and led her through the long passage. Three doors away, she knocked, then pushed the door open.

Standing in the center of a large chamber, her father held open his arms.

"Da!" She rushed to him, colliding with his chest as he embraced her.

"Meggie. Daughter," he whispered into her hair.

"Father, I knew ye were no' dead. Ian . . . he has declared himself laird and even petitioned the King. We must leave at once for London. We can no' allow Ian to take everyth—"

Morven placed a finger over her lips to still them. "Hush, Meggie. 'Tis no' as simple as all that. Now Devlin has returned we might begin negotiations, but 'twill take time. I have learned much since I've been here."

Her father's words reminded her of their plight. There was still the matter of her father's raid to be dealt with. But she would not rest until her father's release was assured.

"As have I, Da." She read the knowledge of her father's questionable parentage in his eyes. But he didn't look sad or disgruntled by it. In fact, he looked . . . pleased.

"Ravenstone, the elder, was not my father at all, Meggie. It seems as if I did not inherit the title because it wasn't mine in the first place."

She waited for him to continue while he paced

several steps away from her.

"I think I knew it all along." His heavy sigh shook the air around her. "Something about this place didn't feel right. I allowed that to fester into a hatred that never should have been born. My father . . . that is, Lord Ravenstone, did what he thought best." Her father shrugged.

"And Devlin?"

Her father pinched his nose as if his head ached. "I've treated him rather poorly, haven't I?"

"Ye must apologize to him."

Her father drew in an unsteady breath. "I know."

"He's no' so bad as ye made him out to be, Da."

"He never was, Meghan. I blamed him for things not his fault. I blamed him for being born."

"He can be good and kind. I've seen tenderness from him. Mayhap, with eno' sincerity, he will forgive ye for the raid and help us reclaim the clan from Ian."

"Tenderness? Good and kind?" Morven repeated. "Meghan, do ye care for him?"

She turned away, hugging herself as she crossed to a window overlooking the raging sea.

"Tell me, Daughter. I would have the truth from ye."

"I love him. But it matters not. He cares nothing for me, nor will he. But this much I know. He is just and fair. He took Mattie and me to safety when he had no reason to. In fact, he had every reason no' to help us then. He will help us, now, if we ask it of him."

Afraid of what she might see in her father's expression, Meghan steeled herself before turning around. Morven eyed her carefully, as if trying to read her mind. She purposely hid behind a mask of no expression at all.

"Fine then," he finally answered. "But know this. If I find the man has hurt ye, I'll kill him with my own hands."

CHAPTER FOURTEEN

Devlin sank into the tub, the warm water coming to his chin. His body throbbed with the knowledge Meghan did the same in the next room. Only the ladies' solar separated her from him, with two connecting doors between.

The incessant wanting had only been stoked by taking her last night. If he sought to remove thoughts of her by satisfying himself, he'd been sorely mistaken. Instead, every second thought to enter his troubled mind included her naked breasts heaving in desire beneath him.

"Jesu," he grumbled. "Control yourself. 'Tis not helping matters any to dwell."

He closed his eyes and then opened them when he saw only her full lips spreading wide in anticipation.

The chamber door opened, and he turned to find Will leaning against the frame, his arms crossed over his chest.

"What do you want?" he grumbled.

" 'Twas boring at Dunburough. I expect you'll be thanking me for coming, if the King's messenger to Ian Douglas contains what we suspect."

"Don't remind me." Devlin cursed as he dipped his head below the surface of the water, resurfaced, and smoothed his hair back.

"So, how fares your lady?"

"She is not my lady."

"That well, I see."

"She is whole and hearty, if that's what you mean."

"I hardly expected you to cleave her in two, coz."

Something in Devlin's expression must have changed. Will pushed himself from the threshold and put his hands on his hips.

"You didn't . . ."

"Bloody hell."

"Saints preserve us, Devlin. You did." Will smiled and closed the door behind him. "When? Where?"

"You're worse than a scullery maid, Will. 'Tis none of your concern."

" 'Tis my concern if her betrothed discovers the fact and seeks your head. Both of them."

Devlin stood and draped a long piece of linen around his waist. It was a distinct possibility. If he were this Ian and had discovered his betrothed, if she were even promised to him, had been taken by another man, Devlin would stop at nothing to hunt the man down and hang him from the ramparts by his own entrails.

Such an ending for himself did not sit well.

"I'm sending both Meghan and her father away in the morning." He hadn't realized he'd even come to this decision until he spoke the words aloud. " 'Tis the only solution."

"You love her."

Devlin's head snapped around. "Nay."

'Twas easy for Will to become lost in the romantic world of poets and minstrels. He had never met a woman he'd been willing to love for longer than a bedding or two.

Will shook his head as if he felt pity for Devlin. "I don't believe you. I don't think you believe yourself, although you try to lie. Keep her here. Take her to wife."

"You're mad." Devlin laughed aloud. "Have you no concern for the people under my protection? Do you know what kind of bloody war would ensue? Nay, 'tis not worth the lives of these people."

"You have a large army at your disposal. You have right on your side."

Devlin shook his head. "Nay. I will send her away. She may petition Henry for whatever she likes, but she will not do it from here."

"She may have to do so from here, Cousin."

"What do you mean by that?" Devlin fastened his trews and pulled on his boots.

"Henry should be here by the time we've finished our evening meal."

† † †

"I'm sorry, Devlin."

Devlin raised an eyebrow at the words Morven uttered.

"I allowed weakness brought by hatred to sway my actions and lead me astray. I should have been well pleased with all I had, and I allowed Ian to convince me otherwise."

"How is it you've come to this conclusion, Morven? You've never apologized for anything in your life. Why now?"

"Sometimes a man must lose everything he has before he can appreciate he had aught to lose."

Devlin's thoughts fell on Meghan, seated beside her father on a bench in his counting room. She looked as if she might cry should he refuse to release her father. He'd already decided he would, but couldn't yet bring himself to say the words.

"And if I free you, Morven, where will you go? You have no home left."

"To London." Morven sucked in his breath. Devlin knew how difficult this discussion must be for him. He all but begged for his release, as well as forgiveness. "To petition the King for aid. Ian is a foul beast who destroys all he touches. Henry should know this before he grants any requests."

"If I know Henry, he's already granted them. He has no love for you, Morven, you know that."

"Aye. But I've ever been loyal to him, and he knows this as well."

Devlin stretched in his chair, more to relieve the ache in his loins than any other reason. If he released Morven, he and Meghan were free to leave at any time. He sighed.

"Well, you will not have to travel to see him. He will arrive this evening, or the next."

"Devlin." Meghan spoke for the first time, her large eyes shining with what could only be hope. "What say ye then?"

He ran a hand through his hair and gritted his teeth over the words. "I'm saying, your father is free to go."

† † †

Meghan breathed a sigh of relief as she entered the feasting hall. She'd left her father and Devlin alone in the counting room. She still couldn't fathom Devlin had actually released him. He'd seemed so adamant about not releasing him; she had to wonder what had changed his mind.

She found Lady Ravenstone overseeing preparations for the feast, which should start any moment, and smiled.

"He's agreed, my lady."

"Thank God," Lady Ravenstone replied, crossing herself. "I prayed he would but see reason."

"He says ye expect the King?"

"Aye. We received word about the same time Will arrived."

"Will is here?" Meghan felt her ire grow at the mention of Devlin's cohort in deception.

"Aye, my lady," came Will's voice from behind her. She spun toward him, not bothering to hide her displeasure.

"Now, now, Lady Meghan, I but followed orders. Devlin forbade me to reveal his status to you."

"Ye should have told me."

"Aye. *He* should have told you, my lady. On this we agree. But for the moment, all is as it should be, is it not? I understand your father has been released."

"Aye," she grumbled. "There is that."

"Let's walk about the garden for a time before supper, shall we?" Will offered his arm, and Meghan hesitated a moment before taking it.

He offered his other arm to his aunt, who sighed heavily and inspected the readiness of the hall before accepting.

He led them into the garden behind the scullery.

Fresh flowers bloomed in every available space, and small patches of herbs grew in and amongst them. She spied several rose bushes in full bloom. It would have been nice, milling about in silence, if she hadn't been troubled by thoughts of Devlin.

The roses reminded her of the care he took to provide the petals for her bath. His care with her comfort reminded her of kindly spoken words.

Kindly spoken words reminded her of last night.

Was it only last night? Only one day since she'd lain with him in passionate abandon? She felt the blush creep into her cheeks and hoped the others did not notice. The remembered sensations flowing through her blood at once pained her and caused her to smile.

"Do you see that blush, Aunt, gracing the fair lady's cheeks?"

"Aye, I see it, Nephew."

" 'Tis my opinion she thinks of none other than your son."

Meghan gasped. "Will, stop it at once."

"I agree." Lady Ravenstone nodded her reply, as if Meghan had not spoken at all.

"What are ye about, Will?"

They had reached a part of the garden housing several stone benches and a shade cover. Will escorted her to one of the benches, and Lady Ravenstone sat beside her.

"We've been talking, Auntie and I, about our Lord Devlin."

"Have ye, now?" What were they up to?

"And we've come to the conclusion the man is in love."

Meghan suddenly felt like crying. Devlin had made love to her when he loved another? 'Twas worse than she thought.

Lady Ravenstone nodded her agreement. "Aye. I've seen enough young people in love to recognize it. The question is, what shall we do about it?"

The Jewel and the Sword

How could they say such terrible things to her? Of course they did not know she loved him. How could they? But why would they speak to her of other women in his life?

"I do no' ken why ye speak to me of this. What have I to do with anything?" She hoped they could not hear the tears she barely kept at bay.

"Oh, child." Lady Ravenstone took her trembling hands in her steady grip. "Don't you see it? Devlin is in love with you."

Nay!

He did not love her. He hardly tolerated her. Loving her last night had come from the basest of man's existence. Need. Wanting. Never love. Only she had supplied the love in their coupling. Willingness to accept this as fact had been part of her decision to lie with him. This discussion of fancy and love only made her carefully checked pain soar ever higher in her consciousness.

"She is speechless, Aunt. See, I told you she had no idea."

" 'Tis no' true. If Lord Devlin loves, 'tis another woman he craves."

"Do you love him?" Will crossed his arms over his chest, implying he would not desist until he had an answer.

She bit her lip, staring up at Will's firmly set jaw and dancing eyes. A lie hovered upon the tip of her tongue.

'Tis simple eno' to lie.

Then she looked at Lady Ravenstone, who all but held her breath beside Meghan. Flashes of her life to come consumed her. Marriage to Ian, should the King decree it. Marriage to another if he did not. Some man she'd yet to know touching her the way Devlin had touched her. Her stomach turned upon itself.

Nay.

If what they believed held a shred of truth . . .

She dared not hope. Could she?

What if he did love her, or could grow to someday?

"What do ye propose, Will?"

"Nay, my lady. First you must answer my question. Do you love Devlin?"

She swallowed as a tear escaped her eyes. "Aye, Will. Very much."

"Then we must make him admit he loves you in return. And we must do it quickly, else 'twill be too late."

† † †

Devlin sat behind the high table. His mother would say he sulked. In fact, she had said that very thing twice since taking her seat next to him. He pushed his trencher away and poured another cup of ale.

He did not sulk.

"Are you not going to partake of this feast, Devlin?"

"Nay, Mother. I'm not hungry."

For food.

THE JEWEL AND THE SWORD

Ever since Meghan and her father had taken their places next to him, as befitted visitors of importance, with Will on Meghan's far side, he'd been unable to form a clear thought, much less digest the tender venison stew filling his trencher.

Meghan.

She fairly glowed, and drew more attention from his men than he felt comfortable with. Such open appreciation on their part further dampened his mood.

"Meghan, do you find the meal to your liking," his mother called to her.

"Aye, my lady. 'Tis very fine fare, indeed."

He should have known her cheerful nature would return upon the release of her father. Had he not hoped for that very thing? But to see her lively and happy, when he brooded in misery, only confirmed her foul use of him. She but wanted the safe release of her father, no matter how she obtained it, or from whom. The fact she didn't know his identity when they'd made love did little to quell the feelings of betrayal he experienced.

The meal wound to an end as his soldiers returned the tables to the walls and the maids cleared the floor for dancing. The minstrels tuned their lutes, the pinging noise enough to make Devlin want to scream for silence. Finding their notes, the three young men played off each other, creating a melody to soothe the soul. When enough revelers gathered, they switched tunes to a lively reel, and his people danced.

He couldn't help but notice Meghan, smiling broadly at Will. The hair twitched on the back of his neck.

"My lady, will thou honor me?" Will offered her his hand.

"My lord." She smiled, accepting his hand in hers. " 'Tis I who will be honored."

Devlin's gut twisted as Will led Meghan to join the other dancers.

A heated stab of jealousy crept into his blood, dampening his ardor more effectively than an icy bath.

"Do ye no' like Will dancing with my daughter, I would suggest ye claim her," Morven stated around a mouthful of venison, as if he indicated a coming storm cloud on a wet day.

Devlin narrowed his eyes. "You jest."

"Nay, 'tis a fine match ye would make her, Devlin. Truly. Besides, 'tis only a dance they share."

To have his greatest, unspoken desire voiced aloud, and by Meghan's own father no less, frightened him. To the soles of his boots, it terrified him.

"You're mad," he grumbled.

He pushed his chair back, nearly toppling it to the floor, and left the table.

He made his way through the hall, accepting the well wishes of the villagers who'd been invited to dine in the keep, until he exited the main doors.

The night air cooled him as a hard breeze swept through the bailey. At least it cooled his face and his hands. He crossed the bailey to the stable. It did little to cool the fire in his loins. He never should have touched her. Her passion drew him, tempted him more now that he knew her than it had before.

Midnight whickered a quiet greeting and swished his tail when Devlin approached the stall.

"Greetings, boy," he whispered, scratching the horse's muzzle.

"Good eve, my lord," the groom called from his stall.

"Why do you not celebrate with the others?"

A feminine giggle met his ears, and he smiled. "Never mind, groom." He couldn't help but chuckle. "I'll leave you be."

"My thanks, my lord," the boy called.

Devlin raised a hand in response and left the two lovers to their own devices. The sun had set completely now, and a chill covered the keep. Foggy mist settled around the base of the walls. The sea crashed against the shore hundreds of feet below.

He'd never thought of his home as a lonely place. Until Meghan. Looking back over the years since his preposterous union with Allyson, he saw how empty his life had become. He'd spent so much time keeping people out of his heart. 'Twas for the best. He obviously lacked a certain ability to judge character.

The mist crawled closer, curling around his boots when he climbed the steps to the chapel. The doors had been repaired, but as his gaze settled upon the altar, the iron display for his father's sword remained empty.

As empty as his heart. As empty as his home would be the moment Meghan left him.

He knelt before the altar, his knees cushioned by the

down pillows set there for this purpose. Prayer escaped him.

"My lord?" The soft voice surrounded him.

Meghan.

"What do ye here? And do no' tell me ye pray," she chuckled softly, "for I will no' believe ye."

He beckoned her forward.

She knelt beside him, her scent furthering the comfort brought by her voice.

"I wanted to thank ye for releasing my father."

"There seemed no more reason to keep him."

"My thanks just the same."

She reached one slender hand to his forehead and brushed away a lock of his hair. He felt her touch to the fiery depths of his soul.

"Will ye return to the feast and dance with me, Devlin?"

How he wanted to. But holding her now would be the end of him. And he needed at least a part of him to lead his people. He could not afford the luxury of losing himself completely to her charms.

"Nay. I cannot."

Her breathing grew shallow. He recognized it as a sign of coming tears, and he hid a sigh. A man limited by his weaknesses could do only one thing.

Avoid them.

He rose, crossed himself, and escaped the confines of the chapel before the first tear fell.

† † †

Ian crumpled the parchment in his hands and tossed it into the flames.

He'd not expected a second messenger from the King. His clansmen had prepared to ride for Ravenstone Keep; had, in fact, mounted to depart when the King's man arrived.

The message was simple. Do not leave Scotland. Normally such an edict would be met with laughter on his part, but he still needed to prove his loyalty as the new Laird of Clan Douglas. Were he to leave Scotland's borders now, he invited the wrath of the monarchy upon him.

He spat into the fire and retreated to his chair behind the high table.

"Bring me ale," he shouted to the maid, who jumped at the fierceness of his tone.

These people feared him. At least he'd achieved part of his goal. For too many years the clan had been ruled by a weakling, bent too much upon his own miserable existence. Under Ian's rule, discipline would reign and power prevail.

"Get yer hands off me, ye traitorous beast," a familiar voice echoed through the hall. He sneered at the sound.

Lachann replied, "Shut yer mouth, wench. Laird Ian will no' stand fer yer insults."

Mattie spat on him as she limped upon a cane, barely allowing her leg to touch the floor.

She came to a stop before his chair, followed by a priest.

"Where is your lady?"

"I will no' tell ye, Ian. No matter what ye will do to me."

"Loyal till the end, Mattie?"

"Aye," she growled back at him. This one had passion. He hardened at the thought of taming her.

" 'Tis no matter. I know where she is."

"Then ye know ye'll no' get her back."

His face hardened as well at Mattie's defiance. "Take her to my chamber."

"Nay, milaird," the priest gasped. "Ye can no' mean to defile the maiden."

"Aye, Father. 'Tis exactly what I mean. Who are ye, and what do ye here?"

"I but escorted the maid to her lady, when these men accosted us along the road. They insisted we come here before continuing our journey, they said."

Ian laughed. "Yer journey ends here, Father. My journey will no doubt end in hell."

CHAPTER FIFTEEN

"Get up," Devlin barked as he kicked Will's bed frame. "You sleep too much."

"What time is it?" complained Will from beneath his cover. His cover happened to be the baker's daughter. Did everyone have a willing partner last eve except for him?

" 'Tis dawn. Get dressed."

"Dawn? You truly are mad, you know? I would sleep for several hours more and wake to this fine, willing woman. Not your surly face."

"Get up," Devlin repeated. "I'll await you in the tiltyard."

"Give me but a moment." Will sighed as he threw the covers back, exposing not only himself, but Constance as well. Still more than half-asleep, she offered him a sultry grin.

Devlin didn't know what offended him more: that she would make such an invitation from his cousin's bed, or that his body made no reaction to the offer.

"Your father will wonder of your whereabouts, Connie, if you do not hie yourself home ere he wakes. The sun rises now." He pointed to the window with the tip of his sword.

"Put that thing away, Dev. You're going to scare her."

"I'm not scared of *that* sword, my lord. Mayhap the other . . ."

"Get you gone, wench, or you'll have no one's sword tonight." Will tossed her kirtle from the floor to the bed. Constance took it and scurried into the next room to dress.

"She's a comely wench," said Will. "I needs may invite her to stay again tonight, after all."

Devlin sat on the edge of the bed. Constance was a beautiful girl, but the way she moved through his garrison, he doubted she would remain so. The fact she had not a single bastard clinging to her skirts spoke only to her inability to conceive, not to her lack of trying. "Hurry," he urged. "At the rate you move, the sun will set before your boots are laced."

"What demons hound you this morning, Dev, that I must be wakened before the devil himself finds his bed?"

"Nothing," he replied too quickly. "I have not trained in weeks. 'Tis past time I test my skills against someone worthy."

The Jewel and the Sword

He could tell by the incredulous expression upon Will's face, the lie did not have the desired effect.

He'd tried everything to get Meghan out of his head. He'd drunk himself into a stupor at Dunburough. 'Tis obvious that plan failed.

He'd ignored her. 'Twas like trying to ignore a fly insistent upon landing on one's nose.

He'd lashed out at her. Such behavior only made tears cloud her crystalline eyes. He'd sooner cut out his own heart than cause her pain.

He sighed.

He'd lain with her. He hardened at the memory. 'Twas the most profound failure of them all, for now he craved her as deeply as he craved food or air.

"Are we going, or not? If not, I'd much prefer to climb back into yon bed."

"Aye, we go." Devlin pushed all thoughts of Meghan to the back of his mind. He needed only a good fight to be rid of her. He slapped Will on the back. "To the armory, Will. You'll be needing mail and a very large breastplate so I do not damage you too greatly."

Will scoffed and then laughed as he chased Devlin to the bailey.

Once Will had been properly attired, Devlin and he met in the center of the tiltyard. Word of the fight between the cousins had spread amongst the men. Dozens of soldiers lined the yard, each of them shouting encouragement to either Will or himself. Coin changed hands as the men placed wagers on the outcome.

Aye. He but needed to fight, to sweat her out of his system.

Will made the first lunge from overhead. Devlin raised his sword deftly, knocking the blow aside with little effort.

"C'mon, Will. Even after having your life force drained from you by our dear Constance, you should have more fight inside of you than that." Devlin smiled broadly. The men cheered at his jest. Many of them knew exactly how well Constance drained a man.

Will smiled in reply. "I merely do not wish to kill you, Dev, and be forced to fight your mighty garrison." Another cheer split the air of the tiltyard.

It felt good to let go. Devlin released another parry, and within moments he and Will exchanged blows like old times. They danced around no more, instead met each other with full force of their equally matched strength. They fought until Devlin's arms trembled with the weight of his own sword. Sweat poured from his flesh; the stinging rivulets blinded him. Still, Will countered each thrust. His body must also scream for release.

Devlin smiled.

If he knew his cousin, he would never surrender. And Will should know Devlin wouldn't either.

"Have you had enough, old man?" Will bantered, his lungs heaving.

"Nay, pup. 'Tis but a warming of the muscles, a fight with the likes of you." Devlin would have laughed, had he been able to draw a full breath.

The sun beat down upon him from its zenith.

"Drink?"

"Aye." Devlin lowered his weapon and followed Will to the well. One of the soldiers raised the bucket and offered Devlin the ladle. He drank his fill and then offered it to Will.

"We've lost our audience, my lord." Will indicated the decreased number of spectators to their fight.

"Aye. They lack patience." He swallowed another mouthful of water with a second ladle.

"Truce then?"

He narrowed his eyes. "You yield?"

"Nay. I can remain well for this task for the remainder of the day. 'Tis you I am concerned for, my lord."

"Bah." Devlin waved his gauntlet. "I could swing this sword at your head for hours more. At least until the sun withholds its light."

Will laughed and shook his head. "Truce then?"

Devlin poured an amount of water over his head and shook the droplets free. "Aye." He laughed. "Truce."

† † †

Meghan watched Devlin and Will as they conversed beside the well from her position high upon the ramparts. From here she discovered she could see in one direction the village and the rolling fields planted with hay, grain and wheat, and the dense forests. In the other direction, she looked upon the sea, with its white peaks and deep blue depths. She'd spent several moments at dawn picking through the myriad shades of the sea for each color of Devlin's eyes. Inside its tormented depths she found the bright blue of his ire, the translucent blue of his laughter, and the deep blue found only in his passion.

The sounds of excitement had then drawn her attention to the tiltyard. Mesmerized, she'd been unable to take her eyes from Devlin as he strode proudly to the center and commenced to exercise his skill in the art of war.

She would never grow tired of it now she'd seen it. His powerful arms raised in defense of himself, even though she knew Will posed no real threat. Still, 'twas with sharpened swords they played like boys, and several times during the mock battle she'd feared for one, the other, or both of them. They seemed to have stopped now, having tarried longer at the well this time than during the previous breaks in the fighting.

Lady Ravenstone joined her then, leaning against the wall next to her. " 'Tis a handsome sight they make, is it not?"

"Aye, my lady." She blushed.

"I think Devlin may need a bath after such a battle."

"More than likely." Meghan swallowed.

"Aye, Meghan. I've already ordered the water heated. His muscles will be sore, likely as not."

"Aye, likely."

"He works himself too hard, I think, when he spars with Will."

THE JEWEL AND THE SWORD

"Aye. He did work hard."

"He'll need someone to attend his bath."

"Aye." Meghan glanced at Lady Ravenstone to find her blue eyes fastened on Meghan's face with raised eyebrows. "What? Why do ye look at me so?"

"He will need someone to tend his bath," she repeated slowly and with great attention to each syllable.

Of course he would. He would need a very good scrubbing after a sword match of such ferociousness. He would need his hair cleaned, his body cleaned and a long soak in the soothing water. What had that to do with her? The woman must be a bit daft to make such a point of telling Meghan, who resided within the castle walls as a guest, that Devlin would need someone to . . .

Heavens!

"Dear woman, I could no' possibly—"

"Aye, Meghan. Have you not attended a man's bath before? 'Tis simple enough."

"Of course I have. But no' *his* bath." Her heart raced as a sheen of sweat appeared on the palms of her hands.

"I suppose I could send one of the maids instead," Lady Ravenstone offered with a sigh.

"Nay," Meghan answered too quickly. "I mean, I suppose I should earn my keep, my lady. Mayhap I should attend the lord of the manor and repay yer good kindness to me."

Lady Ravenstone patted her hand before walking away. "I thought as much."

Attend his bath? Could she really do such a thing,

knowing the power he held over her heart? She shook her head. She had spoken to him not once since he left her in the chapel. But, oh how she'd dreamed.

Aye. She would attend his bath, and with the help of his own Lady Mother, and perhaps some divine intervention, she would make him hers.

✝ ✝ ✝

Devlin entered his chamber and removed his sword belt and scabbard. He'd left his sword with the smith to repair several chips in the blade from this morning's sparring. He smiled when he saw the copper tub, already filled with steaming water set before the fire. His mother always arranged for a bath when he exercised with his men. 'Twas encouraging, this familiarity.

He stripped without benefit of his squire, who seemed to have taken leave of his duties. But a linen cloth lay beside the tub with a bar of freshly molded soap and . . .

Rose petals?

Who would place rose petals in his bath? He thought of the young maid the day of his arrival. Mayhap she had helped pour the bath and sought only to please him. He smiled. He'd have to point out the difference between a man's bath and a lady's.

He climbed in, releasing a groan. The water soothed his aching muscles well enough, and thankfully, one very important part of him had quieted as well. From his reclined position in the tub, facing the window, he could empty all thoughts from his head and concentrate only upon the blue sky dotted with bright white clouds.

The door behind him opened. A maid entered on silent feet. He could hear water sloshing about in a bucket. She brought him heated water to refresh his bath.

He leaned his head back and placed a square of linen dipped in the water over his eyes. His arms draped over the sides of the tub. He thought he might actually melt into the copper, so relaxed was he. Finally.

"Pour it at my feet, please," he sighed.

She did as he asked. The newly heated water burned at first, but tempered when mixed with the cooling water of the tub.

He heard the bucket scrape the hearth as she set it down. Then he felt her fingers kneading the muscles of his neck and shoulders. At first he considered sending her away. Then, as her fingers increased the pressure upon his sore arms, he decided she could stay. The position of her hands changed, and he knew she knelt behind him. When her breath cooled his heated flesh, he opened his eyes and removed the linen cloth. Soft lips brushed his temple.

She kissed him.

And despite his desire to forget, and the belief he'd already forgotten, he recognized those lips. His loins twitched. Then hardened fully.

"Meghan?" His voice sounded hoarse.

"Aye, my lord," she whispered between feathery light kisses and nips on his ear.

He groaned aloud.

"What are you doing here?"

Send her away.

"I but attend yer bath, my lord."

Another nip.

"Many a maid has attended my bath, Meghan. I remember naught of this in the practice."

"For that I am most grateful, my lord."

"Who told you to attend to me?"

"Yer Lady Mother."

He choked and sat upright, sloshing water over the edge of the tub and onto the rush-covered floor. "My mother?"

Meghan appeared before him then. Standing between him and the window, she did not block out the sun, merely out shone it. She wore only her shift, and her dark nipples were visible through the thin fabric. He allowed his gaze to roam over her until it settled on the equally dark triangle between her thighs. Her hair fell loose about her shoulders in wave upon wave of riotous curls.

She pulled one shoulder free of her shift, taking her arm out of the sleeve. Repeating the movement with her other arm, she dropped the shift to pool at her feet. Gloriously naked, she stepped out of the material and approached the tub.

His entire body jolted when she stepped over the edge. He could not have spoken if he'd tried, so tight was his throat. His feet shifted, making room for her to sit.

She leaned forward until the tips of her breasts barely touched the surface of the water, and her tempting mouth hovered above his lips. Then she kissed him, and he surrendered.

She tasted sweet, her tongue swirling inside his mouth where she took control of the kiss. He encircled her with his arms, pulling her toward him. He did not want to wait this time. He needed her as badly as he needed his next breath. If he still breathed at all.

As if she sensed his craving she pulled away, settling her legs on either side of him. She reached below the surface of the water and wrapped her hand around his shaft.

He closed his eyes as his head tilted back of its own accord. What divine pleasure she wreaked within him. Could a man be made of wax and molded unto the desire of a woman? He believed a man could when she touched him thusly.

She impaled herself on him then, rising and falling upon his manhood. Her breathing became labored. He raised his eyes to her face and found her gazing down upon him, her bottom lip tucked neatly between her teeth.

"Oh, Meghan." He sat up enough to cup her cheek with one hand. Then he wrapped her in his arms and moved his hips against her. He suckled first one breast, then the other as she continued to ride him, caring not the measures of water wasted upon the floor.

She moved her hands over the hard muscles of his arms, and then held his head tightly to her bosom. Her screams filled his heart unto bursting and fired his passion.

When she found her peak, her body trembled violently in his arms. He released himself inside her a moment later and joined her slow descent from the heavens.

"Jesu, woman. You were sent to kill me, were you not?"

"Nay, my Lord. I was no' sent to kill ye. I was sent to love ye."

† † †

Meghan lay with her head cradled in the small of Devlin's elbow. He finally slept. The sun had hidden itself beyond the horizon before they'd finished making love. The sounds of the bailey drifted into the night.

She pushed herself up, leaning on her elbow as she studied him. She traced the planes and valleys of his chest with her eyes, amazed anew at the love buried in the warrior.

"I can feel you when you look at me, Meghan. 'Tis as soft as a caress."

She smiled as he opened one eye to peer at her from behind full, thick lashes.

"I thought ye slept, my lord. Ye should no' be so furtive."

He chuckled. "I have no desire to sleep when you lie with me."

She felt the heat of her blush. "Nor I."

He raised his hand to stroke her hair. "Henry is overdue."

She tilted her head. "Aye," she answered.

"When he arrives, I mean to ask him for you."

She couldn't contain the squeal of excitement as she threw herself onto his chest. He curled his arms around her and held her tightly against him. After a moment, the power of his embrace relaxed.

"Hold, Meghan. I'm not saying Henry will agree. And I'm sure your father will have a say in the matter as well."

"My father will agree, of that I'm no' the least bit concerned. But why would Henry . . ." She caught her breath. "Ian."

"Aye. If Henry has already granted Ian's request—"

"But he would have based his decision upon lies. We'll tell him that, and he will be forced to change his mind."

She watched his eyes. He withheld something from her. "Tell me what ye think, Devlin. Do no' coddle me from the truth."

He sighed, releasing her completely and moving his legs over the side of the bed as if he would rise. She crept to her knees behind him, pressed her naked breasts against the hard planes of his back, and leaned her chin on his shoulder.

His voice rumbled through his back when he spoke.

"Kings do not like to admit they've been duped. And Henry, despite anything else he may be, including friend, is a King."

"He would prefer to keep to his original decision and risk war with a rebel laird?"

"Aye." Devlin stood and pulled on a new pair of trews. "He would."

" 'Tis just silly."

Devlin laughed.

"Well, 'tis."

Devlin's hand caressed her cheek, and she leaned into it, covering his hand with her own. "Ah, my Meghan, would that thou be the ruler of the world . . ."

† † †

The jingling of harnesses rose on the wind. He crossed to the window and looked down upon the bailey.

Henry.

No sooner had he thought the name did the man appear. Leading a column of more than a hundred horses, Henry, King of England, rode his dappled gray charger directly to the stable. There he was met by a score of grooms who, based upon their manner of dress, had prepared to bed down for the night.

"I must go and greet him, Meghan. Shall I send a maid?"

She blushed, and his heart skipped more than one beat. "To my chamber, my Lord. I think I shall feign an ache in my head to excuse my absence this day. I'll dress and join you below-stairs."

He chuckled. He loved her so.

He pulled on his boots, kissed her tenderly upon her lips and made his way to the bailey.

"Ravenstone! I had hoped to find you in residence."

Devlin fell to one knee. "Where else would I be? I do live here. Welcome, Your Highness."

"Posh. Enough of that." Henry climbed the stone steps two at a time. "Reclaim your feet. 'Tis good to see you, friend."

Henry's smile lit his face as he clapped Devlin on the back.

Devlin had no time to answer before his mother, Will, and Morven joined them.

"Morven Douglas." Henry directed a pointed glare in Morven's direction. "What is this business I hear of you raiding across my borders?"

Morven squared his shoulders, apparently in preparation for the King's wrath. Meghan stepped from the door as Henry approached Morven with studied steps. "I do not tolerate such behavior from my subjects, Morven. Well you should know this before now."

Meghan's quiet moan caught Devlin's attention as if she'd screamed it. He rubbed a hand over his face, hoping a light mood graced Henry this night. "My liege." He slapped Henry's back. "Mayhap we should retire to the hall, pour a cup of ale, and discuss the goings on of your northern kingdom? Before you start cutting off heads?"

Henry turned and leveled a dire glare at Devlin. He felt the impact of that glare to the soles of his boots.

"You know, Ravenstone. 'Tis you, and you alone, who could jest so and live *not* to repeat it to anyone." Henry laughed. "Very well. Show me the way to your ale, and the wenches who will serve it."

Devlin's mother escorted the King to the feasting hall while Devlin remained outside with Morven and Meghan.

"My thanks, Devlin. Think ye Henry will believe our tales of his newest laird?"

"Henry may loathe the ground upon which you tread, Brother, but I once saved his life. Let us hope that counts for something, hmm?"

CHAPTER SIXTEEN

Devlin studied Henry's expression. He found it difficult to read the half-lidded eyes, or the loosely set jaw. He glanced at the others around the table. Morven, sitting tall and straight, revealed nothing of the nervous tension he must feel. Will leaned his chin on his hand, as if sheer boredom threatened to strangle the very life from him. 'Twas misleading, his lack of interest. His cousin heard every word, followed every movement around him. His eyes settled again upon Henry as the King cleared his throat and finished his cup of ale.

"Dev, what say you of this whole matter?"

Devlin straightened. Four hours of sitting on a bench had taken its toll on the small of his back. He preferred movement, action, to discussion. " 'Tis as Morven has explained, Your Highness. Ian, though I have never met him, seems the epitome of the unjust lord. I have heard of his ruthlessness from not only Meghan, but her maid, Mattie."

"And where is this Mattie, that I may speak with her?"

"In Scotland. She endured a broken leg. I left her in the care of a priest."

"And then traveled here, in the company of Lady Meghan, without chaperone or escort?" Henry's brows rose so slightly Devlin almost missed the movement.

"Aye."

"I have granted Ian his petition to rule Clan Douglas. As well, he is betrothed to Lady Meghan."

Even the hounds before the fire seemed to hush at the fateful words. Devlin frowned, "I had suspected as much, Your Highness. 'Twas only reasonable, based upon the misleading information provided you. However, I would ask you to reconsider. Based upon the information provided you now."

Henry sighed. "I do not wish to be made the fool here, Devlin."

"I understand. Nor do I wish to make a fool of you. But–"

Devlin closed his mouth upon Henry's raised hand. "However, it seems to me, if I can not trust my own knights, who can I trust? You have served me well over the years, Devlin. I count you among my friends."

"You honor me, Your Highness." Devlin nodded.

"I would have difficulty reinstating Morven to the lordship of Clan Douglas, however." Henry stood and crossed to the fire, his bootsteps heavy with what appeared to be regret. "You were easily led astray, were you not? What kind of leader would allow such to befall him, or his people?"

Morven displayed no emotion as he rose and followed Henry to the hearth. "I ruled my clan with fairness and a strong hand for many years. 'Twas after the death of my wife, when I found myself lost and without a reason to live, that Ian maneuvered his way into my old hatred. I am no' burdened with any of that now, Yer Highness. If ye asked my clan who they wished to lead them, I believe they would take me back."

Henry crossed his arms over his chest and rocked back on his heels. "I'll consider it, Morven. If Devlin has seen fit to forgive your raid, and proper restitution can be made for the lives lost, I suppose I can at least give the matter some thought."

"Does this mean you will reverse your decree, Your Highness?" Will mumbled without raising his head.

Henry stared at him, openly bewildered. "Will Barnett, you show the least respect for my reign than any man in Christendom, do you know that?"

" 'Tis because I remember well cutting off Lady Margaret Hamilton's plaits when we were all but two and ten. And if I remember correctly, you spent as much time as we did shoveling shite from his lordship's stable for it."

Henry laughed and clapped Devlin on the back as he circled the table. "Aye, Will. I reverse my decree. Lady Meghan is released of her obligation to wed this

Ian person, and I will consider reinstating Morven as laird."

Devlin breathed a sigh of relief. "So Lady Meghan is free to wed whom she chooses?"

"For as much as any woman is free to choose. Her father retains that right. I have no mind to see to such matters myself. Where is that wench with the ale?"

"So when is the wedding?" Will asked, perking up a bit at either the mention of ale, or wenches. Devlin couldn't be sure.

"As soon as the proper documents are prepared, I should imagine." Morven laughed.

"Wedding?" Henry inquired.

"Aye. Devlin here fancies himself in love with Lady Meghan and would wed as quickly as possible. Before the young lady comes to her senses and refuses to have him."

Devlin scoffed. "Which could be any moment."

Henry cleared his throat, bringing Devlin's attention back to him.

Devlin gripped his cup until he feared his fingers would break, a dark shadow falling in the region of his heart.

"I'm afraid I can not allow a union between these two houses."

† † †

"But why no'?" Meghan ranted in Devlin's apartments. She looked as if she were on the verge of throwing things again, so high was the color in her creamy complexion.

"He did not explain himself. He would only say he would not allow it." Devlin's mind raced with his own assumptions, but none of it mattered. He'd been denied happiness, and he didn't blame Meghan for her rancor.

"That's no' an answer, Devlin, and well ye know it."

He sighed. "We have time, Meghan. We can make him see reason. But for now, the matter is removing Ian from power. I've committed my forces to aid in the attack, and the King has committed his own troops. We'll more than outnumber and outmatch Ian this time."

She stilled when he mentioned the coming battle. Now instead of a heightened pink, her face held no color at all. He reached for her, and she stepped into his embrace. He held her until both of their hearts beat in unison, rocking her gently in his arms. "I will be fine. 'Twas only superior numbers that caused my defeat. I will retake the keep, and the clan. When your clansmen champion your father's cause, Henry will grant him leadership. You'll see."

"Then everything will be as it was?" she whimpered into his chest, holding him ever more tightly.

"Nay." He placed a tender kiss atop her head. "Then we will convince Henry to allow us to wed. Everything will be so very much better than it was."

A knock sounded on the chamber door, followed by Morven and Will as they entered.

"Father." Meghan rushed to his side and embraced him.

"Meggie. Have ye yet broken yer fast?"

"Nay, Da. I waited fer ye to awaken. Will ye come, now?"

"Nay. I have a matter or two to discuss. Ye go on now. We'll join ye."

Once he'd closed the door behind her, Morven settled his gaze upon Devlin. "I want ye to send her away. I ken I've already lost her to ye, and she'll no' leave until ye send her."

"I've already considered it, Morven. The King's messenger leaves this morning with his new decree. Ian will be less than pleased upon its receipt."

Will stepped to the bed and reclined against the pillows. He rested his forearm on one upraised knee. "Which means we have less than a fortnight to train, march, and attack. Before the bastard comes here for your head."

"Precisely. Which is why Meghan and our Lady Mother should both be sent to safety. There is no telling what Ian has already planned, revised decree or no'."

Devlin leaned against the bedpost, his arms crossed. Had all of this truly come to pass because of one red-haired, fire-eyed vixen? Did he stand in his own chamber, plotting to reclaim the house of his enemy? He nearly laughed aloud at the irony of it all. He would ride to the lance of the devil for Meghan, and he would ride to Scotland for her as well.

"Aye. I'll send word to the sisters to expect our

women within the week."

Morven nodded, his expression grim.

Will groaned. "The sisters? You would send them to the convent? To be beaten daily by that wicked nun?"

Devlin laughed. "Mother Elizabeth is not wicked, Will. Had you not been so wicked, she might not have beaten you thrice weekly."

"She hated me, that beastly creature. I could do no right in her eyes, my soul damned to hell from the moment I burst from my mother's womb . . ."

† † †

Meghan refused to believe her ears. Like a spoiled child, temptation to cover them with her hands and hum a loud lullaby threatened to overtake her mature state.

"Nay, my lord. I will no' leave ye when ye are plotting yer own death."

"I'm not plotting anything of the kind. And you will go where I tell you."

"Father, tell him I do no' have to listen to him." She searched her father's eyes for any indication he would side with her. She found none.

"Oh." This time she did stamp her foot. "Devlin Barnett, ye do no' own me. I do no' have to 'obey' ye, or any man."

"Child. Ye will obey me, then."

"Ye wish me to leave, Father?" The all too familiar sting of tears burned in her throat.

Meghan understood perfectly well why Devlin and her father wished her to leave. But the thought of being so far away from Devlin made her heart clench in her chest. She hungered for him even now as they argued in his counting room. Her fingers itched to hold him, but such would hardly present the determined front she tried desperately to maintain.

" 'Tis only for a while. Until we know 'tis safe for ye to return to Scotland. Lady Ravenstone goes as well."

"A convent, ye say?"

"Aye. You'll be safe there, until we are finished with this bloody threat."

She nibbled her lower lip for a moment. "And ye promise ye'll come for me? As soon as ye can . . . after?"

"The devil himself could not keep me from you, my Meghan." Devlin opened his arms to her, inviting her to share his warmth.

She kicked the rushes beneath her feet before running to him. Where had her strength gone? Before she'd given her heart to her knight, she'd been willful and unrepentant for it. Now, she wanted nothing more than to lose herself in his arms, willing to give over her whole existence to him.

"I love you, Meghan Douglas. And nothing will ever take me from you."

"Good, my lord, for I should be very cross with ye if ever something did."

† † †

The Jewel and the Sword

Ian led a column of his clansmen as they marched toward England. Most of the men traveled on foot, but a fair number rode pilfered horses. A rider approached from the south, wearing the King's colors.

Another messenger.

Still in Scotland, he had yet to be in violation of the King's order, but any fool could see he made for war. The only war along this road lay in England.

The rider pulled sharply on his reins, skidding the lathered animal to a stop before he reached them.

"What say ye, messenger?" Ian called.

The rider approached him then. "I have a missive for Laird Ian Douglas. Be you he?"

"I am." Ian spat on the muddy ground.

When the rider retrieved the sealed letter, Ian took it and opened it, his manner rigid.

He cursed as he read it. 'Tis to be expected from an English King to change his mind like a woman.

"What does it say, milaird?" Lachann leaned over to see the letter for himself. Ian handed it to him.

"But this makes no sense, Laird Ian. Meghan was promised to ye."

Ian grunted. "From where did ye ride?"

"From Ravenstone Castle, across the border. And it makes perfect sense if the message contains a reversal of your betrothal to Lady Meghan. The lady is more than a little taken with Lord Ravenstone, himself."

"But, Devlin is Meghan's own uncle," Lachann scoffed.

Ian gripped his reins, leveling his eyes on the messenger.

"The King is in residence at Ravenstone Keep then?"

"Aye, for three days now."

Ian glanced at his captain and delivered a barely perceptible nod. Without any spoken command, Lachann drew his long sword from the sheath on his back and ran it through the messenger.

Ian's horse pranced. The messenger's corpse fell to the ground with a quiet thud. "Take the horse," he told the clansman behind him. "Take the men back to the keep."

"Ye will no' fight for her, Ian?"

Ian felt like running the man through for the comment. But he needed him for the moment. "Nay, ye dolt. Myself, ye, and three others of my choosing will ride to England and discover the threat, if any. And I will take her back."

† † †

"I suppose if we must travel, 'tis a fair eno' day for it." Meghan sighed as she rode in the coach beside Lady Ravenstone.

They had been riding along the bumpy roads for several hours, escorted by a full contingent of guards. Each of them had brought a maid, who rode atop the carriage with the driver. But inside the confines of the coach, only Lady Ravenstone kept her company.

"Aye, although I've always preferred to ride, myself."

The Jewel and the Sword

"Truly, my lady? I was thinking the very same thing." Meghan laughed. She remembered the harsh conditions she'd faced with Devlin on their journey to England. She would readily trade the very comfortable carriage for the mud and grime of the dreary journey to be again in his company.

"Aye. Once I rode astride all the way to London with his Lordship." Meghan watched as an obviously happy memory fell upon her. " 'Twas the most enjoyable of days then. Before the burdens of age kept us home."

"I understand yer lord passed only very recently, my Lady. I'm sorry," Meghan whispered.

Lady Ravenstone smiled. "My Lionel was a good man, and he led a full life. He would have much preferred to go as he did . . . thrown from his horse while chasing a stag through the forest, than to suffer the decay of old age. But I do miss him so. As does Devlin. They were so very much alike."

"Were they? I'm afraid Devlin has spoken little of him."

"Devlin does not dwell on the past. At least, he pretends not to. In truth, I think certain parts of his past are dwelled upon too much."

"His wife?" Meghan prompted.

"Why would you say that, dear?"

"Ye mentioned how much he loved her. I sometimes fear I must compete with her ghost. What will Devlin think of me, if I fail to compete well eno'?"

Lady Ravenstone shook her head slowly. "Dear

child. At one time Devlin loved Allyson with all of his being, but 'twas before."

"Before what?"

"Before he learned of her true nature, of course. Before she was put to death for treason against the King."

Meghan nodded. "Will mentioned something of this before."

"Aye, she was a wicked one. In the same murderous plot which nearly cost Devlin his life, his own wife participated, even helped to plot the events which nearly led to Devlin's own death."

She held her hands steady in her lap.

The scars.

"He was beaten, was he no'?"

"Aye. Badly. Those scars healed, but he forever blamed himself for not recognizing Allyson's darker side."

Meghan grew to understand how he'd become so hateful, why he'd pushed her away so many times. Her heart filled unto breaking as she recognized the changes in him over the past days. Mayhap her love had freed him from the demons hounding him after all.

Meghan opened her mouth to speak, only to have her attention drawn outside the carriage walls. An odd whistling sound met her ears only a moment before she witnessed an arrow imbed itself into the door.

They were under attack.

"My lady!" Meghan squealed. "Lower yer head."

Meghan threw herself over the older woman and

pulled her to the floor of the wagon, a moment before the vehicle lurched and then sped along the forested road. The loud shouts of the men died behind her, followed by the piercing scream of one of the maids. All too quickly, the vehicle stopped and the door opened.

"My ladies, if ye would be so kind." A rough hand grasped her arm. She winced at the bolt of pain in her shoulder as a man dragged her from the coach. Lady Ravenstone followed, a second brigand holding her.

"What is the meaning of this?" Meghan glared at the man, obviously a Scottish raider intent upon robbing them.

"We but follow orders, my lady."

"Whose?" she questioned as she struggled against the hold.

"Mine."

The voice sent a tremor of fear through her limbs. Her heart raced in her chest. She couldn't breathe.

Nay. It couldn't be . . .

Ian.

" 'Tis time to come home, Meggie."

"Nay. I will no' go with ye."

"Ye have little say in the matter. Bind them," he told the men with him, never taking his piercing gray eyes off her face.

Her hands bound, bile rose to her throat as she watched Ian's gaze move slowly over her body. Devlin had been right. One can feel another's eyes upon them. But no heat flowed through her at his studied perusal. Only the cold, grim hand of hate.

Ian broke off his insulting display and mounted his charger. Meghan gasped as his rough, dirty hands pulled her onto a saddle in front him. He sped away, but Meghan could hear the soft cry of Lady Ravenstone as she, too, became the prisoner of yet another rider.

The putrid scent of unwashed man turned her stomach. She tried to fight, but Ian's grip proved too strong. Lying face down across his lap, she felt his arousal pressing against her belly. Sudden terror of what lay ahead for her, and Devlin's own mother, choked her.

And Devlin would have no way to know of their fate for days.

† † †

"Would you please try to concentrate, Dev." Will used his rook to tip Devlin's king to its side. " 'Tis hardly worth my time if you're not going to compete."

Devlin leaned back in his chair and smirked. "I'm sure if you tried, you could find some other form of entertainment, Will."

"Of course, I but wished to keep you company in your incessant gloom."

"I'm sorry. I'm still not comfortable with the war council this afternoon. We're missing something, I can feel it."

"You worry too much. Our superior forces alone will defeat Ian's untried army."

"They are not untried. If you will remember, they forced us into a retreat a mere month ago."

Will scoffed. "Superior numbers, Cousin. How could we have known he'd employed all the neighboring clansmen? We go prepared this time. This time, 'tis Ian Douglas who will hide inside his keep, praying to whatever god will hear him for deliverance."

"Something is still not right with it. I have a very bad feeling about this whole affair. It's as if—"

"Now don't go getting all maudlin. We will sweep into Scotland like the Angel of Death Himself, Dev. And I shall be at your side to see to it you return to your lovely maiden unscathed."

"Still—" Devlin tried to smile at Will's boasting, but could not.

"Enough! Jesu," Will pushed himself away from the table. "I'm going to find Constance and convince her my life is forfeit. Mayhap she'll grant me a boon on this, my last eve upon the earth."

Devlin watched his cousin as he found Constance and whispered something into her ear. Based upon the come-hither gleam in her eyes, the words proved their purpose.

As he traced their movements into the tower stairs, he shuddered. 'Twas not his imagination. Something was very, very wrong.

Chapter Seventeen

Meghan struggled against Ian's tight grip about her upper arm.

"Be still, woman. Or ye shall feel the back of my hand," he sneered.

The feasting hall of Douglas Keep reeked of ale and smoke. The rushes had not been changed since before Meghan made her escape. One trestle table had been broken down the center and rested awkwardly against the wall. The rich scarlet adorning her father's chair seemed duller than she remembered. Ian had made short work of tainting the structure with his wickedness.

And now he would hold her prisoner in her own home, or what remained of it. They reached the tower stairs, and Meghan lost her balance more than once as

Ian dragged her behind him. Her legs would show bruises come morning.

If morning ever comes.

"Where does he take us, Meghan?" cried Lady Ravenstone, several feet behind her and in similar condition.

"To the tower," growled Ian. "I haven't the time to deal with either of ye now."

True to his word, Ian threw open the door to an unused room inside the north tower. A shocked gasp echoed in the dim light.

Meghan found herself falling to the worn wooden floor.

Lady Ravenstone fell beside her as she, too, was pushed through the door.

"Sleep well, Meggie. Very soon yer knight will be dead by my hand, and yer father beside him."

"Nay," she screamed as the door slammed shut.

"My lady?" Meghan could see very little in the darkness. Only one window, set high above them in the tall room, offered what moonlight it could.

"I'm here, Meghan," Lady Ravenstone grasped her arm. "Someone is here with us, I think."

"Aye, milady. 'Tis I, Mattie. Give it a moment and yer eyes will see more clearly."

"What do ye here, Mattie? What of the kind Father Monroe?"

"I can only think he may be dead, milady." Meghan could hear the tears caught in Mattie's throat. "By Ian's hand the very day his men found us."

"Oh, Mattie." Meghan could finally see the outline of her friend huddled against the wall. She slid closer, and her hand went to her open mouth.

Mattie's eyes were badly bruised, one of them swollen shut. Her lips were both cut, dried blood flaking on her quivering chin. "What happened, Mattie? Did . . . did Ian do this to ye?"

"Aye," she sobbed. "When I refused to lie with him."

Tear-filled eyes met her own as Mattie raised her chin in defiance of some memory Meghan could not see. "I am no' a maiden, milady. I ken ye knew that already, but I am no man's whore, neither. And I lie with whom I choose. He tried to force me, but I hid my eating dagger among my skirts and stabbed him well with it."

"Of course ye did, Mattie." Meghan gathered the trembling girl in her arms, afraid to hold her too tightly for fear of causing her pain. "I'm glad ye did so, too."

"He did this to me then. Said if I could not find it in my black heart to love with him, he would show me the meaning of hate."

Lady Ravenstone stood over them, and Meghan looked up into her stunned expression. "My lady?"

"Aye, Meghan. I know. We must pray we are found and the evil that is your Ian is sent to the pits of hell."

† † †

"What vexes ye, Devlin?" Morven handed a pitcher of ale to Devlin as they sat before the fire. The combined garrisons of his own troops and the King's forces camped around them. The familiar sounds of an army on the move comforted him some, but he still felt at odds with himself. "Ye seem more distracted than ye should from just the lack of Meggie's company."

"Nay, 'tis not that." He took the pitcher and poured himself a small serving. "Does something bother you about this whole plot, Morven? I have more than one doubt about our success."

Morven scoffed. "Aye. Of course. We're fighting a man so evil, Devlin, I doubt another before him could match the hatred. He hates everything English. He despises me and my daughter. I have no comprehension why he wishes to wed with her, other than lending credibility to his claim to lead Clan Douglas."

"He said as much in his petition, as a matter of fact, Morven." Henry sat next to Devlin and helped himself to the ale. "He said a great many things in his petition. He indicated 'twas you, Morven, who craved Devlin's sword so you were possessed to kill for it."

Morven's expression dimmed.

"It no longer matters. I fear the sword is lost." Devlin tried to ease Morven's obvious pain at the memory.

"Ian keeps it, of that I'm certain. 'Tis no' the value of it in gold he craves, but in power. I do no' ken why, but he's ever hated ye as much as I did." Morven sighed.

"Why would he hate Devlin?" Will scoffed. "He's never even met the man."

Morven shrugged. "Who kens what the devil thinks when he raids human souls? 'Tis rumored Ian once attempted to usurp the throne of England, so powerful is his greed. The man is mad with it."

Henry smiled. "Only one man has ever attempted that, Morven. And Devlin here bested him."

"You have a keen memory for the parts of history you like, Henry. I'd say we were, perchance, even at best."

Morven's voice held a note of warning. "Be that as it may, we have every right to fear Ian."

"I do not fear him, Morven." Devlin sighed. "I've looked evil straight in the eye, if you'll remember. I have the scars upon my back to prove it, yet I lived then."

"I ken ye've faced Lucifer and won, though for reasons we both ken, I've never heard the tale of it. 'Tis ironic ye should face him again."

Morven's words sunk into Devlin's mind like mud oozing from the moor.

Face him again.

His palms itched for his sword. "You say Ian involved himself in a plan to invade England?"

"Aye, 'twas a rumor, cast about by Ian himself, I should imagine, to boost his own standing among the men. I never took the tale seriously."

Devlin looked at Henry, who returned his gaze with fire reflected in his eyes. "When?"

Morven sat up and stretched his legs toward the flames. "I do no' ken, exactly. 'Twas before he insinuated himself so fully into my life. Before Elspeth died. Mayhap, ten years ago?"

"A plot did exist then, Morven. A design that nearly succeeded in taking not only Henry's throne, but my life as well."

"Truly?" Morven's eyes narrowed on him, and a foreboding shiver crawled slowly down his back. "Tell me."

" 'Twas the reason for these scars I carry. The tale you've never heard."

Devlin explained over the course of the next hour the horrible details of his capture and confinement, finally ending with his own wife's traitorous death.

"Are ye suggesting that Ian is the same man who held ye captive, Devlin? The same man who seduced yer Lady Wife into helping him?"

"I suggest that very thing. I know I'm right, Morven, as mad as it sounds." Devlin's fisted hands ached to find this . . . Ian.

" 'Tis too unlikely." Morven waved a dismissive hand. "The chances are no' in yer favor."

"Aye, you're right about that. But still, I sense something amiss, and for the devil I cannot place it. 'Tis maddening."

"Ian is many things, Devlin, but I can no' see him having the gall to try what ye've described, regardless of the rumors."

"I've learned well not to underestimate any opponent."

"Would you recognize this man, if you were to see him again?" Will asked.

Devlin closed his eyes. The soulless grey orbs of the man responsible for his torture appeared without summons. "Aye, Will," he replied, lifting his lids to level a fierce gaze upon him. "I would."

Morven placed a hand on Devlin's shoulder and squeezed. "Then ye shall soon have yer answer. For at first light, we ride to meet with the man himself."

† † †

Ian walked the ramparts of Douglas Keep. His fist clenched tightly as he watched the horizon for any sign of Henry's army. Confidence danced in his blood. He numbered more than two hundred, an equal if not better match against the invading forces.

He still couldn't believe his good fortune. Finding Meghan outside of Devlin's hands had been a blessing he'd not expected. His loins hardened at the thought that he would soon have her to his own.

"Laird Ian." An archer nodded in his direction.

"Any sign of them?"

"Aye. A patrol returned an hour ago with news. They camp six miles through yon forest. The men were drawn by the fires. 'Tis odd they would reveal their position."

"Nay, no' so odd. They ken we expect them. 'Tis their confidence will be their defeat."

He continued circling the ramparts for a few more

minutes before descending the stairs to his chamber.

Lachann awaited him there with a pitcher of mulled wine.

"They will attack with the dawn, Lachann. Be the men ready?"

"Aye. They fairly shine with the chance to best the English. And ye will have yer vengeance as well as the clan."

"'Tis no' vengeance I seek. I but mean to complete what I started."

"Killing Henry on the morrow will complete what ye started. But killing Ravenstone? That must be a sweet taste indeed."

"Aye. Call it what ye like," he snarled into his cup.

"I do no' ken how ye've done it all these years, Ian. Had I been thwarted in a bid for the throne of England by a whelp, I would have hunted the man down and fed his liver to my hounds."

Ian grimaced. Mayhap he would do that very thing. Devlin Barnett deserved nothing less. 'Twas Ravenstone who bested him those many years ago. But Ian had the satisfaction of knowing Allyson for what she truly was.

He knew many things that his opponent did not. He'd learned of Morven's true parentage several years into Morven's reign when an old woman claiming to be Morven's paternal grandmother arrived at the keep–desperate, filthy, and in ill health. How she knew the truth, he neither ascertained nor cared to know. He'd turned the woman away, but retained the knowledge for future use, keeping the information from Morven to further the man's hatred of the one he thought to have sired him. And it had worked.

Everything had gone according to his plans. Right until the moment Ravenstone refused to die for the second time.

But no more. Devlin and Morven be damned. He would succeed this time.

He frowned. "Go find yer bed, Lachann. The hour grows late."

He needed his rest this night. For, despite his denials to Lachann, tomorrow he would achieve his ultimate revenge.

† † †

Devlin woke the morning of the attack with the same sense of foreboding that had haunted him since Meghan left his side nearly a week earlier. The sounds of camp breaking around him did little to quiet his nerves. He pushed the nagging thoughts to the back of his mind and rose from his pallet. Mayhap Morven was right. He but missed Meghan's company.

"I see you've finally crawled from your bed, old man." Will poked his head into the tent. "Your squire is anxious to help you dress for the battle, Dev."

"Send him in then. How fare the men this morning?"

Will stepped further in and admitted a lad of around ten and two who struggled mightily with the weight of Devlin's armor. "Some are nervous. Others anxious to get to the fighting."

"Fine then. Tell them they will not have to wait overlong. We will attack upon the sunrise."

Henry joined them, wearing a white cape over his brilliantly polished armor. "You know, Devlin, some people assume I am in charge here."

"Not wearing that, they won't," Will teased. "Do you plan to fight, Henry? Or will the blood stain your cloak?"

Henry smiled. "One of these days, Will, I will make you suffer for your insults. Mark my words."

Devlin normally enjoyed the banter among his friends before the seriousness of war stole their good graces. But not today.

By the time his squire completed his task, and Devlin stood prepared for battle, the others had left him. He didn't blame them. Neither did he enjoy his company, so why should they.

He found them standing by their chargers, apparently waiting for him. As he moved closer, he noticed a priest weaving unsteadily in the center of the tightly formed group.

The man boasted several bruises upon his face, and his vestments hung in tattered strips, caked with mud. He looked as if he'd been dragged behind his horse or, more likely, beaten and left for dead.

Not until he reached them did he recognize the good Father Monroe.

The feeling of dread he'd managed to keep at bay for the last hour returned tenfold, eating at his gut with chiseled fangs.

". . . and I can no' be sure, but I thought I saw the Lady Meghan among them."

"What say you, Father?" Devlin's ears perked at the mention of Meghan's name.

All eyes settled upon him then, and he noticed the one emotion he could never abide in Will's gaze.

Pity.

"What happened to you, Father?"

"I escaped yon keep within an inch of my life."

"The good father was just telling us he witnessed the return of Ian and a small contingent of men just last night. He rode hard and appeared to have done so for days."

"Aye, my lord. The poor beasts were lathered and woefully thin."

"And he thinks they carried with them two women."

His heart leapt to his throat.

"One of them black-haired, the other red. I can no' be sure, but she looked very much like the lady who accompanied ye the day ye . . ."

Devlin turned away. He couldn't hear anymore. He'd known something had been wrong. Why did he not send a messenger to ensure their safe arrival at the convent? 'Twas his fault.

His own mother, captured by that foul creature.

And Meghan. If Ian so much as laid a finger on a strand of her hair . . .

"Devlin. We'll get them back." Henry rested his hand on Devlin's shoulder. "But I need you whole, man. 'Tis you the men will follow."

He stiffened his back. His muscles bunched, itching to enter the fray.

"Then we ride," he said through clenched teeth.

He gave the order to mount, and more than fifty heavy horse formed a line behind him. Will took his place on his right, while Morven brought his mount to the left.

Devlin spurred Midnight forward and raised his sword above his head. The jingling of harnesses mixed with the excited shouts of both his and Henry's troops as they ran the animals across a fallow field.

They were met by superior forces midway to the keep. Archers posted upon the ramparts rained arrows down upon the melee.

Devlin drove his way through several soldiers as Will, never leaving his side, did the same.

A few moments into the fighting, Devlin stood in his stirrups and released a bellowing battle cry. In a crashing flurry of horse and armor, the remainder of the heavy horse, nearly doubling their numbers, burst from the tree line. The frightened faces of his enemy told Devlin the tactic had worked.

Ian had no more forces in reserve.

"They run, Cousin," Will panted as he made short work of a Douglas clansman intent upon pulling him from his mount.

"Aye. Make for the rear of the keep, Will. We finish this."

With no significant force between himself and the keep, Devlin turned Midnight toward the far edge of the walled castle.

Morven must have seen his intent. Before Devlin and Will rounded the first corner, Morven joined them.

"Where are we going, Devlin?" Will called. "The fighting is the other way."

"I am well aware of that, Will, but the women reside inside the keep."

He pulled Midnight to a halt and leapt from the horse's back before the destrier ceased stomping his feet. He dashed for the postern gate through which he and Meghan had escaped the castle. He found it readily enough, considering it had been the middle of the night when last he'd been here.

Morven helped him pull open the rotted wood. "We use stealth, then? Do ye ken how many soldiers he may have inside, Devlin? What if we encounter many times our number? Did ye think of that?"

Will caught up to them, having secured the horses. "What are we doing? And will it be fun?"

Morven scoffed. "Aye, Will. We are entering the keep, just the three of us, an old man, a madman, and a boy."

"Neither of you have to follow me. But I go for Meghan and my Lady Mother." Devlin's jaw ticked with his pulse as he drew his sword.

The grim tone of his voice, though not meant to chastise Will, sobered him. His cousin reached his gloved hand to rest upon the shoulder of Devlin's armor. "I will follow you to hell, Cousin. Lead on."

Devlin led them through wet passages. The odor of mold reached his nostrils. Will stifled a sneeze. When they reached the door leading to the keep itself, he stopped.

"After this, there will be no turning back. We take the keep, or die."

"Do you have to always be so maudlin, Devlin? Really, as if I didn't already know that."

Morven rolled his eyes. "What is our plan then?"

Devlin finally felt his mouth turning into a rueful grin. "We kill everyone on the other side of this door."

He backed a step away from the thick wood, raised one booted foot, and kicked the door from its rusty hinges.

CHAPTER EIGHTEEN

Devlin burst into an empty chamber. He narrowed his eyes as he scanned the interior for any signs of the enemy. Finding none, he made his way to the opposite door.

Morven pushed past him. "Let me pass. I'll take us to the feasting hall. If Ian is about, that's where he would be. Sitting in my chair as laird of the bloody keep."

Will scoffed. "Did you not see him on the field?"

"Nay. He is a coward. He only fights when he must. Otherwise, he's content to let others fight in his stead." Morven sneered. "I can no' believe I allowed such a man into my council."

Devlin felt the stirring of compassion in his heart. Not since the days before he married Allyson had he known such empathy for another. He, too, had trusted in the honor of another only to find betrayal at great cost. His trust had nearly cost Henry his throne. Morven's had cost him his clan. He clapped his brother on the back. "Fear not, Morven. All will be set to right this day."

Morven returned the gesture.

Devlin searched Morven's eyes for any sign of insincerity. Could he have been wrong about Morven all these years? Was the man before him filled with the same honor Devlin's father had instilled in his son? He found nothing of the enemy he had known the whole of his life in the deeply set blue eyes.

"Are we going to stand here all day, mooning over one another like lasses, or are we going to save the damsels and return Morven to his rightful place as laird? Because if we're not going to save the day, I'd prefer to wear something a bit less cumbersome."

"Aye," Devlin replied. "As you say, Will. Morven? Lead on, Brother."

They approached the door leading from the scullery to the feasting hall. Morven cracked it open and peered into the hall.

Devlin's nose twitched.

Smoke?

And not just the smoke one would expect inside a keep. It wasn't the tangy scent of a peat fire, or even a smith. Something, a very large something, burned.

"Do ye smell that?" Morven whispered.

"Aye. 'Tis a fire," Will stated plainly. "A large one,

by the sound of it. Now we're closer, can you hear the flames? What do you see, Morven?" Will asked.

"The whole of the hall burns. The trestle tables have been lighted. The flames have reached the tapestries and make their way to the ceiling."

"Damn," Devlin cursed. "We'll need to divide our forces then. Morven, you search for the women on this side of the hall, while Will and I take the sleeping chambers."

"Very well, Devlin. If ye find them before I do, take them immediately outside. Do no' wait for me."

"Aye." Devlin's mouth set in a determined frown.

"Be you ready?" Will coughed as thick billows of black smoke reached them.

"Aye."

Devlin turned the corner with Will close by his side. His sword at the ready, he scanned the room looking for possible threats. Finding none, he made his way quickly through the heat.

The trestle tables lined the walls, each one engulfed in flames. From there the rushes spread the fire throughout the room. The high table did not burn, and Morven's chair behind it had yet to catch. Will kicked the burning rushes away from him, creating a path to the stone steps. At the very least they could make their way to the upper level.

He lifted his gaze to the beams above. One of them already burned, the amber fire crawling slowly toward the center of the ceiling.

"Ware!" Will shouted from his position by the stairs.

Devlin spun on his heels, raising his sword just as a man brought his own sword down upon his head. He deflected the blow with a sure stroke and set the man back several paces.

Gray eyes stabbed him with familiar intensity.

"You!" Devlin growled, moving several steps to his left while the man mimicked his movements.

"Welcome to my home, Ravenstone." An evil smile did not reach the gray eyes.

"So you're Ian? To hear Meghan tell of it, I expected a much more formidable opponent. I bested you once, coward. I shall enjoy doing it again."

Ian sneered as he attacked again.

Devlin deflected Ian's thrusts, twisted his body and landed a solid hit on Ian's armored back. The impact sent a shock of pain up his arms. The heavy steel dented, but did not break.

"Go, Will. Find Meghan."

"Aye, Devlin. I'll find them and we'll make our way to safety. Don't take long, mind you."

The sound of clashing steel became lost as the flames continued to roil around him. He heard the crackling of the fire and the beating of his own pulse. On the offensive, he drove Ian further into the center of the room.

Ian raised his sword above his head and brought it down squarely upon Devlin's shoulder. Losing his balance, Devlin landed on one knee, but quickly regained his feet.

"Ye know, Ravenstone, Meghan tastes nearly as

sweet as honey. Did ye know that?"

Devlin twisted his head toward the mocking voice, hidden in the smoke. "Bastard," he growled.

"And I must say, she is ever sweeter than Allyson. But then, Allyson had been well used by the time I took her."

Blood pumped through Devlin's veins like the fires of hell. Smoke choked him, stinging his eyes until they wept of their own accord. Ian's voice came from somewhere in the blackness.

"I wonder if ye believed the babe yers? When yer own family hung yer wife from the tower walls, did they ken she carried a babe? Or did they indeed know it for certain and meant to spare ye the chore of raising another man's bastard?"

Hell.

Wrath.

The roof above him creaked until a portion by the stairs surrendered its fight and crashed to the floor. The flames found their escape though the hole, taking much of the smoke with it. He found Ian in the center of the room, his stance wide and his sword raised.

"Your cause is lost, Ian," Devlin sneered. "Today, you will die."

Ian laughed through a gagging cough. "I do no' think so, whelp. Today, I will finish ye, and yer King. Today marks the beginning of the end of yer precious England. How does it feel to ken ye were a part of it all over again? Ye were duped again, by yet another woman who would betray ye for my sake."

"Meghan has not betrayed me, you bastard. You have lost what little remains of your mind." Devlin's heart raced and his breath came in heaving gasps.

"But can ye be so certain? How do ye trust yerself after Allyson? Meghan will rule by my side, Ravenstone, and there is naught ye can do to stop me."

Rage filled him. Devlin's mind swam with Allyson's memory. He'd loved her as deeply as he'd loved anyone, and she had betrayed him. He'd lived with the knowledge for too many years not to recognize the differences between her and Meghan. Meghan possessed a light and fire he'd never before encountered in anyone, man or woman. He wanted to trust her, but he couldn't trust himself. The realization felt like a knife in his gut. He turned that fury away from himself and leveled a glare in Ian's direction.

He would not be defeated again. Not by Ian. And not by a woman with fire in her eyes. Not again.

He released a battle cry as he rushed toward Ian. Ian—who had held him captive for those hellish, tortured days. Ian—who had threatened his liege and his country. Ian—who encompassed the very treachery that cost Allyson her life. Ian—who dared put his filthy hands on Meghan.

The room fell into a blurry haze, and he felt as if he moved through water. With every step of his armored heels against the stone floor, he came not one inch closer to his target. His vision narrowed to a black tunnel until all he could see was the sum of all his pain in the form of Ian Douglas.

His own voice echoed in the back of his mind, distant and as crazed as the world around him. His body trembled beneath his armor, and sweat poured into his eyes and mouth beneath his metal helm. The salt, mixed with the smoke, threatened to choke him.

Steel met steel as swords collided. His boot slid from under him as Ian's weapon gained the upper hand. Laughter, sinister and mad, ricocheted off the walls of his heart, and he fell beneath his opponent's sword.

Meghan cradled Lady Ravenstone against her breast, as Mattie leaned out the window and breathed in deeply what fresh air she could manage. After a few short moments, which seemed to last forever, she ducked back inside. " 'Tis yer turn, milady."

"Nay," Meghan choked. "Help me hold her up. She needs the air more than I."

Meghan lifted Lady Ravenstone from the left, while Mattie struggled with her other arm. If someone did not find this room soon, they would surely perish in the coming flames. Devlin's mother had already succumbed to blackness. Her breathing rattled in her chest, and Meghan feared soon she would not breathe at all.

When she could stand the pressure in her chest no longer, Meghan leaned outside the window and gulped several deep breaths. Even with the outside air, she knew they would not survive long.

Hope rose in her like a wave from the sea as something, or someone, crashed against the door.

A muffled voice came through the thick wood. "Meghan? Are ye inside there, lass?"

"Aye, Father," she screamed as she raced to the door. She pounded upon it with hands already torn and bleeding from trying to escape. "Aye. Ye must open the door, Da. Please," she cried.

"The key is no' here, lass. Back away from the door. Cover yer eyes." Morven's voice sounded several miles distant, as if he spoke from the heavens.

Meghan ran back to where Mattie leaned against the wall, holding Lady Ravenstone against her. Flames shot through the floor, which began to creak beneath their weight. Holding her breath in already seized lungs, she spread her arms around Mattie and Lady Ravenstone. She shielded them from . . .

She didn't know what. Only that her father planned some form of release for them.

She closed her eyes, whispering a silent prayer.

She heard the wood splintering behind her and several jagged pieces struck her back. She turned to find her father pushing his way through what boards remained.

"We must hurry, Daughter." Morven's features were set in a grim line.

"Mattie can no' walk, Father. Her leg has no' healed. And Lady Ravenstone sleeps from lack of air."

"Help Mattie. I'll carry Mother," he replied, already hoisting the small woman into his arms.

"Where is Devlin? Please tell me he lives."

"Aye, when last I left him, he did."

"Where, Father?"

"He made to cross the hall and search for ye. I'm certain he is outside by now. Come, we must hurry if we are to avoid the worst of the flames."

Reluctant to leave when Devlin could very well still be inside the keep, she did as her father instructed. He led them through the hall, clouded with thick smoke. Her eyes burned and watered, sending tears over her face. Mattie's face blackened, her own tears leaving white streaks in the soot.

Moving down the tower stairs proved difficult with little light, more smoke, and Mattie's injured leg. Her father maintained the lead, ever watchful for Ian, Lachann, or one of the other guards.

The distant sound of clashing swords wound its way through the stairwell. Panic reared its head inside Meghan's heart. She pictured Devlin as she'd seen him the day he sparred with Will in the tiltyard and forced faith in him to the front of her mind. Talented and strong, he wielded a sword like no other. If the fight included him, he would not be defeated.

When she reached the feasting hall her worst fears were realized. Before her, in the midst of flames and thick, black smoke, Ian held Devlin on his knee, a sword arcing toward his neck.

"Nay!" she cried, leaving Mattie against the wall and racing to the center of the room.

Ian turned his head toward her. Hate covered his expression with a mask of rage. Devlin twisted his armored form from one knee to the other, raising his own sword in defense. Deflecting the blow, he pushed Ian back and regained his feet.

In a frenzied assault, Devlin forced Ian backward, until he leaned his back against the high table. With a twist of his wrist, Devlin sent Ian's sword flying across the room to land harmlessly against the blackened remains of a trestle table.

Ian scrambled backward over the table to land in a heap in Morven's chair.

Her father's chair.

The laird's chair.

Devlin approached the table with measured, heavy steps. "I will never allow you to threaten my family again. You want to be laird here? You will die laird here."

With one mighty arm, Devlin heaved the table out of his way. Meghan found her gaze riveted to the light reflected from his sword. Only when it found its mark in the center of Ian's exposed throat did she close her eyes.

When she opened them again, Ian lay dead where he sat. Pierced through the neck, his blood spilled over his armor to seep into the scarlet velvet of the chair he had so craved.

She met Devlin's soot-covered face as he moved toward her with staggering steps. Her heart nearly burst with joy.

He is alive.

The heart-wrenching creak of splitting timbers

filled the feasting hall. Devlin's face shot upward at the same time she looked toward the ceiling. All of the beams burned with dancing, bright orange flames. Three of them sagged ominously under the weight above them.

"We must leave. Quickly," Morven called from the front door where he'd somehow managed to carry Lady Ravenstone while helping Mattie to walk.

"Mother," Devlin whispered.

Devlin grasped Meghan's arm and led her through the ashy remains of the rushes. Once outside, he continued to lead her through the bailey until she finally pulled away from him.

Something was wrong with Devlin. His brow remained furrowed despite his success. At first, she thought it the fire and the fact all were still in danger. But his scowl continued even once they had escaped the flames.

" 'Tis safe eno' here, Devlin." She turned around and watched her home fall to ruins. Tendrils of fire escaped from every window, and the roof sagged with several gaping holes.

Lady Ravenstone sputtered twice and then awakened as several soldiers plied her with water. "Oh, Meghan," she cried through her fits of coughing. "Your lovely home."

She straightened her back as her father placed his arm around her. " 'Tis only stone and wood, Meghan."

"Aye, Father. I ken it."

A horse neighed frantically from the far side of the

keep as a lone rider raced toward them, the leads of two other chargers in his grip.

"Will." A smile touched her lips. How like him to be the last to escape, ever gallant and charming.

The beasts slid to a stop not far from them. "At what point were you good people going to tell me we could leave the castle? I've been upstairs all this time trying to save the bloody thing."

He dismounted and narrowed his eyes against the sun. She followed his gaze to find it settled upon Devlin, wandering among the injured from the battle. He conversed with a lad no more than two score of age whose bloody face revealed the intensity of the battle just won. She stood amazed at how the boy's expression changed from fear and anguish to a relieved smile with only a few spoken words from his lord.

"You love him well, my lady?" Will stood beside her, his breathing still heavy beneath his armor.

"Aye. I do no' ken how, but I have faith he will find a way for us to be together."

"Henry be damned?"

She laughed at Will's ability to ignore the fact Henry happened to be the King of England. "Aye."

" 'Tis over, is it no', Will? The senseless fighting?"

"Aye, for now, my lady." He turned his attention toward the men lying about the battlefield.

She took a deep breath and wiped her sweaty palms upon her skirts. She made sure Lady Ravenstone recovered well before she helped the soldier tend to the wounded.

Her father walked beside her, and with each clansman they found among the fallen, his steps slowed. He stumbled, and she reached a hand to his arm to steady him.

"Be ye well, Da?"

"Aye." He took a breath. "So many dead."

For the first time in her life, she saw her father as an old man. Weary. Worn. He would be a long time haunted by these deaths. " 'Twasn't yer fault. Ian did this, no' ye."

"Nay, Daughter. My hand is covered in the same blood as Ian's. Were I the leader I should have been, this would not have happened."

"Ye were misled."

"Exactly my point." He offered her a smile that did not reach his misted eyes. "I should have known better."

He squeezed her hand and moved away, alone.

By the time the sun had set, her limbs ached and her heart with them. Henry had been kind enough to offer his own pavilion to herself and Lady Ravenstone. The older woman already lay abed, sleeping soundly, when Meghan entered. Withered with weariness, she climbed into the bed beside her and drifted to sleep.

† † †

"He abused her, Will." Devlin spat into the fire, the flames reminiscent of the hell he had so recently fled.

Will ran a hand over his two days growth of beard and scratched his chin. "How do you know?"

"He said as much, before I killed him." Devlin sat down and placed his head in his hands. He wanted to rip his hair out, so deep the frustration coursing though him. He'd failed to protect her. How could she ever forgive him?

"But how can you be certain he did not bait you, Dev?"

"He was evil, Will. He had Meghan in his grasp for days. Nay, I believe him."

Will shrugged. "I'll ask her."

"You will not," Devlin growled. "You will not say a word to her about this vile topic."

"I think you're mad, Dev, to assume such a thing."

"Assume what?" Morven joined them by the fire.

" 'Tis no matter, Brother. How fares Mother?" Devlin leaned against the trunk of a tree, hoping he appeared relaxed. Still, doubts circled his mind.

"She is well. She sleeps now, as does Meghan."

"How is she?"

"Tired. She worked herself like a soldier this day, tending to the men. She will make someone a great Lady Wife."

But not him.

The words were a knife in Devlin's soul.

Chapter Nineteen

The fire burned for two full days and nights before Meghan and her father journeyed through the ruins of their home. The roof had fallen and turned to ashes; what walls remained standing cried with blackened tears. If not for heavy rains, the whole of the keep would have been lost. As it was, only two of the four towers remained standing.

Singed remains of her mother's tapestries lay strewn about the stone floor of the once grand feasting hall. These had been in the solar above the hall, for none of those delicate fabrics hanging in the hall itself had survived.

Gray smoke still wafted from several piles of scorched wood the men had piled in a corner. She picked up a platter, miraculously untouched and released a rueful laugh. She allowed the object to fall from her fingers and land loudly at her feet.

'Twas no use. The keep would have to be rebuilt completely. Her clan did not have the rich backing of English nobility to complete such a project. She hugged herself. All was lost.

Mattie leaned against a cane Will had fashioned for her as she limped toward Meghan.

" 'Tis a fine thing, milady, to ken what is truly important. Ye live, and yer man lives as well. 'Tis a fine thing, indeed."

Her man.

She hadn't seen Devlin more than a handful of minutes in the past two days. He avoided her as if she carried a plague. He had not come to her, and when she sought him out, an excuse played easily upon his lips why he must leave.

Try as she might to find one, an explanation for his distance eluded her. Even Will had taken to changing the subject whenever she asked for his thoughts.

"I'm going into the tower, Mattie. Mayhap something of value remains."

† † †

"I have good news, Ravenstone." Henry clapped him on the back as they searched the forest for remnants of Ian's renegade forces, most notably Lachann MacGregor.

"And what news is that, Henry, a new shipment of

silk has arrived at your palace?" No news was good unless it concerned his lady.

She must be on the verge of madness. Uselessness settled over him, heavy and cumbersome. His nature did not allow for the delicacy needed to help a woman so abused. She would be best placed in a convent, where no man might cause her distress again.

"Nay. 'Tis much better than that," Henry continued, ignoring Devlin's hint he wished not to converse at the moment. "I have received a missive from Lord Marlow. It seems his daughter has run away from home again."

"And this is good news?" His curiosity bested his doldrums, and he looked at Henry.

"Aye. It seems as if the young lady took to throwing things and screaming like a banshee when her father told her of a marriage contract we'd signed for her."

He recalled the fury in Meghan's eyes the morning after they'd first made love. He cringed inwardly even as his body hardened with wanting. She'd been wild, like some fey creature of the woods, in her displeasure.

"In any event, he writes his wishes to be released from the contract, for the benefit of the poor soul to whom she would be bound for mortal existence." Henry laughed.

Devlin's patience wore thin as he brushed his hair away from his face with a sigh. "What has this to do with me, Henry?"

"Not much. Only that 'tis you whom I arranged for the shrew to wed."

Devlin's ears perked at this. He tightened his grip

on his reins even as he did so with his temper. A marriage contract? How could Henry have entered into such a thing without so much as consulting him? They were friends, not just liege and subject. He remained silent, waiting to see what Henry would reveal next.

"I chose you, Dev, because I rely on your loyalty. This girl is one of the wealthiest heiresses in Christendom, and only the strongest of men could tame her."

"I have no interest in taming some irascible child." Devlin's temper threatened to expose itself.

Henry sighed, as if this whole design were no more important than choosing . . .

Devlin didn't know what. He could scarcely form a complete thought.

"That's why I came to see you. To tell you of the contract and bring you back to London to be wed."

"And?"

"Given the fact the woman has disappeared, it seems more than unfair to saddle you with a runaway bride."

Devlin pulled Midnight to a stop and waited. The interminable silence echoed among the soft forest sounds created by a small breeze.

Henry continued several feet, as if he hadn't noticed Devlin no longer rode beside him.

"Oh, bother it. And so, Devlin–" he turned slightly in his saddle, "I am once again forced to rescind an order. You are free to wed your Lady Meghan."

For a moment, Devlin's heart raced with more joy

than any one man could ever hope for. Just as suddenly, despair followed.

"What is it now, Devlin? I thought you would be pleased." Unmistakable bewilderment sounded through Henry's voice.

"I cannot marry her, Henry."

"Why the devil not? You have my blessing, for the love of Peter."

"She has been ill-used." Devlin's jaw ached from gritting his teeth for two days from the knowledge.

Henry's expression became serious. "Ian?"

"Aye. He claimed to have taken her. I can only assume 'twas against her will."

"Of course, of course. But you would cast her aside for this? 'Twas not her fault, and while it is certainly within your rights to repudiate her for it–"

"Nay," Devlin insisted. " 'Tis not for my benefit I can not marry her, Henry. But I have heard from women, when something so vile happens, they . . . prefer to remain as far from men as possible. They withdraw. I can not subject Meghan to fear of me for the rest of her life."

"Have you discussed this with her?"

"Of course not." Devlin sighed. Why did they continue to ask him that? He could no more broach such a subject with a lady than he could spear the moon.

"Ravenstone. If you do not, you are a bigger fool than I thought."

† † †

Meghan pushed open the last door left unscathed by the inferno. To her pleasure, she'd found the northernmost wing of the keep untouched by the fire. Inside she found several trunks, locked of course. Except for one, set into the far corner. She opened it and smiled widely.

Alone in the box lay a sword and scabbard.

The sword.

She picked it up with trembling fingers. 'Twas wickedly heavy, and she brought her other hand to the hilt to steady her grip. Jewels caught the light from the tower window, winking with pride.

She heard a party of men return and peeked outside. Devlin, Henry, and several others brought their mounts to a halt before Henry's pavilion, where a meal had been laid in anticipation of their return.

Her heart filled with longing. How she loved him. Her knight.

Would she allow him to cast her aside? Her cheeks, flamed with passion at his remembered touches. Ire filled her soul.

Nay. She would not.

He walked toward the ruins of the feasting hall. His hair, caught by a breeze, whipped about his head. Several others laughed and teased around him, but he remained intent upon his course. So it was not only her he kept at bay.

Leaving the belt and scabbard where they lay, she took the sword with her and made her way quickly down the steps and through the burned-out hall.

"Devlin Barnett," she called when she met him in the center of the roofless chamber.

He raised his eyes to her and visibly paled.

"My sword." He choked on his bread.

"Aye." She leveled it at his throat, causing him to take a step back. He held his hands wide.

"What do you, Meghan?" His shocked gasp would have been comical, had her anger not consumed her.

"I take what is mine, Sir Knight."

"And what is that, Meghan?"

"Ye. I will no' surrender ye without a fight. Now, tell Henry ye and I want to wed."

Another step forward.

Another step back.

"But after what you have been through, I thought—"

"What I've been through?" Her confusion must have played out in her expression.

"Aye." Devlin pressed his back against the stones of one remaining wall. "Ian . . . I know he used you, my Meghan. I understand you have no desire . . ."

"Desire," she screamed. "I've lain awake for two nights, Devlin, two nights, praying ye would come to me. Ian never touched me. And even had he, I do no' see why—"

Before she could finish speaking she felt his solid grip upon her wrist. He pushed the sword safely away from him and pulled her to his chest.

"Are you saying that you still want me?" Devlin's voice rasped with emotion.

"Of course I still want ye." Her heart beat so quickly,

she thought it might burst.

He smiled the lopsided grin she'd so missed. His moist eyes danced as she felt her own tears of joy cascade over her cheeks.

"I love you, Lady Meghan Douglas, and if I ever suffer from stupidity again, you have my permission to cleave off my head."

"Oh no, my lord. I like yer head exactly where 'tis."

You've seen Sean O'Brien as the hero on the cover of *The Jewel and the Sword*... Now hear this country western crooner sing for you...

While I'm Dreamin', is Sean's latest album, featuring ten original compositions written by Sean, and several famous song writers from Nashville. There are love songs and up tempo country dance songs, including:

Just for the Heaven of it,
He's Living my Dream and
Touched by an Angel

To order *While I'm Dreamin'* send a certified check/bank check for $14.00 US
($12.00 for CD + $2.00 s/h) to:

Sean O'Brien
Re: While I'm Dreamin'
P.O. Box 216
Karnes City, TX 78118

For the latest news on Sean O'Brien, including appearances, performances, albums, modeling and more, head to:

www.seancountry.com

Helen A. Rosburg
presents
By Honor Bound

A sweeping historical epic filled with danger, courage, love and above all, honor. By Honor Bound is a tale of one woman's heroic journey through the intrigue and beauty of King Louis XVI and Marie Antoinette's France, from Chateau de Chenonceau to the court of Versailles. *Lavishly written and breathtakingly poignant.*

ISBN 0-9743639-1-X

Leslie Burbank
brings you a beautiful novella duet

To Tame a Viking

Silke Thorganson, Viking queen and warrior, is tamed by Ambrose Steele, the Scotsman she has set out to destroy. Her brother, Aragon, is likewise ensnared by Irish woman, Lady Thunder, who is doomed to marry another. Separate destinies become one through love and magic.

ISBN 0-9743639-2-8
www.medallionpress.com

Nan Ryan
presents
The Last Dance

Lucy Hart is setting out the first adventure of her life.

Blackie LaDuke is taking a vacation from a life overflowing with adventure.

When these two very different worlds collide, can a life begin together agater the last dance?

> "There are good books, there are great books, and there are books that live in the heart forever. ***The Last Dance*** is one of these. Travel in Nan Ryan's turn-of-the-century Atlantic City with the unforgettable Lucy Hart and a part of you will never come back."
>
> —Award Winnin0g Author, Helen A. Rosburg

ISBN 0-9743639-3-6
www.medallionpress.com

JEWELL MASON
PRESENTS
LADY DRAGON

ISBN 0-9743639-5-2

Tragedy has dogged Lady Celeste Brystowe all her life, and she is left with only her ancestral home, and the devoted villagers who help the lady protect a dark secret. Devon de Grenfeld, liege Lord of Ambellshire, arrives to collect his due, only to become entangled in a web of intrigue, and clash between love, and lies.

Tracy Cooper-Posey
Presents
Heart of Vengeance

In order to find her father's killer, Helena of York is forced into a desperate charade that takes her directly into the lion's den, the court of Richard the Lionhearted. She is forced to share her secret with the most despised man in England, the Black Baron. Together they become outlaws, and with Robert of Loxley, Robin Hood, they race against time to reveal a murderer and save the life of the King of England.

ISBN 0-9743639-7-9
www.medallionpress.com

Attention Booklovers

Look for these exciting titles from
MEDALLION PRESS
wherever your favorite books are sold!

Gold Imprint

Breeding Evil by Liz Wolfe
ISBN 1932815058 *Suspense*

By Honor Bound by Helen A. Rosburg
ISBN 097436391X *Historical Fiction*

Charmed by Beth Ciotta
ISBN 193281504X *Contemporary Romance*

Daniel's Veil by R.H. Stavis
ISBN 0974363960 *Paranormal*

Heart of Vengeance by Tracy Cooper-Posey
ISBN 0974363979 *Historical Romance*

The Jewel and the Sword by Marjorie Jones
ISBN 1932815066 *Historical Romance*

Jinxed by Beth Ciotta
ISBN 0974363944 *Contemporary Romance*

Lady Dragon by Jewell Mason
ISBN 0974363952 *Historical Romance*

The Last Dance by Nan Ryan
ISBN 0974363936 *Historical Romance*

Gold Imprint continued...

More Than Magick by Rick Taubold
ISBN 0974363987 *Science Fantasy*

The Soulless by L.G. Burbank
ISBN 0974363995 *Paranormal Vampire*

Wintertide by Linnea Sinclair
ISBN 1932815074 *Fantasy*

Silver Imprint

All Keyed Up by Mary Stella
ISBN 1932815082 *Contemporary Romance*

To Tame a Viking by Leslie Burbank
ISBN 0974363928 *Historical/Paranormal Romance*

Illustrated Fairy Tales
for Adults

Ellie and the Elven King
by Helen A. Rosburg
ISBN 0974363901

www.medallionpress.com

WIN FREE BOOKS!

Head to **www.medallionpress.com**, and take the **READER SURVEY** and you will be entered for a chance to win prizes in our monthly contests.

Books, goodies, and more...

ALSO ON OUR WEBSITE...

➤ Author Interviews & Bios
➤ News
➤ Upcoming Releases
➤ Reviews
➤ Photos

And more...

One entry per person per month, please.

SPECIAL OFFER!

ROMANTIC TIMES
BOOKclub
THE MAGAZINE FOR BOOKLOVERS

Request your FREE sample issue today!

★ **OVER 200 BOOKS REVIEWED & RATED IN EVERY ISSUE**

Romance, Mystery, Paranormal, Time Travel, Sci-Fi/Fantasy, Women's Fiction and more!

★ **BOOK NEWS & INDUSTRY GOSSIP**
★ **BESTSELLING AUTHORS FEATURED**
★ **PREVIEWS OF UPCOMING BOOKS**
★ **WRITING TIPS FOR BEGINNERS**

CALL TOLL FREE 1-800-989-8816
E-MAIL INQUIRIES TO: RTINFO@ROMANTICTIMES.COM
MENTION CODE: **Medallion0304**

Or send to Romantic Times BOOKclub Magazine
55 Bergen Street, Brooklyn, NY 11201.
Please be sure to include your name, address,
day time telephone number and/or email address.

Romantic Times BOOKclub is a magazine, NOT a book club.